Dear Romance Reader,

Welcome to a world of breathtaking passion and never-ending romance.

Welcome to ***Precious Gem Romances.***

It is our pleasure to present *Precious Gem Romances,* a wonderful new line of romance books by some of America's best-loved authors. Let these thrilling historical and contemporary romances sweep you away to far-off times and places in stories that will dazzle your senses and melt your heart.

Sparkling with joy, laughter, and love, each *Precious Gem Romance* glows with all the passion and excitement you expect from the very best in romance. Offered at a great affordable price, these books are an irresistible value—and an essential addition to your romance collection. Tender love stories you will want to read again and again, *Precious Gem Romances* are books you will treasure forever.

Look for fabulous new *Precious Gem Romances* each month—available only at Wal★Mart.

Kate Duffy
Editorial Director

THE RAREST FLOWER

Candice Kohl

Zebra Books
Kensington Publishing Corp.
http://www.zebrabooks.com

ZEBRA BOOKS are published by

Kensington Publishing Corp.
850 Third Avenue
New York, NY 10022

First Printing: July, 1999
10 9 8 7 6 5 4 3 2 1

Printed in the United States of America

To the LHX ladies:
Here's to the "afterlife!"

And to my dear friend, Rosalie Whiteman—
thanks for everything.

ACKNOWLEDGMENT

My thanks to Craig Cockburn of Edinburgh, Scotland, for his swift translation of English into Gaelic.

One

August, 1588

He strolled across London Bridge, with its fine timber-framed houses lining the sides, just as dusk was falling. Soon the gates in the city walls would be secured for the night. The Bow Bell would sound, and the bellmen would walk the streets, calling the hour and singing:

Remember the clocks,
Look well to your locks,
Fire and your light,
And God give you good night,
For now the bell ringeth.

But as yet the sun still glimmered golden on the western horizon, providing enough light to see the gory heads of criminals and traitors displayed on pikes above the tower gate.

Robin had dressed suitably for a nocturnal visit to the unsavory Southwark district; his plain white shirt, black leather jerkin, tights and boots, even his unadorned flat hat, set jauntily on his head, connoted no class. He might have been a wealthy lord seeking anonymity while attending the theatre. Or he might have been a professional thief, looking for a rich nobleman to rob.

Robin was neither.

Hand on the hilt of the dagger sheathed at his waist, he strode with a leisurely sense of purpose. Ignoring the noisy bearbaiting and cockfighting rings he passed, shouldering his way through the rowdy crowds celebrating England's victory over the Spanish Armada, he soon located the brothel he sought. Three bawds sat on the stoop, attempting to entice customers into their establishment. Robin thought no man, either poor or pissing drunk, need settle for the fat whore with her flabby breasts or the skinny one with no chest at all. But the third, the shapely blonde with the huge blue eyes . . .

He stopped before the trio, and the stout woman declared, "We got ourselves a live one!" She grinned, exposing missing teeth, and winked at Robin lewdly.

"Is this Fat Fanny's stew?" he inquired.

"Aye, covey, it is. You heard of us, ha' you? We got quite a reputation for pleasing a man, and none o' us be Frenchified, that's a fact." She spread her knees so that her skirt draped across her plump thighs.

He quickly diverted his gaze toward the pretty wench who had risen and now loitered behind the other two. Though she wore a low-cut blouse and tight-waisted skirt just like her companions, unlike them she exposed neither her breasts nor her nether regions—rather modest for a bawd working out of a Southwark stew. Yet if ever he felt inclined to pay for sex, Robin decided he wouldn't mind paying this fair-haired wench with eyes so huge they seemed almost too large for her delicate face.

"What's your name?" he asked her.

"I—I'm not available," she announced instead of answering his question.

"I didn't ask your price," he pointed out. "Only your name."

She shook her fair head mutely.

"I didn't come here for sport," he went on, determined to engage the wench in conversation.

"What, then?"

"I came to ask about a—a friend who was here the other night. Seems someone made off with his clothes whilst he was occupied with one of Fanny's bawds. Was it you he found himself enamored of that evening?"

Her mouth dropped open, and though she remained silent, the pair of bawds beside her shrieked with laughter. "Occupied with the likes o' her?" the skinny whore cried, wiping tears of mirth from her eyes. "Even seein' a pizzle would scare her back to wherever she come from. She'd not be letting a man push it between her legs, that's a fact."

"Shut your mouth, Moll," the blonde ordered.

Moll sneered but held her tongue.

"Do you know about my friend?" Robin pressed. Sensing that the girl intended to bolt, he kept his voice low and even, hoping she heard him above the din of revelers.

"Nay."

She was lying and Robin knew it, so he met her wary gaze with a cocked eyebrow. That look as good as pinned the wench to the wall at her back.

"You're—you're speaking of that little fellow?" she inquired reluctantly. He was, indeed, and when Robin nodded, she admitted, "Well, I—I heard . . . I heard he had his clothes taken. But they were returned. Weren't they?" She dragged her gaze from Robin to look at her friends, who nodded their confirmation.

"I know that bit. Who returned them?" Robin demanded.

"I—I don't know! I told you. I wasn't with your friend, I don't know him."

"The information would be worth something to me." Taking some coins from his purse, he held them out to her.

Before the fair maid could grab the money, if in fact she considered grabbing it, the fat whore snatched the currency from Robin's open palm. " 'Twas a couple o' coves what went after the thief," she explained. "Yer puny friend caused such a stir when he found himself without a stitch, two lads hanging about, awaitin' their turn upstairs, chased the culprit down the street. No doubt they expected to be rewarded for their efforts."

"Were they?"

She shared a snicker with Moll. "I'm sure they was. Probably took their reward before returnin' the fellow's duds. Scots, like your friend, are famous for their deep pockets—and short arms." She laughed.

"Who was it first stole the clothes?" Robin asked, his gaze flicking between Moll and her chubby friend. When neither seemed inclined to name the culprit, he flashed more coins at them.

This time, the skinny bawd cleaned Robin's palm faster than a cat could lick up a drip of milk. After biting one coin to ensure its authenticity, she opened her mouth to respond.

But the fair-faced, golden-haired wench cut her off. "Moll, no!" she pleaded.

"He paid me, dearie," Moll said. "The gent deserves an answer."

"Moll!" She cried the name plaintively. "Nellie!" She added, turning slightly to blink at her other compatriot.

Then, with a despairing glance at Robin, which almost made him feel bad for asking any questions, she turned full around. To his consternation, she didn't stomp through the stew's front door into the house. Instead, after a moment's hesitation, she leapt off the stoop and ran around the dwelling, disappearing into the dark between Fat Fanny's stew and the building beside it.

She wrenched open the rear door and dashed inside, sidling into a shadowy corner behind the back stairs. Pressed against the wall, she breathed deeply, trying to calm herself.

Who was he? Dark and handsome, the black-clad stranger wasn't the sort to frequent Fat Fanny's. He could have nearly any woman he chose, and he needn't pay for the privilege.

Yet he hadn't been looking to take his ease with Moll, Nellie, or even herself. He'd come around only to ask questions about Flea. Damn the little fool! Why had he plied his trade here the other evening? She couldn't fathom it, Flea stealing from one of his own aunt's customers, and in the very place he lived. Good flicks always found their marks far from home, and Flea was a very good flick.

The back door creaked open and thudded closed as the culprit entered the house. "Flea," she whispered sternly, angry with him, worried for him.

"Lady, what'cha doin' hidin' back here?" the lad demanded. " 'Tis where I should be!"

He joined her in the tight space beneath the back stairs. Pressed between him and the wall, Lady scowled down at Flea. A few years younger than her own nineteen, he was a short, slight, but handsome youth with a shock of sandy hair and eyes as green as clover. In the dim light, she could see his smooth, freckled cheeks looked ruddy, and a sheen of sweat covered his brow.

"Who'd you rob now?" Lady asked. "And is he after you?"

"I didn't rob no one," Flea replied, raising his empty hands at his sides. "Do you see any booty here?"

"Then why are you running and hiding?" she demanded.

"There's a cuffin out front—"

"The stranger? The dark-haired man in black?"

"Aye. You saw him, too?"

She nodded. "I was on the stoop. Fanny asked me to help Nellie and Moll bring in some customers."

"Fanny likes the coves t' think she has bawds what look like you. By the time they're ready to do some swiving—"

"What about the stranger?" Lady interrupted. "He told me about his friend, the one whose duds you stole. He wanted to know who lifted them."

Flea's face paled, his freckles darkening. "You didn't tell him anything?"

"Of course not. But I—I left, Flea. He frightened me. I think Moll might have told him you were the one who took the cove's clothes."

"I don't understand. The gull got his duds back. No harm was done. Why is this fellow here, askin' about me?"

"I don't know," Lady admitted. "I don't know why you stole his clothes to begin with. They couldn't have been much to look at. Nobody who frequents Fanny's wears fine clothes."

"I took 'em because he was me size!" Flea blurted, his voice rising well above a whisper.

"Your size?"

"Aye. He was a mite heavier, but not any taller, if you recall. An' I ain't had a new suit o' clothes for a long while, Lady. I noticed him goin' up the stairs with Alice, an' I thought it would be a good jest, leaving the fool without a stitch to wear home to his wife. Besides, he wasn't just a stupid lout like most o' the coves what come to Fanny's. He was a foreigner in the bargain." Flea chuckled. "Can you imagine it, Lady? A short little Scot."

Lady could see the humor, for Scots were all notoriously large, big-boned men. But she refused to smile.

"I'm glad you find this so amusing, Flea. You broke your own rules, the ones all flicks live by, and it went bad, didn't it? Those two coves chased you down, took the clothes back, and you ended up with naught except that stranger asking around about you."

Mentioning the mysterious—and potentially dangerous—man again, Lady conjured up his image in her mind: brown eyes with lashes so thick and curled a woman would wish them for her own, dark hair falling to his shoulders, a neatly trimmed mustache and goatee, and muscled thighs to which his black leggings cleaved . . .

Her breath hitched, but Flea brought her back from her musings, saying, "I know it's all my fault, but there's no undoin' what's already been done. Thus, I'll be takin' meself off from here, at least for the darkmans. Come mornin', I'll be 'round again. Will you find out if Nellie and Moll gave me up to him? If they did, I may have to leave the city for a bit. But if they kept their mouths shut, we'll go to St. Bartle's Fair on the morrow, just you an' me. It's time for you to practice at your cony-catchin', Lady."

"All right. But go, now. And be careful, Flea."

"I'm always—" he began. Then he thought better of it, closed his mouth, and shook his head. A moment later, he was out the door and into the night.

Lady knew Flea was right. She did need to practice her cony-catching, her stealing and cheating. Flea had arranged for Lady to do the stew's laundry in exchange for a cot in a room no bigger than a stall. But she still needed white money to pay for life's other necessities. Since she had no desire to earn silver coins on her back, Lady felt glad to be learning Flea's trade.

Robin sat in his superior's office, facing an ornate desk. Behind it sat the drably garbed, dour-faced secretary of state.

"How went your visit to Southwark last eve?" the old Puritan inquired. "The crowds more debauched and unruly than usual, I suppose, what with the celebrating. As if those whoremongers had anything to do with England's victory over Spain. 'Twas the old sea dog, Drake, who routed Philip's fleet and sent the Spaniards slinking home."

Robin knew Sir Francis Walsingham felt nothing but contempt for those who lived and sported in that borough on the other side of the Thames. But he agreed, saying, "That's true, my lord. 'Twas a noisy affair there last eve. Yet every Englishman's the right to feel joyous over the event, don't you agree?"

If Walsingham did, he seemed disinclined to admit it. He merely grunted and asked, "What did you find at that madam's stew?"

A comely wench who caught my eye, Robin thought. Aloud he confessed, "Very little, my lord. I only confirmed what you already knew. A Scotsman referred to as 'little,' obviously short in stature, was temporarily deprived of his clothes. The pilfered items were returned by two others seeking reward. That's all."

"You did not find him there?" Walsingham asked, and Robin shook his head. "What of the thief and the bawd who entertained him?"

"Naught. Those I spoke with were not about to give either of them up. Not yestereve."

"Damned Scots," Walsingham muttered, scowling at a small scrap of parchment he plucked from the clutter on his desk. "Their queen is dead. They cannot bring her back. And now her son, James, is not only Scotland's king but destined, one day, to be England's. They'll have what they want in time, their monarch sitting upon our throne. Why in damnation must they continue to plot against our queen?"

Because Elizabeth ordered the beheading of her cousin and their queen, Mary. Methinks you'd do the same had circumstances been reversed.

Robin kept his thoughts to himself, as his superior seemed to consider his question rhetorical.

Walsingham turned the torn bit of paper, which had first been discovered in the bawdy house customer's clothes, toward Robin. He asked, "Can you read the signature there? In Gaelic, it means 'Loyal Knighthood.' I can only wonder if they are truly knights or a pack of crude ruffians bent on mayhem."

Robin wondered as well. Yet he had to do more. He had to find out the truth behind that missive, which suggested a great deal but provided no real evidence.

Walsingham nodded, pressing his mouth into a tight, grim line above his beard. "You do understand that whoever is behind this brief epistle wants Elizabeth dead. Assassinated. *Murdered.*"

Robin frowned. He was not so certain, but if his superior believed it to be so, it probably was. Walsingham had almost never been wrong. His network of spies, along with those reporting to Baron Cecil, the Lord High Treasurer Burghley, managed to prevent the queen from being harmed by traitors who would see her removed from power.

"Mark my words," the older man continued. "Though it would do them no good if they succeeded, they'll try for only one reason: revenge. 'Tis what Scots do, you know. An eye for an eye, a limb for a limb."

"Have you spoken with Her Majesty?" Robin inquired. "What does she say?"

"Ach!" Walsingham shook his head again and sat down once more. "I haven't even bothered her with this. There's too little to bring to her attention right now. Besides, she's riding the wave of glory our defeat of the Spanish Armada has brought her. And I know, though she would most certainly deny it, Leicester's poor health has her worried. She sways between high spirits and low."

Sir Robert Dudley, Earl of Leicester. The queen's love nearly all her life. If she'd but wed him when she was young and he widowed, there would be an heir ready to govern England when Elizabeth passed on. All these years of contention between the Scottish and English queens would never have been. There'd be far fewer conspiracies.

Yet Elizabeth hadn't wed her beloved; she'd produced no children from her womb. So there were conspiracies, an endless lot of them. Those conspiracies kept Robin employed.

"I'll return to Fat Fanny's," he volunteered.

"Aye. And seek information in the other, usual places.

St. Bartholomew's Fair is open today. That would be a good place to make discreet inquiries.

"We must determine the identity of the traitor who carried this message in his clothes," Walsingham reiterated. "Is he a laborer or a gentleman, an artisan or yeoman? We *must* know." He pounded his fist smartly on his desk.

Robin took that as his cue to leave. "I shall report back to you the moment I learn anything," he vowed.

"Good. I am depending on you.

Sighing the moment he was beyond Walsingham's door, Robin wished to the saints he had more to go on. He hoped the secretary's suspicions were overblown and that the cryptic message, inadvertently intercepted, meant naught. But it wasn't for him to dismiss potential dangers to the queen of England. So Robin hurried to his apartments, changed his attire, and headed directly to the fair.

"What have you there?" Lady asked Flea the following day. They had just rendezvoused near St. Bartholomew's Church, the entrance to the fair, after several hours' separation.

"A meat pie." He grinned, dribbling gravy from the corner of his mouth.

"You lifted it without paying, didn't you?"

Flea narrowed his gaze. "Did you pay a penny for that tart in your hand?"

"I did."

"Then you're a fool, wench. Why should you pay for somethin' when there's no need?"

Flea had her there, so Lady did not argue. Instead, she licked the clotted cream from her fingers and nodded when Flea motioned to a plump young man in dowdy clothes. "There's a fine-looking cony," he declared.

"That bumpkin?"

"Aye."

Lady swallowed the last of her pastry and ran her hands down the length of the cloak. Inside were many pockets, all of them filled. "I can't fall down in front of him wearing this," she informed Flea. "I'll dent all the pewter I pilfered before we have a chance to sell it."

"Give it to me." Impatiently, he held out his hand and waited for her to lay it over his arm. "All right. Do it now. Don't dawdle. Timing's everything."

Knowing she dared not hesitate, Lady promptly slipped on her lethally sharp horn thumb, the one she used to cut purses, and stepped directly into the path of her unwitting prey. Feigning a swoon, she fell to the ground.

"Gawd! Mistress? M'lady? Are you ill?" the fellow asked anxiously.

Lady rolled her head back and forth on the stones and muttered inaudibly.

"What's that? What's that you say?" he inquired, leaning his earnest and pudgy face much closer to hers.

The country lad's purse dangled from his waist. He hadn't even bothered to hide it beneath his shirt. Lady wondered how he'd managed to hang onto it this long. She relieved him of it now, cutting the cord and discreetly tucking the pouch down her bodice.

"Many thanks, kind sir." Giving him her hand, she let him help her to her feet.

"Are you quite steady now? Mayhap you could use some refreshment. I'd be pleased to buy—"

"Nay, nay. I'm fine, thank you. Good day, now." Lady

dashed off, hoping her mark wouldn't realize he hadn't the means to buy anything at all until she was well away.

Flea and Lady divided the stolen money, and she settled the heavy cloak on her shoulders again. He complained of a lingering hunger, but Lady insisted they dispose of the day's take immediately. "I tell you what," Flea suggested. "We'll go to the Pig Lady's. I'll have meself some o' her famous roast pork, an' you can deal with her whilst I'm eating."

"Are you sure?"

"O' course. Ursula's a fair enough fence. She won't short you."

Shrugging, Lady agreed. At the Pig Lady's stall, Flea found himself an empty table while she continued on alone through a rear door.

Everybody with a nose knew that Ursula the Pig Lady sold tasty roast pork at St. Bartholomew's Fair. Savvy gentlemen, especially Londoners, also knew that Ursula ran a brothel behind her eating establishment. But only people like Lady and Flea knew she brokered stolen goods as well.

Lady cringed as she passed through the stew on her way to the warehouse. She should have been inured to the goings-on in this makeshift bawdy house, since she lived every day at Fat Fanny's. But she wasn't, and she could never be. Lady's mother, God rest her soul, had instilled in her certain sensibilities. . . .

Biting her lower lip to squelch those sensibilities, Lady kept her eyes straight ahead until a man standing sentry stopped her outside the door of an aging, ramshackle edifice. She flashed him a peek at her cloak lining, and he nodded, allowing her admittance to Ursula's secret domain.

A short while later, pleased with the weight of the

extra coins she'd added to her purse and the lesser weight of her cape, Lady retraced her steps. As she left the brothel behind and pressed on into the eatery, a burly, bearded man blocked her way. "You one of Ursula's bawds?" he inquired, licking his greasy fingers suggestively.

"Stow you!" Lady snapped. It tired her, everyone presuming she worked as a whore. It didn't matter that she brought it upon herself, keeping the sort of company she did. "Stand aside," she snarled, giving the leering man a shove.

He resisted, making a grab for Lady's arm. She whirled, managing to evade him but losing her balance with the effort. She might have fallen, except another man grabbed her arm, steadying her. "Thank—"

She lost her voice. She lost her mobility. She lost, for the moment, all thought. The man gripping her wrist was the dark stranger! The fellow from last evening, in front of Fat Fanny's stew. The one asking questions.

Where was Flea? Lady glanced around the crowded stall and saw her friend still eating. *Flea!* she cried silently, willing him to look her way, to see the danger. But he only had eyes for a pretty maid who was nearly falling out of the top of her blouse as she served him another ale.

Lady looked back at the man holding her captive. She'd have known his face anywhere—she had memorized his features. But his clothes seemed quite different from those he'd worn yesterday. These garments did not fit him so well as his black leggings and leather jerkin had. He wore a laborer's cap, not a gentleman's hat, and his feet were shod in shoes, not boots. A glance at his waist (Lady forced herself not to look lower) revealed no dagger in his belt. He looked like any man who made his living with his muscles, not his mind.

"Forgive me," he said, as though he had caused her to stumble.

Lady couldn't look away again. His dark eyes held hers, and almost immediately, she saw a flicker of recognition in his gaze. Before he could speak another word, she wrenched herself free and bolted, hissing, *"Flea!"* beneath her breath as she rushed past the youth's table and dashed out the front.

By the time she had gained the outdoors, Lady was at a full run. Not until she heard Flea calling her name did she dare stop and turn around.

"What's amiss?" he demanded, his expression both worried and annoyed. "Who you be runnin' from? Not the authorities!"

"Nay, not the authorities," she assured him breathlessly. "The cove, the fellow who came 'round to Fanny's last night asking about his friend and the purloined clothes."

"He was there, at the Pig Lady's?"

Lady nodded.

"Damnation. Moll an' Nellie vowed they tol' him naught about me or Alice, who entertained the little Scot that night. Did he see me, do you think?"

Lady shook her head. "I hope not. But he did see me."

"Did he recognize you?"

"I'm not sure."

"Come on." Flea grabbed her elbow and escorted her briskly off the fairgrounds. "We'll haunt somewhere new from now on. Damnation, I wish I'd never stole that foreigner's duds! 'Tis bringing naught but trouble down on me head, an' I don't even have the gull's clothes to wear!"

They neared the church, on their way to the exit, and Lady saw her former mark, the country bumpkin, wandering in a tight circle, looking at the ground. A pang of guilt pricked her conscience, so Lady freed several coins from her little leather bag and dropped them discreetly near the penniless fellow. She hoped he'd see the money and retrieve it before someone else counted himself lucky.

At the Pig Lady's stall, Robin spent a moment musing over his brief encounter with the pretty bawd. She intrigued him, for all the whores he'd ever known were, to a one, bold and brassy. They had to be, to do what they did with complete strangers. And this one seemed industrious enough to work for not one but two madams, Fanny and Ursula. Yet she was nothing like the others of his experience. In truth, she seemed shy to the point of skittishness.

Robin wondered how well she did at her trade, which shortly reminded him he had a trade of his own, one he had best pursue if he was to earn his monthly wage.

Two

Robin stood across the lane, discreetly observing Fanny's stew. He chuckled to himself, noting that she'd adorned it above the door with an emblem known as a "cardinal's hat," which looked far more like a part of a man's anatomy. As if, in this district, with that group of painted whores lolling on the stoop, anyone might be unsure what business she conducted within.

He looked over the bawds, overtly displaying their wares, once again. The young, truly comely wench was not among them.

Robin strode across the street, making himself known to Fanny's bawds. "I was here the other eve," he said. "Mayhap you'll recall."

"Oh, I recall!" Moll assured him with a grin. "Decided you wanted a piece o' me after all, did you?"

He graced her with a look that transformed her smile into a scowl.

"What d' you want here, then?" she demanded.

"Information. You know more than you told me before."

"It'll cost you."

Speedily, Robin grabbed hold of the skinny woman's chin with his fingers, stood close, and glowered down into her face. "I shan't pay you a halfpence, Moll. Tell me what I want to know, or lead me to those who can."

"Al—Alice can, if she be around!"

"Is Fanny in?"

"Fanny's always in."

Robin released her, opened the front door, and strode inside. The bawds followed him, like ugly ducklings in a row.

He recognized Fanny the moment she waddled into the stew's fore chamber. Not that he'd met her before, but she was one of the fattest females he had ever seen.

"I wish to see one of your girls," Robin informed her. "And I shall be very distraught if I'm told Alice is away."

The corpulent madam, with her brassy, frizzed hair piled high upon her head, chortled. "I didn't know ol' Alice had a regular the likes o' you. That chit must know some tricks!"

"I'm here on business, and not your sort of business. Now, call for her. I've little time to waste," he snapped.

Robin exuded an air of authority few would defy. A bawd near the foot of the stairs promptly dashed up the steps, screeching Alice's name.

Lady heard Bea shouting for Alice as she entered the rear door, carrying in a basket of linens she had just taken off the line. Setting down her load, she passed through the back rooms and headed to the fore to see what the fuss might be about. But Lady stopped cold before entering the main parlor. Through the open doorway, she saw him, the handsome, dashing cove, back here again! And again he was garbed mostly in black, as he'd been on his last visit to Fanny's.

Her breath hitched as her heart did a little flip-flop. But Lady had already sidled close to the wall so that she could peer into the front room without being seen.

"Who are you?" Fanny demanded of the stranger. She crossed her ham-like arms over her udder-like bosom.

Robin tilted back his head and folded his hands in front of his belt. "My name is of no concern to you. What may be, however, is the fact that I can make a good deal of trouble for you should you fail to cooperate."

Fanny pursed her rouged mouth, apparently weighing the potency of his threat. She shrugged before her eyes flicked toward the stairs. Robin turned and saw the bawd who'd run up them returning with another female. He felt, first, a wave of disappointment that Alice wasn't the pretty creature he'd seen here before and at St. Bart's. Then he felt relieved. If he had learned that angelic face and figure had been the ones pleasuring a traitor, it would have soured his stomach.

"You're Alice?" he inquired, and she nodded, looking more defensive than frightened. "I have some questions about your recent activities."

" 'Tis none o' your damned business where I go or what I do!" She raised her chin defiantly.

"I'm afraid it is my business if you're consorting with a traitor."

"What!" Alice gasped and blinked. "I'd ne'er do such a thing! I'm a law-abiding, loyal subject, I am. We all are, aren't we, Fanny?"

"Indeed," the madam confirmed.

"Then tell me. Was it you who had a cove in your cot last week, a short, Scottish cove . . ."

In the adjoining chamber, Lady whirled as Flea appeared, asking, "What're you about there, Lady?" Before the youth could utter another word, she covered his mouth with her hand and drew him close to the wall. Gesturing for silence, she motioned toward the front room. Flea's eyes widened when he saw who occupied it; she knew he understood the man was the stranger who'd shown such a keen interest in him.

Together they hid, observed, and listened.

"Oh! The cuffin our resident flick tried t' send home in his braies!" Alice was saying. She chuckled, glancing at Fanny, who returned her gaze with a warning look.

"Your resident flick?" Robin repeated.

"The lad don't actually live here," Alice amended quickly. "He's just a regular in this ward, you understand."

"Has he a name?"

"Truth be told, I don't know it. Do any o' you ladies?" Alice looked to the others in the room.

Robin saw Fanny exchange wordless communication with them all before the women chorused, "Nay," and shook their lice-infested heads.

Still unseen by Robin and the rest, Lady turned and noticed Flea's sweat-beaded brow. She felt his tension mounting and grabbed his wrist to prevent him from running.

"What of the Scot?" Robin continued. "Is he a regular customer, Alice? Has he been here before or since?"

"Nay."

"Did you catch *his* name whilst he was here?"

Alice snorted and shook her head. "The coves what come 'round here give no names. Or if they do, they're false ones. Bruce, I think, was what he said. It might've been Bert or Billy."

Robin felt sure it was Bruce. A good Scot's name, was Bruce.

"Did he tell you anything about himself?"

"Pshaw! He didn't come here for talkin', m'lord! Gettin' his cods off was his only purpose for bein' here.

Mostly he grunted an' moaned, 'cept for when he was shoutin' at the flick fer tryin' t' make off with his hose."

"What did he look like?"

Alice looked pained. She glanced at her madam, who merely stared back at her. "I dunno!" she told Robin finally. "Don't much look at the squires' faces."

"Where you do look, what did you see?"

Her face suddenly broke wide with a yellow-toothed grin. "I don't know as that could help you. Not unless men strut about with their arses bare!"

Robin scowled. "I thought you claimed yourself a loyal subject. What you know could be of import even to the queen."

"Oh, could it?" Alice returned skeptically. "You mean t' say, sir, that now the Earl of Leicester's dyin', Queen Bess is lookin' to replace Dudley with a wee bit o' Scot? Tell her to look elsewhere, if you got Her Majesty's ear. The one who paid me fer me trouble wasn't worth the effort, even for the coin."

When Robin moved forward abruptly, Lady and Flea ducked away from the doorway and pressed their backs to the wall. Alice also backed away, so threatening was his gesture.

But Robin did not intend the bawd any injury. When they stood toe-to-toe, he peered meaningfully, even menacingly, into Alice's eyes. "I shall return," he warned. "By then you'd do well to either remember or learn more about this Scotsman."

"I thought the cuffin was yer friend?" Moll called to him, apparently having remembered their earlier conversation. She cocked her head to one side and peered at Robin as though she had bested him somehow.

"We're not that close," Robin responded as he turned and strode toward the front door. When he passed Moll, he gripped the handle of the dagger sheathed on his belt. She saw the motion, for her eyes dropped to his gloved hand. The smug expression on her face dissolved.

After hearing the door close and the women begin chattering, Flea and Lady stepped out from their hiding place. Immediately, Fanny pounced on her nephew.

"What did you go an' do there, Flea?" she demanded. "Those sticky fingers o' yours be gettin' the lot of us in trouble here, 'twould seem."

"I'm sorry!" the youth apologized. "I ne'er thought there'd be so much commotion, then or now. How could I know?"

Fanny slapped Flea's cheek soundly. "I don't care what you did or why you did it, lad! You're bringin' trouble to me doorstep, an' I don't like it. If it gets any worse, kin or no, you can find yourself somewheres new to sleep!" The madam glanced over Flea's shoulder at Lady, who hovered behind him. "An' you can take yer lady love, there, with you! 'Tis only 'cause o' my good heart I let the pair o' you live here on my charity!"

Charity, my arse! Lady opened her mouth to contest Fanny's assertion and took a step toward the massive, jiggling woman. But at the same moment, Flea freed himself from his aunt's meaty fist, whirled, and caught Lady about the waist. As she sputtered incoherently, he backed her out of the room, on through the next, and then out the rear door.

"That—that—!" Lady had the perfect word in mind for Fanny, but her sensibilities prevented her from uttering it.

"I know, Lady, I know," Flea agreed. "But you mustn't get in her way or she will throw us out. An' then where would we go?"

Anywhere. Ideally, far from London. But as yet, Lady

hadn't enough coins secreted under a floorboard in her cramped little room.

"I need to make more money, Flea," she announced. "You, too. If we had money, we could get away from here."

"You're right," he agreed. "You work damnably hard for me auntie, an' she doesn't pay you a penny over that room you sleep in an' your meals. An' my room under the eaves, well, 'tis all I can do not to sleep standin' up, there's so little space! Aye, you're right, Lady. We need t' save up more white money so we can strike out on our own together. Besides," he added, "I should like t' get clean away from that cuffin who's askin' all the questions 'bout me an' Alice's customer! Next time, if not the girls, then Fanny'll give me up to him. I know it."

Not long after daybreak, Lady and Flea set out across the river by ferry, having paid their pennies for a ride to the opposite bank of the Thames. No one at the house had seen them go; it was too early yet for Fanny or her women to be awake.

Today they hoped for big pickings at St. Paul's Church. Anticipating the various deceptions they would play on those of the upper classes whose purses they hoped to lighten, Lady had donned the only gown that remained from that long-ago life she'd led before moving to Southwark and Fat Fanny's stew. It sported wide, jewel-toned stripes and a white ruff, and its tight bodice ended in a V below her waist. Lady even wore long, draping necklaces of the sort Queen Elizabeth favored. Though the "gold" links tended to turn green overnight, and the "jewels" gleamed only dully, she didn't intend to allow her quarry time to notice she was anything less than authentic. She'd become quite the actor these days, and lying was now her second language.

Once on solid ground again, Lady looked up and spied the church's angled roof. Though it presently lacked a steeple, St. Paul's was such an elegant, impressive edifice that it attracted everyone's eye. It also drew inside almost every Londoner, at one time or another. Though services were held there, it wasn't to hear scriptures that most people came. They filled the aisles because of the church's almost palpable energy, a force that hummed like a steady heartbeat. Hope lived in St. Paul's Church, and that was a commodity most people could not live without. Hope they'd pinch some money or meet someone who'd buy them a meal, hope they'd find a job through a posted listing or negotiate a shrewd business deal. No matter how downtrodden, everyone felt better after spending a bit of time in St. Paul's.

Lady's heart pounded. Striding past the booksellers in the churchyard, she lowered her eyes so she wouldn't see the gallows. Once inside the sanctuary, she led Flea immediately to "Paul's Walk," the central cavernous aisle that stretched beneath the vaulted ceiling. The passage teemed with people, fully half of them there for the same purposes as Lady and Flea. The rest were their potential victims.

Flea whistled beneath his breath. "We chose a good day to come," he said softly. "We should nip-and-foist a few heavy purses before we're done. Then it's a tavern for us, not an alehouse. What d' you say, Lady?"

"Aye. Let's get to it," she urged, scanning the well-dressed gentlemen and countrified gulls.

* * *

Robin also scanned the folk congregated in St. Paul's, looking for that diminutive Scot who had briefly lost his clothes at Fat Fanny's stew. If he ever got his hands on the bugger, Robin intended to skewer him with his sword. But so far, he'd had no luck. Despite the belief that everyone who ever came to London soon came to St. Paul's, he knew his chances of finding the elusive outlander this day, or any other, remained slim. Still, he had no other leads, and ofttimes patience paid off.

Voices pricked his ear, voices gilded with a broad Scottish brogue. Robin's pulse leapt. Good fortune at last!

As though by accident, he insinuated himself among a trio of Scotsmen. They broke off their discussion and studied him seriously from beneath their bushy eyebrows.

"Feasgar math, a chairdean," Robin greeted them in perfect Gaelic. Then he apologized, expertly burring his r's just as they did. "Pardon me fer intrudin' on yer gatherin'. 'Tis just that it made me a wee bit homesick, hearin' familiar speech."

"An' who might ya be?" one of the men asked stiffly.

"Is mise Robin MacDougal, o' the clan MacDougal."

"Where's yer tartan, then?" another inquired.

Robin shrugged. "Safe in me cupboard, ya ken, fer when Ah return to Kiscardine."

"Tha's where yer from, then? I wis wonderin'."

"Born there, aye. An' you?"

"Lorne, near the firth." The third man, whose clothes were the least fine of the group, eyed Robin with open suspicion. "Whot ya' doin' here in London, laddie?"

"Same as you, mos' likely."

"Ah see. Makin' a livin', an' wishin' you was back home."

"O' course. But is no sae bad when one meets countrymen." Robin grinned.

"Me name's Fraser, Horace Fraser. This here's Murdoch an' Gowan."

"Pleased t' make yer acquaintance. Mind if Ah ask whot ya do t' make yer livin's?" Robin inquired.

"Ya kin ask," the balding Gowan said, but neither he nor the others told Robin what trades they practiced. Instead, Fraser began to extol the beauties and glories of Scotland, never mentioning even by vague reference that country's recently executed Queen Mary.

Eventually, Robin had the Scots laughing at jests he told, because the ribald humor focused on Scottish women. Like a river, the conversation flowed, meandering lazily. He hid it well, but Robin did not feel the least bit relaxed. He felt as though he'd stumbled into a nest of snakes. They were a devious lot, these snakes. He hadn't learned anything of them but their names, and he couldn't be sure those were true.

"We been lucky," Flea muttered, grinning crookedly. "Let's go, now. I'm hungry."

Exhilarated by their swift and bountiful successes, Lady shook her head and pleaded, "Not yet, Flea. Let's not go yet! I feel lucky. Let's do one more, a simple foist. Then dinner will be on me."

The youth shook his head and rolled his eyes. "I've created meself a monster, now, haven't I? All right then, Lady. We'll have one more go. But I'll choose the gull meself."

He led her through the throngs milling in the aisles. "There!" he announced, coming to a sudden halt. "That cove standing about by himself, lookin' lonely an' lost. He's the perfect cony."

"How shall I do it? Faint?"

"Nay, don't do that again today. You're all put out in your best duds. Cover his eyes an' play the game, why don'cha?"

"Very well." Lady grinned at Flea. "Still wearing your horn thumb? Come on, then."

Lady approached their victim from behind. Decently dressed, the young fellow appeared to be a gentleman whose purse surely contained a few coins. Standing on tiptoe, she slapped her hands over his eyes. Giggling, she put her lips close to his ear. "Greetings, dearest," she sang. "Have you missed me? Do you know who I am?"

"What!" he gasped, delighted to have a young woman teasing him. "Of course I've missed you, you wicked girl! What man wouldn't?"

"Prove it."

"I would, if you set me free so I could turn about and take you in my arms."

"Nay. I shan't let you go 'til you guess my name rightly."

Lady peered straight ahead at Flea. Why didn't he hurry and cut the gull's purse? She couldn't carry on like this for long!

Belatedly, Lady noticed two sheriffs strolling along, eyeing the crowds very near to Flea. Damn! She'd have to let go of this cuffin now, with no profit for her efforts.

But wait. Finally, Flea approached, sauntering nonchalantly, drawing little attention to himself.

"Lucille?" the young man blinded by Lady's hands volunteered. "Theresa? Jane?"

Flea was almost on top of them when Lady noticed a man turn and peer their way. She felt like a sparrow frozen in a winter's snow, so still did she go upon recognizing the stranger! All dressed up he was today, in trunk-hose and doublet, his jacket's slashed sleeves revealing inserts of bright-colored silk. But Lady would have known him naked or garbed in king's robes when his deep brown eyes looked straight at her, straight at—

She hadn't time to warn Flea off. As she watched, the handsome stranger pounced on her copesmate.

"What?! What's happening?" her startled victim asked when she dropped her hands from his eyes. Swinging around, he blinked at Lady before turning back and gaping at the stranger struggling with a kicking, flailing Flea. "Damnation!" he exclaimed. "That lad stole my purse!"

Though he hadn't yet connected Lady with the theft, she recognized her cue to run. But she ignored her instincts, instead lunging at the stranger to try and pull his arms off Flea. They might as well have been iron bands for all the effect her tugging did, until suddenly the man raised one hand of his own accord—and grabbed hold of Lady herself.

Heart hammering and blood pounding in her ears, she met his gaze as she had that first night in Southwark, and the next day at St. Bartle's Fair. "Please," she whispered. "Please!"

He seemed to be debating his options when Flea bit his arm. "Damnation!" the gentleman cried, and though he released Lady, he maintained his hold on her partner.

"Go!" Flea shouted.

"Not without—"

"Go!" he ordered again, and she went.

"I have her!" Lady heard another masculine voice declare from some distance away. She presumed it was a sheriff speaking, but she dared not look back to confirm her suspicions.

Whatever the distance between them had been, the official closed it shortly after Lady exited the church. Overpowering her, he tied her wrists together roughly. "I did naught!" she insisted tearfully. Though she lied, her tears were sincere.

"Damn you if you didn't, you little wench," the sheriff swore, pushing her roughly ahead of him. "Dressin' like a lady don't make you one, you connivin' little thief!"

People stared at Lady. Dropping her head in shame, she watched her feet. She didn't need to look where they were going. She knew: the gaol.

Robin escorted his prisoner directly to a chamber in the Tower and manacled him to a wall. Yet as he sat on a stool, Robin wondered if he needed to interrogate the little thief at all. The lad looked so ashen, his freckles appeared like mud spatters on his cheeks. Any moment now, he thought, the cony-catcher might soil himself. Surely the boy would begin blurting out everything he knew about the conspiracy against the queen.

But as the slow minutes passed, the lad remained silent. He was just a thief, Robin told himself, a mere youth who made his way cutting purses and picking pockets. He and the bawd, the comely, fair-haired bawd.

Robin knew he shouldn't have let her go, but those eyes of hers proved more persuasive than her whispered pleas. If he'd held firm and brought her to the Tower, she would have talked. Robin nurtured a compulsion to talk with her, if only because every time she saw him she quickly ran away.

But the wench wasn't here, the boy was. And he was saying naught.

"Let me tell you a story," Robin began, deciding to

break the silence. "Several nights past, a short little man went to Fat Fanny's and paid for some time with a bawd, name of Alice. Whilst he was in bed with his whore, someone made off with his clothes. Fortunately for him, two Samaritans chased the thief down and reclaimed his clothing. But unfortunately, they didn't trust him to reward them for their efforts. Before returning his jacket and shoes, the men searched his pockets and helped themselves to both money and a missive. They kept the coins but not the letter. Suspecting it suggested someone's plans to harm the queen, they brought it to Sir Francis Walsingham. Do you know who Sir Francis is?"

The lad nodded, visibly swallowing. "He protects Her Majesty."

"Aye, that he does, with the help of many men like me."

"He—he put Throckmorton on the rack, they say," the thief continued, " 'til his bones cracked and he confessed to the Babington Conspiracy."

"Right again, boy." Robin stood, studying the lad curiously. He was short enough to be the fellow who'd frequented Fanny's. And he was in league with a wench who worked at Fanny's. But he didn't sound at all Scottish. "Have you ever heard of something called the Loyal Knighthood?" Robin asked.

The prisoner shook his head.

"Then you did not write the letter found in your clothes."

"Write! I can't read or write, m'lord."

"Were you given the missive to carry elsewhere?" Robin asked evenly.

"Nay! Those weren't my duds, I'm tellin' you! I weren't the fellow cavortin' upstairs with ol' Alice!"

Robin canted his head to one side and narrowed his eyes. "Then who was?"

"I don't know. I only stole his damned clothes," the boy confessed.

Straightening, Robin stroked his goatee. "You're the thief?"

"Aye. I'm the thief."

This did not come as a great surprise to Robin, who'd begun to suspect as much. Yet he couldn't ignore any clue or any suspect, for not only Walsingham, but Burghley also, would relieve him of his head, or at least his employment.

You did let a suspect go free, a silent voice reminded. Robin shook himself. He'd make up for it.

"What's your name, lad?"

"Flea."

"Flea's no proper name."

"It's the only one I got."

"Tell me, Flea. How did you come to be in Fat Fanny's, enabling you to make off with that fellow's clothing?"

"I live there. Fanny's me aunt."

Robin raised both his eyebrows. "And the wench, the one put out like a lady who aided you today in crimes against your betters?" Robin pressed.

"She's got naught t' do with any o' this!" Flea insisted, pulling his chains taut.

"I didn't say she did. I only asked her name."

"Why?"

"Because I want to know!" Robin roared, pounding his fist on the plain wood table, the only furnishing in the room besides the stool.

"Lady! She goes by Lady."

"Lady what?"

"There's no what. Only Lady."

"That's no name," Robin said again.

"It's a sight better than mine." Flea's chin came up defiantly.

"Why are you protecting her? Is she your sister? Your . . . lover?"

"Nay, o' course not! She's my copesmate, my friend."

"I see. If she was with the cove whose clothes you stole, I'd merely like some information from her."

"W-w-with him!" Flea sputtered. "Lady wouldn't be with him. She's no whore."

"Oh. She merely lets a room at Fat Fanny's," Robin said, his voice dripping with sarcasm.

"Aye! That's so!"

"Don't lie to me, lad," he warned.

Flea looked tempted to try again. Then he glanced at the chains anchoring the irons on his wrists to the wall behind him. Shaking his head, he muttered, "Lady cuts purses with me."

"That, I believe. I saw it with my own eyes, same as I saw her on Fanny's front stoop and leaving the Pig Lady's crib." Crooking his mouth to one side, Robin paced the width of the small chamber before returning to Flea. "What else do you know about the little man who lost his clothes?"

"Nothin'. I never seen him afore or since. But he was short, like me. 'Tis why I took his clothes to wear."

"I see. Did you have a chance to inspect them whilst they were in your possession?"

Flea shook his head. Abruptly, though, his chin came up. "A scrap o' cloth fell out of his jacket, m'lord. I don't know if that means anythin' . . ."

Robin clamped a hand on Flea's shoulder. "What did the cloth look like? Describe it."

"Patterned, it was. Stripes going up, down and across.

A reddish hue, mostly, and black. Mayhap a touch o' yellow. M'lord, I don't know for certain. 'Twas dark, an' of no use to me. I think I dropped it on the ground."

A tartan plaid. Robin knew it; he knew the clan it belonged to. This proved valuable information. It confirmed what Walsingham suspected about the conspiring traitors and narrowed down the list of possible culprits. Like a hound, Robin had finally caught the scent of his prey.

The boy looked more weary than frightened now. Yet when Robin reached up to unlock his manacles, Flea flinched as though he expected to be cuffed.

"Don't piss in your leggings, lad. I'm not going to beat you. Tell me this: Can you recall what the fellow looked like?"

Flea shook his head. "I mostly saw his bare arse, pumping away, and only for an instant."

The boy looked up at Robin, waiting . . . for the worst. Robin let him stew a moment, and then he shook his head. "You're not going to the gaol, Flea. 'Tisn't my business if you've filched a purse or two. But I would suggest that you and your friend, Lady, give it up. You're both young and strong. You could make an honest living, the two of you."

Even as he spoke, Robin wondered if it were true. A lad named Flea, a wench called Lady—they weren't likely to be taken on in service in any nobleman's house. Yet he felt compelled to give the lecture just the same. He doubted the boy would last long, if arrested and sent to Newgate. He felt sure the girl with the huge blue eyes would fare even worse.

"You could indenture yourself, learn a trade," he added.

"I got meself a—" Flea began indignantly. Then he

scowled and lowered his head. "I—I could, m'lord. Aye, I could. But Lady, she couldn't. She needs me."

Lady needed a man, not a boy, Robin found himself thinking. A man mature enough, strong enough, monied enough, to protect her. But he didn't say so because he wouldn't be volunteering for the position, no matter how she intrigued him.

"I'll escort you out," he announced, opening the chamber door. If you remember anything else you think I might find interesting, or if that Scotsman returns to Fanny's, I want you to get me word."

"How do I do that?"

"Go to Whitehall, approach any guard posted near the tennis courts, and tell him to get word to me. He will, and then I shall find you."

"Who are you?" Flea asked as they made their way down narrow, spiraled steps to the ground floor.

"Sir Robert Moreton."

Three

Lady was in hell. She had thought, working for Fat Fanny, living in a stew, making her spending money by stealing, she lived at nearly the lowest level of human existence. She had been wrong. But then, she had never visited the inside of any of London's prisons. The one she was now privileged to know personally was called the Counter.

During her trek from St. Paul's to the gaol, Lady had choked on emotion that left her both frantic and defeated. She did not think to object when the sheriff helped himself to the purses she had hidden inside her bodice and pockets. Nor had she understood why he returned a few coins. She'd almost refused them.

How foolish she'd been! She should have fought like a cat to keep all her silver, for Lady soon discovered that even in prison, accommodations did not come without cost.

She had her first hint when the tipstaff inquired, "What'll it be for you, wench? Master's Side, Knight's Ward, or Hole?"

These phrases she had heard before, but they meant nothing to her, except for the Hole. The term was synonymous with hell and sent a thick, sluggish feeling of dread down her gullet into her belly.

"Not—not the Hole," she begged, staring warily at the

official, who looked like he belonged on the other side of any locked door.

"That narrows it down a mite. So which is it to be? Master's Side or Knight's Ward?"

"Master's Side," she declared impulsively. Even knights had masters, so accommodations there had to be better than any other.

"Where's my garnish?"

"Your what?"

"Money, wench, money! It costs good coin, and lots of it, to keep yourself on the Master's Side."

"I . . ." She remembered the money the sheriff had left her. Retrieving a purse, she scooped out a few coppers. Innocently, she held them out to the man with her open palm.

He laughed. "That's all you got? Won't last you long, dearie, not long at all. I suggest you don't lodge on the Master's Side. Takes half a crown just to open the door. You'd best settle for the Knight's Ward as long as you can pay. Least then, when you're in the Hole, you'll know what you're missing."

The tipstaff took a few pence from her, leaving Lady to clutch the rest of the money in her fist. Then he led her down a narrow corridor to a door that opened without any funds greasing its hinges.

The stench assaulted her like a blow to the head, making her dizzy. Lady knew the source of the fetor was offal and piss, and the stench of unwashed bodies, even though she could barely see anyone in the thin light of a few candle flames. She reeled before managing to steady herself, and the keeper who met them at the portal grabbed her arm and pulled her into the Hole.

Arms and legs assailed her, grabbing, tripping. Lady felt as though she were negotiating a nest of serpents until she and the keeper reached another door. He stopped before it, dangling his keys instead of using one to open the lock.

"Wh—what? What is it you want?"

"Me garnish." He held out his hand.

Wiser now, Lady unclenched her fist and parted with another of her precious few coins. Accepting it grudgingly, the keeper opened the rusty lock, and the heavy door yawned wide, creaking in protest. Beyond, Lady spied light slanting through a few high-placed, shallow windows. The Knight's Ward appeared less ghastly than the Hole, but not by much.

"You goin' on through?" the keeper asked.

"Through?"

"To the Master's Side," he explained.

"Nay! Nay." She shook her head. "I—I'll stay here, thank you."

The man snorted. "You won't be thankin' me for this on the morrow. You'll be cursin' me!" He laughed, left her, and secured the door behind him.

Lady remained where she stood, eyeing the Knight's Ward's inhabitants. All were disheveled and damnably dirty, so she couldn't determine what sort they had been outside. But if they were inside, she deduced they must all be criminals like herself.

There were stools and a table in this ward, but Lady didn't dare approach them. She hunkered down against a wall, sitting on a thin pile of mite-infested straw strewn across the floor.

"Hullo, there. I'm Abby. What you in for?" a woman nearby inquired.

"Foisting. At St. Paul's. You?"

"Couldn't pay me debts. 'Tis good I've a brother helping me in here, or I'd've starved t' death already. You got money?"

Surreptitiously, Lady slid her fistful of coins under her skirt. "Aye."

"Good. You'll be needin' it. Suppers coming 'round soon."

"We have to pay for our supper?"

The woman nodded. "Christmastime, folks bring us baskets o' food. Otherwise, if we wish to eat, we pay the keeper."

Christmas. If someone didn't rescue her by Christmas, Lady suspected she'd be dead or raving mad.

She knew no one would rescue her. Which would happen first, she wondered, madness or death?

Robin sat in Baron Cecil's home, Burghley House on the Strand. The secretary, Francis Walsingham, had joined Robin and the high treasurer, and Robin had already shared the sparse information he had gathered with both his superiors. Now the three men were discussing the implications.

"You didn't see the bit of tartan?" Burghley asked Robin.

He shook his head. "Nay. 'Twas described to me by the thief who tried to make off with the naked Scot's clothes."

"You're certain he described a Scottish plaid," Burghley said, the statement not quite a question.

"Aye. Methinks it's the clan MacKinney's. They are staunch supporters of the Stuarts. It makes sense that they would be vengeful."

"They have oft been involved in plots to free their

queen during her years of imprisonment in England," Walsingham put in.

"You are correct, Francis," Burghley agreed. "But their efforts always came to naught because they're far from subtle. They are more the sort to swing maces and swords than to sneak about with encoded messages. A bloodthirsty lot, they are."

"The sort to seek retribution since Mary was beheaded," Robin said softly.

Both Walsingham and Burghley nodded. And Robin's mind drifted. He wondered if Lady, when she got clean away from the sheriff in St. Paul's, had returned to Fat Fanny's. Most likely. Where else would she go?

"I thought to send Sir Robert to Scotland," Walsingham explained, directing his comment to Burghley.

"I disagree. Robert can continue to investigate the conspiracy in London." Burghley turned from Walsingham to Robin. "You did say those Scots you met at St. Paul's might be involved, did you not?"

"Aye. But I've no proof. 'Tis only a feeling."

"Agents often have to go on their instincts," Walsingham assured him.

Burghley added, "You've unearthed a few slugs, sir, and I think their trails ought to be followed. You may always hie up to Scotland later."

He could hie over to Fat Fanny's meanwhile. Perhaps Lady knew more about the incident at the stew than Flea assumed.

"I can do that, my lord," Robin assured the treasurer. As he rose from his chair, he asked, "Are we finished, or is there more we need to discuss?"

"Nay, go," Burghley ordered, waving his arm dismissively. "It must be nigh on midnight."

"Then I bid you good eve." Robin bowed politely before quitting the chamber.

Outdoors, he strolled the Strand, intending to take the bridge to Southwark. He thought about his assignment, feeling his frustration rise at having so little to go on: a short-statured Scot who indulged in cheap bawds; a missive from a "Loyal Knighthood" that implied something sinister; a tale about a scrap of tartan; and his own inklings regarding the Scots he had met at St. Paul's.

St. Paul's . . . Flea . . . Lady. The events of earlier that day whirled in Robin's mind. Damnation, the wench had looked every bit the lady, garbed to trick the foolish young men at the church. Anyone as beautiful as she should have aspired to being a courtesan, not settled for being a bawd in a low-class brothel. Better, she should be some rich man's mistress. It was unfortunate he was neither rich nor interested in taking a mistress, at least a mistress he would feel compelled to support.

The night air around him teemed with voices, the clamor of carriage wheels, and the clatter of horses' hooves. Lost in his thoughts, Robin had been indifferent to the noise until all three distinctive sounds crescendoed when a coach neared and a female voice called, "Robin? Robin, is that you?"

He stopped and looked up. "Olivia! How is the widow Crane this evening?"

"You, better than any man in London, should know." The youthful, raven-haired matron smiled seductively, revealing all her even, white teeth. "But perhaps you shouldn't, since you've left me to find my own amusements so often of late."

"And where did you amuse yourself this eve, Olivia?"

"The theatre and a late supper with friends." She raised one delicate eyebrow that arched like a raven's wing, and leaned forward so that her bosom plumped like ripe melons above the stiff bodice of her gown. "Mayhap I should have invited one of my friends home to spend the rest of the night with me. But as I did not, 'tis fortunate I spotted you walking alone." She paused and considered Robin thoughtfully. "Are you done with whatever business kept you from me tonight?"

He smiled. "Aye, I'm done."

"Then perhaps you would like to join me to make the most of the time we've left this eve."

Going to bed with Lady—with *Olivia*—was, he decided, just what he needed.

"Aye, perhaps I would." Robin doffed his plumed hat with a rakish smile and then climbed into the conveyance beside Olivia.

Lady could wait, he told himself. He had work to do in the morn, and right now, he deserved to indulge in a bit of mischief.

Four

Lady was just getting good at enduring life in the Knight's Ward when she was ousted from it. During the time she'd been an inmate at the Counter, she had learned whom to be wary of, whom to be cordial to, and whom to trust. There was only one person she trusted, and that was Abby. Following her advice about everything had proved advantageous. And eating sparingly, Lady had made her coins last.

Yet those coins were not like the biblical fishes and loaves; so finally, her money was spent. Though Lady told no one, not even Abby, the keeper took note after several days of her foregoing food. He questioned her, she answered, and without any ceremony, the guard tossed Lady out of purgatory into hell.

Once, years before, she had been to Bedlam to see the lunatics. She'd attended with cousins, in from Bristol, who wished to see what they'd heard of. They enjoyed it immensely, her cousins had, as they participated in taunting the madmen chained just beyond their reach. But it had sickened Lady. She'd had no desire to visit the asylum in the first place, and she had determined never to return.

Stepping down from the Knight's Ward into the Hole proved, however, to be a return to Bedlam. Only instead of being an onlooker, she was the lunatic, and instead of the spectators being out of reach, these had full access to her.

No sooner had the guard disappeared through the far door than someone grabbed Lady's arms and ankles. Though she kicked and flailed, her attackers managed to put her up against a wall and hold her there, face pressed into the stones. She screamed, and someone grabbed her hair, rapping her forehead hard against the wall so that the pain was blinding and she almost lost consciousness. Certainly, she stopped struggling. When they were finished with her, she was naked except for her smock.

Crumpling to the slimy floor, she cowered with her head in her hands and drew her knees up to her chest. Lady knew there was no point in trying to get her clothes back. She knew there was no point in registering a complaint. There was even no point in kicking off the rat she felt scampering over her toes.

Soon enough, this would all be over. She would be dead.

Lady didn't die. She could feel herself growing weaker as time passed, but she hung on, malingering in spite of her desire to be freed, at least in spirit. At night she shivered, blanketless, on the wooden floor that served as the Hole's communal bed. Or she sat with her dizzy head lolling, her back propped against the wall, while her empty stomach seized and shrank. Occasionally she attempted to eat a crust of moldy bread, the only food provided, and to drink a sip of scummy water from the bucket near the slops. But it seemed easier to eat nothing, drink nothing. Besides, she did not wish to thwart the death she felt creeping up on her.

"Visitor! Visitor comin' in!" the guard announced one

day. Lady had no idea what day or even which month. She was even fuzzy on the year. Not that she had any interest in a visitor. She had no one to aid her, so she didn't make the effort to lift her head off her arms, which rested on her knees. In fact, the guard's announcement barely penetrated the drowsy dream state she preferred to dwell in.

"Visitor!" he declared again as the door creaked open and closed immediately with an echoing thud.

"Lady! Lady, are you here?"

Involuntarily, her head snapped up, and she peered through the gloom at the fellow wading through the pack of prisoners. She thought she must be dreaming. No one in this place knew what she was called. She could not have heard correctly.

"Lady! I know you're here. Answer me!"

She blinked, attempting to recognize the cove crouching to peer into the faces of her pathetic compatriots. Their bodies obscured him; she did not know who he was. Though Lady kept silent, she continued to watch as he suddenly lunged and dragged a prone woman upward—a woman in a striped dress or a dirty ruff, she supposed.

"Where is she, mort?" the cuffin demanded, shaking the woman's shoulders. She was, Lady saw, wearing her own striped dress. It fit her because they were about the same height, which made the female prisoner a head taller than the youth before her.

"Flea?" Lady's voice was barely audible even to her own ears. It had been a long, long time since she had spoken aloud. "Flea, 'sthat you?"

"Lady? Lady!" Flea let go of the woman, shoving her aside and literally jumping over bodies lying in his path as he scrambled toward her. He dropped to his knees and cried, "God in heaven, Lady, what've they done t' you?"

"Took my clothes." She giggled like a drunk. "I thought you were in a place such as this. Newgate or—"

"I got off. Never went in, really. I'll explain it all t' you later." Flea sat on the floor, crossed his legs, and opened a bundle he had been carrying. "Here. Drink this."

He handed her a blackjack, but he had to help Lady raise it to her lips. The ale was good, so good! It dribbled down her chin.

"Not so much so fast now, dearling," he cautioned. "You'll make yourself sick. Got t' eat somethin', Lady. Little bites, but eat."

He broke off a piece of cheese, and she nibbled it like a mouse. Then a piece of bread—fresh bread, soft bread, smeared with butter—and some ham.

Just a taste of the ham increased Lady's thirst. Greedily, she sucked down more ale.

"Ho, there! Be careful, Lady. You don't want t' be bringin' back up what you just got down, now, do you?"

The edibles Flea had spread out on the cloth before her looked like a feast. But already Lady felt a bit nauseous. Shaking her head, she waved the food away until he wrapped it up again.

"How—how did you find me?"

"'Twasn't easy. I never thought you'd been pinched by the sheriff, Lady, so it seemed you disappeared, like a puff o' smoke. But once I suspected you'd got yourself arrested, I went t' Southwark's upright man, the ruffler, Octavian. He put the word out 'til he learned you be here, in the Counter."

Flea had gone to the top criminal in the borough, and Octavian had gone through channels, all informal connections far more efficient than proper ones. London's outlaws were quite well organized. They took pride in it.

Lady tried to nod in understanding, but her head drooped to her chest. Sleep came so easily these days, despite the hard discomforts.

"Don't be noddin' off," Flea warned sharply, lifting her chin. When she met his eyes, he explained, "Octavian did some investigatin', an' we found you're not bound for trial. If you was, we'd have seen about payin' a fine or somethin', an' gettin' you free. But you're—you're not." He looked down at the stained, splintered floor dejectedly.

Lady touched his shoulder. "Don't worry, Flea. 'Tisn't your fault."

"It is!" He scowled darkly as he looked up at her again. "I dragged you into nip-an'-foistin', cony-catchin', an' all that, didn't I?"

"Nay. You taught me what I wanted to know, what I needed to know. I was starving when you first met me."

"And you're—"

"Dying. I know. You can say it, Flea. Doesn't disturb me anymore."

"Shit!" He leaped to his feet. "I'm goin' t' get you out, Lady. By God, I am!"

"You are. I know you are," she agreed softly, quite sure he would not.

"You wait."

"I'm not going anywhere."

"Don't die on me!" He hunkered down again and pushed the satchel of food into her lap. "Keep that safe. Take this, too." He handed her a stick that looked as though it once had been a spoon handle. Now it had a very sharp tip. "I didn't want to risk tryin' t' bring you a knife, Lady. This'll work just as well. Don't let anyone take your food. Promise?"

She nodded.

"Blast it all! Lady, I searched your room for the money I knew you were savin' t' get yerself out o' the city. 'Tis gone. Fanny took it, I'm sure. An' I been havin' no luck at me trade without you, or I'd have brought money for garnishes. Still, if I'd known you were nearly naked, I'd have pinched some duds for you. I will, before I come next time. An' you shan't be here long enough to need garnishes. This food'll last you, I vow."

Again, Lady nodded.

Flea leaned toward her and without hesitation kissed her cheek. "You have t' trust me, Lady. I let you down before, but I shan't again. Believe that, dearlin'."

"I do," she lied, glad she'd had a word and a kiss from her only friend in the world before she passed on.

"Robin? Robin, dear, wake up."

He wasn't asleep, but he pretended to be. He could feel Olivia crouched above him, her long, silken hair tickling his naked chest as her lips tickled the flesh below his belly. Next she'd have him in her mouth, trying to force him to salute the day. But despite the woman's expert ministrations, Robin didn't think she would be able to make all of him rise upon command. He was going to linger here in bed awhile and do nothing save ponder his current dilemma.

Robin knew he had to accomplish something soon, or he would find himself in serious disfavor with his superiors. Yet his current assignment was proving the most difficult he'd faced since being recruited to be a secret agent for the Crown. He had no firm leads to follow up, no solid clues, only unfounded suspicions. Though Walsingham put some store in intuition, neither he nor Burghley would be satisfied much longer without material evidence. Others might also be trying to ferret out both the conspiracy and the conspirators, but Robin felt the most responsible because he had been the first assigned to the case. As well, Robin could never forgive himself if something untoward befell the queen due to his own incompetence.

Suddenly, he rued his youthful stand against his sire, who had urged his only son to follow in his footsteps and become an instructor at Gray's Inn. At the moment, a teaching position seemed far more appealing than it had been when Robin turned his back on such a goal to seek adventure instead.

Yet there was no efficacy in regretting now the choices of the past. He had a job to do, a vital, critical job, and if he intended to lie about in bed, he should only be using the time thinking of ways to accomplish his task. Yet Robin couldn't keep his mind on the Scottish intrigue, and it wasn't Olivia's tongue distracting him. Instead, a pale, heart-shaped face with incredibly large, impossibly blue eyes crowded his thoughts. Days would pass without him thinking of the wench named Lady. Then, for no apparent reason, he would catch himself recalling their fleeting encounters. At this very moment, Robin found himself wondering where she had gone. He hadn't caught a glimpse of her those times he'd watched Fanny's stew. Had Flea convinced his friend to take up a legitimate trade or to toil in service, as Robin had suggested? He doubted it, but he hoped.

"Ummmm," Olivia crooned, deep in her throat. It was the most sound she could manage.

The woman was obviously giving him her best erotic

efforts; she deserved a suitably potent male response. To that end, Robin determined to set all other matters aside for a time, as he was accomplishing nothing by ignoring Olivia. Squeezing his eyes more tightly shut, he attempted to concentrate on the beauty whose bed he presently shared.

The old men, Burghley and Walsingham, fled Robin's mind easily. So did the trio of suspicious Scots. But not that face, that heart-shaped face with the pair of azure eyes. Nay, it continued to linger before his mind's eye.

Robin again attempted to dispel the image, this time by peeking surreptitiously at Olivia. He hoped the view would both chase away his errant thoughts of Lady and arouse his ardor as well.

Seeing dark silken tresses cascading over his loins should have whetted his masculine appetite, but it failed. Olivia's skilled mouth, tongue, and fingers should have had him on fire, but he felt cold. It was that damnable wench he barely knew keeping him from his pleasure! Damn. If only he might see Lady again, he would pay her price, swive her, and think of her no more—most certainly not while a ravishing, worldly widow sought to pleasure him in bed!

Meanwhile, however, his head remained filled with the girl's distracting image. Reaching down to touch Olivia's head, he begged softly, "Forgive me."

She released Robin and rolled onto her side. Swinging her mane of sable hair over her plump, pale shoulders, Olivia spared his thick but still limber shaft a glance. "Robin," she asked, "what ails you? You're always randy in the morning."

"Is it morning? Or is it past noon?"

"Does it matter? Robin, what is the problem?"

"Not you, I vow. 'Tis only that I am plagued by distractions."

"Work?"

"Aye," he admitted.

"You have things backward, then. I am supposed to distract you *from* your work. Besides, I presumed you had no pressing duties, since you've been so long in town. When you have a mission, doesn't the secretary or treasurer usually send you out of England?"

"Not every time, Olivia. Presently, there's a nasty situation here in London. Unfortunately, it's not been going well. And today, there is a meeting planned where I fear I'll be forced to admit my failure."

Robin swung his bare legs over the side of the bed and began pulling on fresh clothes.

"What are you doing, Robin?" Olivia complained with a frown. "Don't dress so quickly. You must wait for me."

He stopped putting on his waistcoat and looked at her blankly. "Why must I wait for you?"

"Sir Robert Moreton," she replied in a tone usually reserved for incompetent servants, "only last eve you asked to take me out to dinner today, and I accepted. I therefore presumed we had plans."

"I asked you to dine?" He glanced up curiously from the garter he had anchored to the top of his stockings.

"You did. I was looking forward to it."

"Oh, Olivia," Robin chided, "you could not have been looking forward to it for long, if I only invited you last night!" Satisfied with his garters, he plumped out his padded trunk hose before tugging on his shoes.

"Robin, that's not the point. You know quite well I'm leaving—"

"Are you sure I invited you for dinner, not supper this eve?" he asked with a scowl while shrugging on his doublet. "As I only just mentioned, I have a meeting scheduled with those ranking lords from the queen's Privy Council. Mayhap I meant to dine with you on the morrow."

"You did not!" Olivia threw a pillow at him. Robin dodged it. As he plucked his plumed hat from the seat of a chair and set it on his head, she continued, "I shan't be here—"

"You shall be here for me," he interrupted brusquely, planting a kiss on Olivia's cheek. "You'll have to forgive me for dashing off so quickly now, but duty calls. My work must precede my pleasure, and that you know. Don't you, my pet?"

He wasn't at all sure that she did. But as Olivia elected to say nothing, Robin took advantage of her silence and quickly departed, first from her bedchamber, then from her town house.

Later that day, Robin sat in Walsingham's office, but it was the Lord High Treasurer with him, not the secretary of state. Walsingham was ill. He had been unwell a great deal of late, and some thought he would never fully recover.

Burghley gripped the arms of his chair and sat straight, meeting Robin's gaze levelly. "Now tell me what you know."

He'd learned nothing more in the time between his departure from Olivia Crane's and his arrival at the meeting. "I can connect none of those three Scots with the clan MacKinney," Robin admitted. "All are permanent residents of London, two with families here. One's a baker, another owns a warehouse dockside, and the third is a smith. They all appear to be what they claim."

"You do not believe we should rule them out?"

"Nay. There's something amiss, my lord, something askew. Though they're friendly enough when I happen to join them at their weekly gatherings at St. Paul's, I'd not be surprised to learn they've initiated inquiries about me. I'm familiar with the land and the language of Scotland, so I can weave a good tale. But they're cautious—too cautious to be innocent."

Burghley cocked his head to one side. "You've nothing more?"

"There is something," Robin confided. "I followed Gowan, the baker, when he left his shop, and on two occasions saw him take receipt of a letter."

"And?"

"The whole business was queer, my lord. Last week and this, Gowan went to meet a coach in broad daylight. He was not furtive—donned his hat and cape, and set out on foot. I presumed he was meeting someone on the coach, once I saw where he headed. Both times a well-dressed gentleman emerged from the conveyance, though it was a different fellow in each instance. Instead of escorting the traveler somewhere, or taking him home, they did not even exchange a greeting. And both men, both times, passed a letter to Gowan, which he slipped inside his jerkin, slick as you please."

"Damnation! If only we knew what the missives contained!"

"Unfortunately, I'm not much of a pickpocket."

Burghley's gray eyebrows met above his nose. "Fortunately, we have had a bit of luck from another quarter, Moreton."

Robin tried not to scowl. Was someone else doing a better job than he?

"You'll recall that Walsingham was keen on sending

you to Scotland. When we decided you'd be put to better use here in London, Francis sent another agent, name of Dekker. Do you know James Dekker?"

Robin nodded. Another knight, another spy, in service to the Crown.

"He sent word that arrived from Edinburgh yestereve. The plot against England, as you surmised, does involve the MacKinneys. Their plan is to kill Her Majesty. Dekker believes they intend to slay the queen on her Accession Day."

Whistling beneath his breath, Robin said, "That's it, then. Even if we cannot foil the Scots' plans, we can at least protect Her Royal Highness."

"It will not be easily done." Burghley pursed his lips and shook his head. "You know how the queen is about her Accession Day. The tournaments, the spectacle. And we have no idea how the malcontents intend to do their wicked deed, with poison or pistol."

"She'll simply have to cancel the festivities."

"You're daft, Robert! She'll never do it. She would rather expose herself to assassination."

Queen Elizabeth was indeed that stubborn, and Robin knew it. "Then what do you propose?"

"We have time on our side. The seventeenth of November is many weeks away yet. If we can determine who the intended assassin will be and by what method he expects to slay her, we can watch him. If we delay 'til the last possible moment before apprehending the blackguard, we'll deny the other conspirators an opportunity to supplant him with a new man using different means."

"Very well."

"As Dekker is already in Edinburgh, he'll remain

there. You can continue with the leads you have here, especially Gowan and that lot."

"May I make a suggestion?"

"Certainly."

" 'Twould seem to me we must learn what's in those letters the Scottish baker has been receiving. If he's somehow tied to the MacKinneys and their plot, I'd stake my life that those letters are secret messages from his associates in Edinburgh."

"Aye. Are you suggesting we ransack his house and his shop?"

"Nay." Robin shook his head and leaned forward in his chair. "The missives were surely destroyed as soon as he learned the contents. And an official visit from the authorities would only alert him, and the others, that we're on to them."

"What do you propose?"

"If two messages or more have already come to London from Edinburgh by way of public coach, I'd wager others will follow. I should like the opportunity to waylay them en route."

Burghley arched his eyebrows. "You mean to rob coaches? Like a common highwayman?"

"I hope not to be considered common," Robin confessed as he straightened, allowing himself a smile. "But aye. That's what I wish to do."

"How would you know you had the right coaches? There's many traveling hither and yon, public and private both."

"My lord, of England's four true roads, only one leads south from Scotland. Because the other messengers traveled by public coach, I would limit my piracy to such conveyances. As for identifying those from Scotland, I'd not deign to begin practicing 'highway law' 'til I was much nearer the border. And should I be in any doubt, I can ask."

Burghley's pensive expression disappeared as he broke into a beaming smile. In fact, he grinned like a silly old fool.

"Damnation, Robert, you're quite correct! You can ask the passengers, 'From whence do you come?' And they, frightened witless, will surely tell you. Oh, this is a divine scheme. I wish I were young enough to join you on the road!"

They had a good laugh together, the old spy and the young one, both of them trying to ease the tension that came with protecting their queen's life. Burghley poured some claret, and they toasted to their pending success.

"I shall get word to Dekker about your plans to intercept messages carried by coach. If he gleans any information that may help you, he'll devise a way to see you get it."

" 'Tis an excellent idea, my lord."

Robin felt cheerier than he had in a while. The prospect of leaving the city, riding his horse, and wielding his sword instead of slinking about in narrow, shadowed lanes or playing the idle cavalier at St. Paul's appealed to him. Having nothing to detain him, when he left Burghley's company he proceeded directly to his apartments. There he changed into appropriate riding clothes and packed the belongings and the weapons he required to play the highwayman.

Before Robin could reach the stables and his steed, someone accosted him, grabbing his leg and hanging on like a mad monkey.

"Ho!" he exclaimed, seizing the lad by his shoulders and throwing him off. While he held the boy by his shirt, he recognized him with a start. "Flea? Are you daft?

You're damned lucky I didn't run you through! What are you doing, throwing yourself at me like I was a chicken you wanted to catch for your supper?"

"It—it's Lady."

Robin let him go. This was strange, too strange, Flea seeking him out this very day to speak of Lady when he himself had been thinking of her just a short time ago. One might assume his morning musings had been some sort of omen. Or that, perhaps, he and the wench were bound in some way, like a parent and child, close siblings, or . . . star-crossed lovers.

"What about her?" Robin demanded gruffly, gracing Flea with a scowl. "I presumed you'd passed along my earlier advice and that she took it, getting out of her various illegal trades. She's well, is she not?"

"Well!" The youth looked stricken. "By God, she's not! M'lord, she's in the Counter, an' she—she's dyin'!"

Robin stiffened, insisting, "She can't be."

"She is! The sheriff nabbed her that day you caught me at St. Paul's. She's been in the Hole ever since, and now, she's near to dyin'."

A lump that nearly choked him lodged in Robin's throat. More than a month had passed since that infamous day at St. Paul's. If she'd been imprisoned since then, he could easily believe Lady now hovered near death. Jesu! It amazed him she'd survived this long on stale crumbs and polluted water.

"Is she scheduled for trial?" he asked.

"Nay." Flea relayed the information Octavian had given him. "She has to be bought out, m'lord. I haven't enough white money, an' what Lady saved, Fanny took and spent already."

Robin swore under his breath. He glanced over Flea's head at the Whitehall stables, but he did not really consider riding out on the queen's business before taking care of Lady.

"Flea, take this." He handed the lad his bundle. "Go to the stables and ask for Niles. Tell him Sir Moreton sent you, have him keep my things, and—and tell him to have my steed ready to be saddled whenever I arrive. Here," he added, tossing Flea a half crown. "For your efforts."

"I don't want it. If you get Lady out o' the Hole, 'tis more reward than I deserve, Sir Robert."

"Keep it nonetheless. Do what I bid you, now. And, Flea: To you and Lady, and anyone else you know, I am simply Robin. Do you understand?" He cocked an eyebrow at the boy.

Flea nodded solemnly. "I understand. M'lord?"

"What is it?" Robin snapped, anxious to be off, to get that pretty, poor, pathetic wench out of the Counter's stinking Hole.

"Lady's got no clothes. The others stole 'em from her."

Naked and starving. This was not an image of Lady he desired to hold in his mind. "I'll see her decently covered before she leaves the gaol," Robin vowed. And finally, Flea went off in one direction, he in another.

There was no announcement of a visitor. The door to the Hole simply flew open, startling the occupants. Lady, in her usual spot against the wall, had regained a bit of strength with the victuals Flea had brought her. She almost rued her renewed energy, but, alert and mildly curious, she watched the activity as a tall man entered. She expected he was a new inmate, one headed through to the Master's Side, judging by the fellow's well-cut cape and hat. But then she noticed he carried a sword sheathed against his thigh—not even those prisoners quartered on the Master's Side were allowed weapons. And he paused, scanning the abruptly silenced occupants of the Hole.

Suddenly, Lady recognized him. She might have uttered his name, if she'd known it.

He said her name, and she heard it. His dark eyes came to rest on her face. Thrusting his head forward, one hand gripping the haft of his sword, the stranger marched straight toward her like a grounded archangel, kicking off and slapping away those who dared impede his progress. "Lady," he said again, softly, when he stood directly before her. "Oh, Lady, what have they done to you?"

She wept, tears streaming, warm and silent, down her dirty cheeks. Flea had instigated the stranger's appearance here, that much Lady instinctively knew. She couldn't fathom how, and she still had no idea who this man was or why Flea knew him well enough to ask a favor, a huge favor. Though relief and gratitude should have been her emotions, Lady felt only shame. Like all the other times she had met this handsome stranger face-to-face, she felt like running.

She had nowhere to run, and even if she had, her feet would not have carried her away. As it was, she wobbled when he helped her to stand.

"Can you raise your arms?" he whispered. "I need to slip this gown over your head."

Lady peered at the dress that materialized from within the folds of his cloak. It was a simple frock, used but clean. To her, it seemed as fine as a ball gown.

She held her hands above her head, and the stranger tugged the dress on, quickly lacing up the back so that Lady was, after all this time, entirely decent. "Shoes, too," he added, revealing a pair. It occurred to her he had pockets in his mantle lining, same as in the cloak she'd frequently worn.

"Good Lord," he muttered softly as he held Lady's hand so that she could slip her feet into the shoes. "I had thought this gown might be too small, but it hangs on you." He glanced at her feet. "The shoes?"

Silently, Lady raised one foot. The slipper flopped, caught only by her toes.

"We'll remedy that," he promised. "Now, come."

"You're taking me out of here?"

"Aye. Why? You didn't wish to stay?"

In another life, Lady would have returned his remark with a sneering retort. But now she shook her head as her eyes welled with tears.

"Come," he urged gently, escorting her toward the door to freedom with a hand placed easily on the small of her back, as though she were truly a lady and he, her beau.

Five

Robin found Lady so weak, he carried her through the city like a babe in swaddling. Suddenly, he realized he did not know where he would carry her to. He couldn't return her to Fat Fanny's. Knowing the Southwark madams' reputations, Fanny would set her to work again straight away, which would most certainly kill her, though confinement in the Hole had not. Nor could he take her to his own apartments in Whitehall. He had to leave London, and there'd be no one to care for her. Perhaps Olivia . . .

Without further consideration, Robin made his way directly to his lover's town house. Her footman ushered them inside and promptly went to collect his mistress. By the time Olivia appeared in the parlor, Robin had settled Lady in a chair, where she sat, looking dirty, delicate, but demure.

"Robin! What—who—?"

"Forgive our intrusion, Olivia," he begged, taking her elbow and backing her up to the doorway. "I have a tremendous favor to ask you."

"What is it? Who is that girl?"

"They call her Lady. I don't know her Christian name. In fact, I hardly know the wench at all." He thought frantically, wondering how much or how little to tell Olivia. "She's connected to my current assignment, and as you can see, she's rather the worse for wear. I hoped, dearest, that you could keep her awhile. See that she is bathed and properly attired, and that she gets bed rest and some regular meals. I realize it shall prove an inconvenience for you. But, truly, Olivia, I've no one else to turn to."

Olivia blinked her thick, black lashes. She glanced at Lady again before saying softly, but firmly, "Robin, you ne'er listen to a word I say, do you?"

This was not the response he had hoped for. "Of course, I do, Olivia," he countered.

"Nay, you do not. I am leaving for Paris in a few hours. 'Tis why we were to dine together earlier, to share a farewell meal. I got nothing from you by way of farewell today," she added pointedly, arching a plucked eyebrow.

Robin glanced down at his boots, understanding full well that Olivia referred to their aborted lovemaking this morn. She had every right to be miffed, especially since her accusation was sound. He ofttimes listened to her with only half an ear, and half of what he heard he forgot. Robin had critical matters on his mind—the life of the queen, for instance—which prevented him from paying much heed to Olivia's litany of social plans.

That was his excuse, but he dared not voice it. Instead, Robin opted for apology. "Aye, I'm afraid I forgot," he confessed. Then he gave Olivia a look that frequently prompted her to comply with any request he made—usually when they were in bed. And he boldly pressed forward by asking, "Are you sure Lady couldn't stay here whilst you're gone? I'm certain she'd be no bother to your servants."

"Robin, my servants are all taking a month's leave. The house will be closed and unoccupied by tomorrow evening. I'm sorry."

" 'Tisn't your fault. I shouldn't have come here, shouldn't have asked." Now Robin glanced at Lady and saw her chin resting on her chest. Either she attempted to be circumspect, or she'd succumbed to exhaustion or God-knew-what illness she might have contracted in that miserable gaol.

Robin turned back to Olivia. "Could you do whatever you're able before you depart? Food, clothes, and the like? I, too, must leave London. In fact, I should leave this very night. Meanwhile, I—"

He did not know what he could do meanwhile. Perhaps find someone, somewhere, who could take Lady in until she fully recovered from her recent ordeal.

"Of course I will. But Robin, we must have a serious talk upon my return to London. Things haven't been—"

"Thank you," Robin interrupted, so relieved he could have embraced Olivia and spun her around in the air. "I'll reimburse you for any expense you incur."

"You had better not take overlong," she warned. "Upon my leave, the house will be closed and locked. If the . . . girl . . . is still here, she'll be waiting for you on the stoop."

"I shan't dally, I vow." Robin pecked Olivia's smooth cheek and then walked back to Lady. He raised her head by touching his fingertips to her chin. When those huge blue eyes focused on his face, he explained, "Lady, this is Mistress Olivia Crane, a friend of mine. She's going to see you're cleaned up and have a good meal. I have business to attend to, but I'll return for you shortly. Do you understand?"

Mutely, Lady nodded. Relieved to be leaving her in capable hands, however briefly, Robin bid farewell to both women and headed back to Whitehall, wondering all the time what he would do next. Yet he never once asked himself why he felt compelled to do anything.

"Robin!" Flea called when he spied him approaching the Whitehall Castle. "Robin, did you find Lady? Did you get her out o' the gaol?"

"Aye, lad, I did. She's with a friend of mine at the moment, having a bath and a meal."

"Thank you, m'lord!" Dramatically, Flea dropped to his knees, grabbed Robin's calf, and pressed his brow to Robin's knee. "Thank you."

This being the second time today the urchin had captured his leg, Robin growled, "Get up," and shook his foot as though the boy were a small terrier who'd fallen in love with his shin.

"Where is it you've taken Lady off to? I'll have t' go an' fetch her."

Robin almost jumped up and clicked his heels together. Of course! The lad and Lady were friends, in fact, boon companions. Flea would take care of her. How quickly Robin found himself relieved of his unexpected burden, free again to ride out of the city, still on schedule.

But his feet remained firmly on the ground, and he inquired soberly, "Once you fetch her, where would you go?"

"Back t' Fanny's, o' course."

"Of course!" he repeated, irate. "Flea, you told me Fanny stole Lady's money. How could you return her to that woman's house now that she's free of the Hole?"

"Where else would I take her?" Flea asked belligerently. " 'Tis where we both live, Lady an' me."

"And where Lady works," Robin added angrily. "You know your aunt would have the wench plying her trade whilst she's flat on her back, instead of letting her lie in bed alone to recover."

"Lady's no bawd, I keep tellin' you!"

"Watch your tone with me," Robin warned, wagging a finger at the boy. "You may call me Robin as though we are somehow equals, but you know my true name and rank, and what I can do to you, if I so choose."

The reprimand silenced Flea, but he set his chin stubbornly. "She's no bawd," he muttered.

"Thus, there is no reason at all for her to return to that stew."

"Very well. Where's she goin' then?"

"With me," Robin announced before he had decided on it, before he had given the consequences proper consideration.

"But you live in Whitehall!" Flea exclaimed.

"I've no intention of taking her to live in the queen's palace, of that you can be sure. Nay, she's coming with me. I've business in the north country."

"I'm goin' with you."

"The hell you are!"

"Please, m'lord, reconsider," the lad begged. "If you've business, who's going t' look after Lady? She'll need lookin' after for some weeks yet, I'd imagine."

The little mite was correct, Robin realized. Dear God, what was he getting himself into? He—a knight in the queen's service, an agent for the Crown charged with a mission to prevent Elizabeth's assassination. Yet here he stood, on the Strand, resigned already to taking a young thief and a Southwark bawd, just out of prison, on a hard ride to the Scottish border.

If Walsingham or Burghley knew, he'd be relieved of his position and sent to Bedlam with all the other poor souls who'd lost their minds.

"Can you sit a horse?" Robin asked Flea, knowing

full well the boy could not, and knowing, too, he would insist he could.

"Aye."

"We'll get you a mount from the stables. But I'm warning you, Flea. If you fall off, you'll either walk or be left behind. So you'd best be telling me the truth!"

The knob in his throat lurched up and down as Flea swallowed visibly. If Robin's situation had not been so extreme, he might have chuckled.

Olivia Crane did as Robin asked of her. First a servant delivered Lady into a chamber fine enough to accommodate a guest of noble rank. Then she was given a tub filled with steaming, perfumed water. After she bathed, a tray straining under the weight of the food it carried was presented to her. Lady tried to do it justice; every morsel tasted delicious. But her stomach could hold very little, and, as drowsiness quickly overtook her, she crawled into the wide bed with its soft mattress and fragrant linens.

Olivia cut Lady's nap short. Opening her eyes to spy the woman beside the bed, Lady suddenly recognized her. In truth, Olivia had changed very little in the past decade, but Lady did not remark upon it. She merely sat up and bowed her head demurely.

Olivia smiled, tightlipped, and said, "I have here a dress from my footman's wife. She's about your size." She draped the gown at the foot of the bed. "My maid is almost finished altering the frock you were wearing upon arrival. She should have the seams taken in before Robin returns."

"Thank you, madam. You've been most kind."

"There's a new smock for you, too. Well, not new,

exactly, but clean and serviceable. You had no stockings, so here's a pair of my own I can spare. They're rather fine; have a care, or they'll be quickly ruined."

"I shall be careful."

"These boots." Olivia displayed the pair dangling from her fingers. "At a glance, 'twould seem our feet are near in size, so these should fit you. You're fortunate I didn't toss them out. I nearly did."

"Quite fortunate," Lady agreed. "Again, my thanks for your kindness."

"What I do, I do for Robin, whom I adore, despite his shortcomings." Olivia eyed Lady levelly. "Who are you, Lady?"

She didn't know how to reply. She certainly could not tell the woman the truth. If the widow Crane knew that years ago, she and her late husband used to attend suppers and musicales at Lady's home . . . If she knew Lady had been the little girl perched on the stairs, peeking at the handsomely garbed noblemen and gentlemen and their beautiful wives dancing and drinking . . . If she knew Lady made her living as a cony-catcher, or that she'd spent the last several weeks starving to death in the Counter . . .

One truth was as shocking as the other, so Lady would never admit to either. She repeated only what she'd heard earlier.

"I am of some importance to"—his name, overheard, came back to her—"Robin, because of his work. 'Tis in his interest I'm kept alive. Other than that, I'm naught, I am no one. Just a street mort."

She had purposely used common patois so that the woman would have no cause to suspect she came from better than she was or had endured worse than she deserved.

"You look as though you could use some more sleep," Olivia observed. "But since Robin should be coming for you shortly, I suggest you hurry and dress."

"Very well, I shall."

As Lady climbed off the bed, Olivia quit the room.

The dress, a deep forest green, fit perfectly. It was no lady's gown requiring hoops or sporting a ruff. The neckline had been cut square and low enough that the top few inches of the embroidered smock Olivia had given her peeped above the edge of the bodice. Olivia's cast-off stockings were decadently soft and sheer, and even her old boots fit Lady as though they'd been cobbled especially for her. The soles were solid and seamless instead of sporting holes! That notion made Lady chuckle. What a way she had come. A few years ago, she'd have settled for nothing less than the sort of costume Olivia wore today. Now she was pleased to look like a tavern maid.

Lady peered at her reflection in a looking glass. She still wore faded bruises on her cheek and a crumbling bit of scab on her forehead from that terrifying time when the other prisoners had pressed her face into the wall and stolen her dress. But despite her pale complexion and lackluster tresses, at least she was clean.

She did not style her hair. Lady had neither pins nor combs, so she merely ran her fingers through her golden mane, knowing the ends would curl when they dried completely.

A knock sounded at her door. "Aye?"

"Excuse me, ah"—the man beyond searched for an address—"mistress. You're wanted below in the salon."

"Thank you."

Certain Robin had returned, Lady yanked open the door. Then she hesitated. When she made her way down the stairs, she did so slowly.

Their eyes met before Olivia even noticed her because Robin stood facing the doorway when Lady entered the salon. She felt nervous and weak, but the way his dark eyes slid over her, like warm, scented oil drizzling down her skin, gave Lady a thrill. Her heart swelled with gratitude, not only because Robin had rescued her from the Hole, but because he made her feel feminine again.

"Lady," he said, though he remained standing beside Olivia. "You look remarkably recovered."

"I'm feeling much better, thanks to you and—and Mistress Crane."

"I'm always here to help," Olivia said wryly, turning to Lady but casting a sidelong glance at Robin. "Where are you off to?" she inquired of him.

"I'm not at liberty to say."

"Nay, you never are."

"I'm sorry. For everything," Robin told Olivia gently. "By the time you return from Paris, I should have a long tale to tell. Mayhap then you'll forgive me for my thoughtlessness."

Olivia's gaze met Robin's. "I already forgive you. But when I return to London, we must indeed have a long talk."

They were both headed out of the city very soon, Lady realized, yet they were not going anywhere together. But where was she going herself? If it was back to the streets, Robin did not need to escort her. Olivia had merely to open the door. So why . . . ?

"Your second dress is there." Olivia addressed Lady but slanted her chin toward a chair. Over the back lay the blue gown Robin had brought to the prison.

Lady snatched it up, holding it to her bosom. "Thank you." Her glance flicked between Olivia and Robin.

Both of them nodded. Then all three stood in a tableau.

Lady did not know what to say or do next, until Robin took her elbow and escorted her to the door.

"Have a safe journey, Olivia," he said, as a servant opened the door and stood aside. "I'll call on you when I return, to see if you're safe home again."

"I look forward to that."

Olivia presented her cheek, and Robin kissed it. Then he urged Lady out the door and up the lane.

Neither of them spoke at first, but Lady decided to precipitate his departure by saying, "You needn't walk me anywhere. I—I can just . . . go."

"Go where?"

She didn't know. She had no wish to return to Fat Fanny's place. That the witch had actually stolen her money . . . ! But she did need to cross the river and return to Southwark. Flea had to be there, somewhere.

"You shan't be returning to Fat Fanny's stew," Robin announced, as though he had read her thoughts.

"Nay. I think not."

"Have you any kin in the city?"

Lady shook her head. "They're . . . dead. I've no one now."

"I'm sorry."

"You've nothing to be sorry for!" she exclaimed, looking up at his profile. "I can't ever thank you for what you've done on my behalf. I've never known anyone so . . . kind."

"Kindness has little to do with what I've done," he returned gruffly.

Lady disbelieved it. The story he'd told Olivia, to spare herself embarrassment, was pure fantasy. She had nothing to do with his work. She had nothing to do with his friend, the little man whose duds Flea had stolen. She had nothing to do with Robin at all, except that she'd kept bumping into him when, by rights, they never should have met!

"In any event, I should be going. I can take care of myself."

Robin halted and turned to look down at her. "Can you?" he asked, sounding a bit skeptical.

Lady blushed. Of course, he wouldn't believe her capable of taking care of herself, considering the places he'd encountered her before. And even though she felt vastly better this evening than she had that morn, Lady still felt weak and wobbly. Perhaps she couldn't care for herself. For that reason, she needed to find Flea, and fast.

"What say you don't attempt to be on your own again quite so soon?" Robin suggested.

"I beg your pardon?"

"What say you come with me now?"

"Come . . . with you?" She couldn't fathom his meaning.

"Aye. Just accompany me a bit farther, if you don't mind."

Lady nodded and took another few steps. But abruptly, she stopped in her tracks. There, walking toward her and leading two horses behind him—one a regal-looking gelding and one a plump mare—came Flea! He was grinning sheepishly.

"Flea!" she exclaimed, running toward him. "I didn't know what had become of you, and I wasn't sure if I should ask! I suspected you had something to do with His Lordship's—"

"Robin, you may call me Robin," her rescuer interrupted.

Lady flashed him a quick, shy smile before turning

back to her friend. "I suspected you had something to do with Robin getting me out of prison, Flea. Did you?"

"Aye. Did I not promise I'd be gettin' you out?"

"But, how . . . ?" Lady turned from him to gaze up questioningly at Robin.

"Flea, here, tracked me down and demanded I get you released. What could I do, but what he ordered?"

The idea was outrageous, and it almost made Lady laugh. "I owe you both my thanks, then," she said. "But I shan't impose on you anymore. You must know there's little chance I can repay you in coin for the cost of my release. But if there's ever anything I can do for you, please . . ." She left off with a shrug.

"You can accompany me, since I'm set to leave London immediately."

Instinctively, Lady stiffened. Everything that had happened to her of late had been bizarre. But this man's suggestion—despite his many kindnesses to her—did not seem at all innocent. And though Lady led a sordid life, she remained innocent.

"I couldn't, sir. I live here in London." She said the words, but she didn't mean them. In truth, she'd give almost anything, risk almost anything, to leave the city. But dared she risk leaving here with Robin? She shook her head and muttered, "Nay, 'tis impossible."

"Aye, it is," he countered. "I fear I couldn't keep my mind on my work if I had to worry that you might be thrown into prison again whilst I was gone. As Flea, here, isn't inclined to let you out of his sight, he's coming along as well."

"I don't understand!"

"There's no time now for more explanations, Lady. The light's growing scarce, and I do wish to be out of the city before the gates close. Let's be off."

"Here. Give me that," Flea ordered, taking the extra gown Lady had been clutching.

As he stuffed it inside a pack roll on the mare's rump, she asked Robin, "How are we traveling?"

"There are two horses amongst the three of us. How do you think?"

"But Flea can't—"

"—ride?" Robin finished for her, giving the boy a smirk. "Yet he assured me he could, and a fine demonstration he gave coming over here from the stables."

"Flea?" Lady looked at him questioningly.

"Stow it," the youth ordered gruffly. "I'll make do."

"Indeed he will," Robin confirmed as he climbed onto the gelding and reached for Lady's hand. When she was seated behind the saddle, he continued, "For if the lad tumbles off that old nag's back, I won't be stopping to pick him up. I haven't time to nursemaid a novice. There's a lot of road between London and where I need be."

"Where is it you need be?"

"North. Near Scotland."

Scotland! Lady had never been more than a day's ride from London in her entire life. She imagined it would take a year to go the distance between here and Scotland.

It proved, indeed, a long, long ride from London to Scotland. As yet, they were not near the border, and the trio had been on the road for long days already. Frequently, as on this early morn, Lady had time to contemplate her fate and fret about her future.

She felt grateful to Robin. If he hadn't freed her from the Hole, no one would have. If he hadn't taken her away from the city, she'd never have fled—not since she'd been reduced to penury at the hands of Flea's aunt. Yet, why? Why had Robin spent his money on her freedom? Why had he imposed on Olivia Crane to see her fed and decently clothed? And after all that, why hadn't he sent her off with Flea to fend for themselves as they always had? Why had Robin insisted on taking them both along when he left on his long journey?

Lady wanted to accept Robin as an angel of mercy, a good man in a world of wicked scoundrels. She wished she could believe his heart shone as brightly as his molten brown eyes. But she'd lived too long among whores, thieves, and other criminals, both petty and vicious. She had learned the hard way that no one did anything without selfish motives. Robin surely had a secret purpose behind his acts of charity, and Lady could not help pondering what it might be.

She puzzled also over *who* he might be. When Robin first appeared at the stew that fateful evening, he looked as though he belonged in Southwark, with its sinister inhabitants and its vulgar entertainments. Yet he had a "friend" (his mistress, surely) who was wealthy, beautiful, and as much a lady as a titled woman. There was also the matter of his curious clothing, which either connoted no rank or position, or otherwise implied a full variety of stations. Who was this cove called Robin, with no surname, who garbed himself in everything from the simple raiment of a laborer to a courtier's fashionable attire?

The object of Lady's musings now lay not three feet from her, on the ground where he'd passed the night under the stars. He'd awakened when the first birds began chirping but had not opened his eyes. Still less than fully alert, Robin contemplated the wench who lay so near to him; he could hear her breathing.

To his relief, Lady's health had improved with every passing day. A hint of color now bloomed in her cheeks, and her eyes had a sparkle he'd never noticed before. She had a good appetite and ate so well, Robin noticed she had begun filling out her borrowed gown. Certainly he thought her breasts seemed plumper, where the creamy swells rose above the ruffle of white linen peeking out of her frock.

Damnation! Robin felt a part of his own anatomy plumping, twitching, lengthening. He rolled onto his side, his back toward Lady, and willed his stiffening staff to soften. If merely thinking about her attributes did this to him, how was he to endure more days with her riding on his horse's rump, her arms wrapped around his middle? With every jiggle and jounce, Lady's breasts bobbed against his back. Often, he felt her breath against his neck. And sometimes, when she dozed and fell against him, he felt her long hair tickling his cheek. It was almost more than a man could bear!

Yet why did he fancy a whore at all? Perhaps the enticement lay in the fact that she did not appear to be one, for she was modest, and her speech lacked the cant common among her kind. . . . Robin recalled Flea's insistence that Lady was an innocent, but he resisted. Even if, as the boy claimed, she worked as a servant in Fanny's stew, a common-born female with Lady's looks could not reach her age without having intimate knowledge of a man or two. Thus, Robin felt he had every right to expect her to give him ease. God knew he needed some time with a willing woman, or he would never have a decent night's sleep again. And Lady would never say nay if he approached her; she owed him her life. So why had he not already asked her to lie down for him?

Robin knew, and it rankled. As long as there remained the slim chance Flea had spoken true, that Lady wasn't a doxy but a dell, he would not seduce her. A queen's knight did not defile virgins. So until he knew the truth, Robin would play the courteous, if exhausted, gallant.

Squeezing his eyes more tightly shut against the intrusive daylight making its presence known—*bright as a watchman's lantern,* Robin thought in annoyance—he tried ignoring the persistent growth at his groin. It was easier thought than done.

Dear God, is there no relief for me?

Nay. Covering his eyes with one arm, Robin rolled onto his back and rued the fact it wasn't Olivia accompanying him on this journey. Not that he had expected any female companionship, but if he were forced to have some, better it be his lover than Lady. Damnation, he would never have to approach Olivia cautiously—she would seduce him! She would delight him, too, with her expertise. She would—

She wouldn't. Olivia Crane would have naught but complaints on a rough journey such as this. She'd whine about riding horseback, her bruised bottom and sore thighs. She'd detest the food, the dry bread, hard cheese, and game spitted without seasoning over a small fire each night. There'd be squawking about the cobwebs masking her face when she rode through them, and she'd blame him for the assortment of crawling, flying things that might bite or sting her, insisting he *do* something. As for bedding down on the ground, Olivia would never consider it. Robin would be trekking her disassembled bed by mule cart and reassembling it every eve. Aye, she would do that, if she accompanied him.

Lady did nothing of the sort. She never uttered a complaint about anything. Still, she didn't belong with him, most assuredly not on a rough ride through the wilderness. Yet she and Flea were here by his own doing. So Robin found himself not only with a wench but a boy to hold safe! Dear God, but Walsingham would throw a fit if he knew his agent's circumstances! Burghley, too. Hell, even Queen Elizabeth would shake her hennaed head, amazed by her man's foolishness.

Lady surreptitiously watched Robin through her lowered lashes, sensing he intended soon to rise. On impulse, she pushed herself to her feet and hurried over to the still-sleeping Flea. She nudged the youth with her toe, determined to wake him, to get him up and alone. She hoped to finally get some answers to her plaguey questions, and if Robin, as usual, rose before Flea, another day would pass with an opportunity lost.

"Get up, now," she ordered in a loud whisper. "Darkman's gone, the sun has risen. Come on. I know you hear me."

"Lady!" Flea complained.

"Up!"

He did as she urged, glancing at Robin's prone figure. "His Lordship—I mean, Robin—isn't awake yet. Why'd you wake me?"

"Because I wish to speak to you. Let's pick some berries."

"There won't be no berries this time o' year."

"Nuts, then. Will there be nuts?"

Flea frowned but trudged after Lady as she led the way through the forest. "What did you want t' ask me?"

he inquired warily as he paused near a tree to relieve himself.

"Why did Robin buy me out of the Counter? And how did you dare ask him? You did ask him, didn't you?"

"Aye."

"Explain, Flea. When he came to Fanny's that first night, neither of us knew him. Then, at St. Paul's, he grabbed us both, to aid the sheriff. What happened, Flea?"

As the youth approached her, his eyes danced. Lady knew he was thinking up a lie. "Don't bother concocting tales for me," she warned. "I want the truth."

Flea shrugged, resigned. "Robin didn't hand me over t' the authorities. An' Lady, we both truly believed you'd got away. But Robin did take me off to—to somewheres, an' he questioned me about the Scot an' the duds I pinched, an' all that."

"Who is he, Flea? What is he?"

"Just a cove, Lady, but a wealthy one, I suspect. 'Tis why, when Octavian learned you'd been arrested, I went t' him. Robin was the only one I knew who might have enough money t' spare t' buy your freedom."

Lady no more understood Robin's incentive now than she had before. "Why did he do it? I'm naught to him, and neither are you."

"He's a good man, I'm thinkin'. Don't you think so, too?"

She wasn't sure. She wanted him to be, but . . . "Why are we here, Flea, on the road with him? He's got business up north. We must be slowing him down—especially you. Damnation, but you fall off that palfrey half a dozen times a day! I'm surprised Robin has the patience to keep stopping, hauling you up, and setting you back in the saddle."

Flea colored brightly and pursed his lips. "I'm not that bad. I only fall off a few times every day."

Lady very nearly laughed, except Flea still hadn't answered her question. "Why are we here?" she demanded again.

"Because you had nowhere t' go. Robin wouldn't let me take you back to Fanny's."

That surprised her. "Why not?"

"Because he said—" Flea looked away. "He said you couldn't get well there. So he decided t' take you with him." He looked back at her and added, " 'Twould seem t' be a good decision Robin made, 'cause you're lookin' well, Lady."

With this, Lady had to agree. She knew if she had returned to Fat Fanny's, she'd have died in her tiny, cramped quarters. The effects of her weeks in the Hole would not have been the cause. With no strength to go on living in that wretched borough or to make her living on the streets, she would have given up and perished.

But there were no streets in the forest and meadows of England. Lady looked up through the trees at the lightening sky and felt the breeze tousle her unbound hair. Here, there was no stink, no filth, no danger. And it was here, not this particular spot but anywhere well away from London, that she had hoped to come ever since . . .

"What's he going to do with us, Flea?" Lady asked abruptly. "He can't take us in, like a couple of wards. What does he intend for us?"

"I don't know," he replied honestly. "Methinks that when his business is done an' he returns to London, so will we. By then, you'll be fully well, an' we'll be on our own again, as always."

Lady did not mind being on her own, at least with

Flea as her copesmate. But back in London? Not if she could help it.

She still felt bemused and . . . a little besotted. Clinging to Robin day after day as they rode tandem on his huge steed, feeling his taut muscles beneath her fingers and sometimes, when her hands slipped, that bulge in his leggings at the juncture of his thighs—it made Lady want to know Robin the way Nellie, Moll, and the other bawds at Fat Fanny's knew so many coves.

But as she could never act on her feelings, she could never let them show. Robin might still have dark motives for both rescuing and keeping her. If he did, he'd be her foe, no matter what favors he'd done her in the past. If he proved to have a pure heart, she would behave as ladylike as he behaved chivalrously. She could, indeed, behave as well as her name.

"We'd best get back," Lady announced. "I didn't see any nuts, did you?"

Flea shook his head as they made their way to the little clearing where Robin awaited them. "Lady, can you give me some tips for stayin' up on that beast I'm ridin'?"

"Don't fall asleep, for one thing," she advised. "Keep your back straight and your weight in your arse. And always hold your heels down in the stirrups."

"Since you know how t' ride, Lady, mayhap you ought t' ride alone. I could sit behind Robin an' hang on t' him."

She slanted a look at Flea. "I think not," she said firmly.

Six

The north of England was covered in leaves of gold and amber, which the brisk autumn wind fingered in the air and scattered across the land. At the back of his mind, Robin had always known he would come to just this place, for the inn here was an overnight stop for travelers heading south from Edinburgh. In addition, a house in the area would prove suitable not only for himself but for Flea and Lady, who needed sturdy shelter as the season turned toward colder months ahead. Despite being wrapped in his cloak, the girl clung to Robin for warmth while she rode behind him. And poor Flea shivered in his thin shirtsleeves even though the boy clutched a blanket around his shoulders.

"Will we be staying here?" Lady asked, lifting her cheek from his shoulder as Robin halted his steed in the pub's busy yard. She sounded as though he had brought her to a king's castle; the many nights sleeping abroad had apparently been hard on her, although she never complained.

"Nay. That is, we shan't be taking rooms."

"Oh."

"It's too early to stop for the day. But I think it is a good time to have a meal."

"We're goin' t' sup at this inn? Real victuals?" Flea asked excitedly as the mare halted beside his gelding.

Robin surmised the palfrey had merely followed and stopped near the larger horse. Then again, the lad appeared to have reined his placid animal in the correct direction and brought her to a stop. His riding skills were definitely improving—they could not have grown worse.

"Aye, we're going to eat at The Sutter's Sword, here," Robin assured him, watching as the youth dismounted without tumbling onto his backside. "Hurry, now. You're freezing."

Robin grabbed the mare's reins and handed them off to a stableboy, along with his gelding's. After requesting grain and water for the beasts, he tossed the lad enough coins to pay for the horses' sustenance with one or two coppers left over for the stableboy himself.

When the trio entered the public house, they found no tables free. Robin, Lady, and Flea waited in the taproom 'til others finished their meal. Then Flea lunged across the timbered room to claim their vacated table.

"If we hadn't found a spot t' sit soon," Flea declared, "methinks I'd have fainted from hunger."

Lady rolled her eyes before sharing a shy look with Robin. The blaze in the hearth at his back lit her hair with a golden light and made her eyes sparkle, as though they were faceted jewels. Her bones were too fine for a common street mort's, Robin found himself thinking. And then he thought how glad he was that Nature erred. Soon he'd have himself a mistress who looked like a princess. What man could ask for more?

"An' what'll it be fer you folks this fine day?" an aproned fellow inquired when he appeared at the table.

"Mulled wine all around," Robin declared. "What have you got in your kitchens?"

"Mutton stew. Best in these parts. Me brother raises

the sheep himself. Tenderest lamb you'll find. Melts in yer mouth, it does."

Robin glanced at his companions. "Is that all right with you?"

"Aye," they chorused.

"Mutton stew it is, then."

When their meals came, Robin watched Lady clean her bowl and devour a chunk of bread and butter that would have been too much for his own stomach to hold. He hadn't thought he'd been starving the girl. "Would you like something more?" he asked her.

"Nay. I—I'm full up, thank you."

"You're never full up, Lady!" Flea protested. Leaning across the table, he confided to Robin, "This wench is always ready to eat. 'Twas only after . . . her trouble . . . that she couldn't stuff as much down her gullet as she usually does." Flea straightened and turned to Lady beside him. "You'd think she'd be platter-faced and jigglin' all over with what she eats in a day."

Lady whacked Flea's arm, and he howled. Her cheeks flamed bright crimson when she faced Robin again, and she looked down, not at him.

"If you're hungry, eat," he advised.

"I'm not hungry. Not—not anymore."

"I think you are." Robin stood. "Whilst you wait for me, order something else. Another bowl of stew or a pastry."

"You're going somewhere?" She sounded surprised and looked suspicious.

"I have business, if you'll recall."

"Oh. Aye."

"Don't worry, Lady," Flea advised. "He shan't leave us. He'll be back, won't you, Robin?"

Robin hesitated a moment before replying, for he'd

glimpsed something in Lady's expression. Suddenly he understood that not only wouldn't she be surprised if he abandoned the pair of them, she rather wished he would.

Robin knew not what to make of this, but he assured Flea he would return. "Remain where you are, though," he warned. "I don't intend to be long, but whilst I'm away, you're to wait. Understand?"

Both the lad and the wench nodded solemnly. Robin strode off, locating the innkeeper, and paid for their meals. He inquired about the frequency of coach stops, making note of the days those from Edinburgh or Glasgow brought their passengers to spend the night. Then he went out and retrieved his horse, riding off with the hope of securing a particular hunting lodge where they all might reside until the time came to return to London.

Meanwhile, Flea craned his neck, looking around at the press of people crowded into the public rooms. "Don't you think it's queer, so many people here in the middle o' the day?" he asked Lady. "This can't be usual. There must be somethin' happenin' round about. A hangin' or somethin'."

Before she could respond, Flea hailed a cove standing nearby. "Is there some entertainment in these parts?" he inquired.

"Aye, in Briarwick," the man replied. " 'Tis the fall festival."

"And where is Briarwick?"

"Just up the road a few miles."

Grinning, Flea turned back to Lady. "Did you hear? A fair! Let's go, Lady!"

She considered the suggestion for a moment. If they slipped away, they would not be beholden to Robin anymore. And they could stay, far up north here, away from London, and learn to make their way without stealing from innocent folk. More important, if Robin had plans for them, plans they wouldn't care for, they'd no longer be around for him to implement them.

Still, Lady asked, "Do you think we should, Flea? Robin told us to wait here, and we agreed."

"We'll be back long before he returns, I swear we will."

She knew Flea had nothing to base that prediction on, but his enthusiasm proved infectious. "Very well," she agreed, not really so certain she intended to return to The Sutter's Sword at all.

Bubbling with excitement, Flea chattered all the way to town. They took the palfrey at his insistence, to make better time, so Lady sat in the saddle while Flea, behind, clung to her waist. The horse's jogging rhythm immediately renewed sensations Lady had tried to ignore when riding spread-legged on the gelding's hard, muscled rump. She even sat more surely, nudging the mare into a faster pace, while thoughts of Robin—wispy, smoky thoughts Lady couldn't quite define—spun sensuously in her head.

She was glad to reach Briarwick, and happier still to dismount and tether the horse to a slim tree trunk on the edge of town. A bit weak-kneed, Lady strolled the village that today seemed a bustling metropolis, mobbed with people and crammed with tents and stalls that augmented the usual shops.

"We found ourselves a treasure," Flea declared. "Me fingers are itchin' already. Thank the Almighty I happened t' bring me horn thumb along." Discreetly, he displayed the device.

"We do need warmer clothing," Lady agreed. "We can shave a cloak or two."

"We need white money, too! A bit o' nip-an'-foistin' won't hurt."

"We'll see."

The wind gusted, leaves rattled across their shoes, and Flea shivered exaggeratedly. "Let's do a bit of shavin'. There's a booth selling shawls. Would you like a shawl, Lady?"

It had gone against his better judgment to leave Flea and Lady on their own. Robin sensed the wench's unease, and he knew the lad would leap at the opportunity to catch some conies, if Flea heard about the fair. Yet Robin had no choice but to secure permission to use the old hunting lodge he recalled from his youth, so he'd visited Briarwick's vicar, father of his old schoolmate. He also bought supplies to sustain his counterfeit family during their sojourn there.

Thus it was that Robin not only now had a key to the lodge, he had two sacks, large and cumbersome, and no palfrey to use as a packhorse. With no other option, Robin trudged to his steed like a miner carrying sacks of coal on his back, and hoisted a bag over the animal's hindquarters. Lashing one in place, he tied the second to it. The tall gelding resented the awkward load; to convey his displeasure, he cow-kicked, shook his mane, and snorted.

"Behave!" Robin warned the beast, threatening him with his fist. The kicking ceased, and the snorting mellowed to a nicker. "I can see young Flea will be walking to the cottage. The poor little mare shall have to do the peasant work of carrying our supplies. Such labor's beneath you, eh?"

Robin stroked the steed's glossy mane. As he did, he

looked out over the village and the milling crowd, and paused a moment to appreciate the music, laughter, and tantalizing aromas that tickled his nose. It was a pity he couldn't bring Lady and Flea around to enjoy the fair. But he had no time for dawdling. Queen Elizabeth's life might depend on what he learned once he began his ruse.

A flash caught his eye. Nothing bright, but something familiar. Narrowing his gaze, Robin spied Lady, still wearing his mantle. Damnation! After all he had done for them, they disobeyed him to attend the fair with only one purpose in mind—their damnable thieving!

Robin strode toward Lady, his steps so long and sure he did not have to maneuver around anyone—they saw him coming and made way. Grabbing her shoulders, he spun her about. "What are you doing here? You're supposed to be at the inn. And where's Flea?"

"Over here."

Robin's eyes leapt to the boy. Standing behind Lady, the youth sported a burgundy-hued cloak and a jaunty green hat with a feather.

"Where did you get *that?*" He pointed at the cloak. "Did you shave it from one of the merchants?"

"Nay!" Flea did his best to look injured. "I paid good money for it. 'Tis not even new, Robin."

"You have money?" Releasing Lady, Robin stood between her and the lad. He glowered at Flea.

"Aye. Well, nay. Not anymore, m'lord. Ah, Robin. I spent it, see, on these new duds. 'Tis why we come t' the fair. I been cold, you see, an' Lady needed a cloak o' her own, too."

Robin turned to the wench again. She had half turned away from him, and between her downcast eyes and the set of her shoulders, she looked thoroughly guilty. "Lady?" he said tightly.

She jumped and whirled. The edge of Robin's cape opened to reveal a glimpse of what she wore beneath it.

"What's this?" He grabbed both edges of the drab, woolen cloak and spread them wide. Under that oversized garment lay a rust-colored lady's mantle. "And this?" he continued, spying beneath that cape a dark blue knitted shawl.

"Nothing!" Lady stepped back, clutching closed the edges of the outer cloak. She had gloves on now, gloves she hadn't been wearing when they left London.

"Something," he hissed, taking her arm in one hand, Flea's in the other, and dragging them off. "You've been stealing, haven't you? Else why are you hiding your new possessions beneath the wealth of my cloak?"

"Nay!" Flea insisted as he stumbled alongside Robin. "I'm not hidin' my hat an' cape, am I, m'lord? I tol' you, I had coin. I spent it on me an' Lady, so you wouldn't feel you had to. You done enough for us, Robin. But we were cold."

Halting abruptly, he considered the boy speculatively. Then Robin asked Lady, "Is this true? On your mother's grave, is what Flea says true?"

Her head snapped up. For an instant, Robin saw a film of tears soften the light in her eyes. Then she dashed at her lashes with the backs of her gloved hands, and when she blinked at him, her gaze looked brittle as cut glass. "I would think you've an idea of what Flea's word is worth," she said crisply.

"Lady!" Flea gasped. "I surely did buy your things with good coin."

"Coins we picked from people's pockets." Her glance flicked from Flea back to Robin. "You oughtn't be surprised. You know what we are, what we do."

Robin clenched his hands into fists. "Quite right. I

know what you are, what you do. But you shan't break the law if it might bring me notice, do you understand?"

Lady's eyes narrowed. "Why? Are you hiding from someone? Mayhap a wife?"

"I have no wife!" he shouted so loudly, people passing turned to stare at Robin curiously. Then, more softly as he leaned down toward Lady, he added, "If I had a wife, I would not have two thieving children in my care."

"I'm not a child!" she protested.

With a narrowed gaze of his own, he assured her, "I know that about you, too."

Grabbing Flea's shoulder and pulling him closer, Robin demanded, "Where is the mare?"

"Tethered there, near the gates."

"Get her and tie her up beside my mount." He pointed, indicating where he had left the gelding. "You'd best be there when I arrive."

"Aye, m'lord." Flea nodded and scampered off.

Taking Lady's arm, holding it so tight Robin thought he might bruise her and then decided he didn't care, Robin forced the wench to point out the people and peddlers they'd pinched money and merchandise from. Discreetly, Robin compensated them all, leaving coins where they would discover them.

By the time they rejoined Flea, Robin's temper had cooled a bit. He no longer held Lady's arm. But he said to the boy, "Damned fortunate for you that the palfrey remains in our possession. Else you'd have to carry this load." He began transferring the heavy cloth sacks from the gelding to the mare.

"Forgive me, Robin. I—I swear I shan't disobey you again. We meant no harm, Lady an' me."

"Stow it," he grumbled. "You'll pay for your sins by walking."

"That's fine, Robin," Flea assured him eagerly. "I don't mind walkin' at all. Prefer it, actually, t' ridin'."

"We've a fair piece to travel yet," Robin announced as they anchored the heavy sacks to the palfrey's saddle. "We'll see how much your feet prefer walking by the time we arrive at our destination."

Without a word, Robin reclaimed his mottled gray-and-brown woolen mantle from Lady, settled it on his own shoulders, and climbed onto his mount. When he looked around for her, he discovered the wench hanging back.

"I'll walk with Flea," she informed him.

Robin felt half tempted to let her. But he hadn't saved her from death to let her kill herself now. "Get up," he ordered.

She shook her head, sorely trying Robin's patience. "Get up behind me," he ordered again, holding out his hand to assist her.

She continued to balk, though she gave no other sign of resistance. Robin pressed his point by cocking an eyebrow at her. Suddenly she came forward, grabbed his hand, slipped a toe into the stirrup he'd left unoccupied, and swung herself up. Yet all the way to the little house in the woods, she did not touch him. Not only did Lady never wrap her arms around Robin's middle, he never felt a whisper of cloth graze his back.

Part of him hoped the little tart would fall off, bumping her bottom hard on the ground. But another part of him felt amazed she could stay seated, with naught but balance keeping her on his horse's hindquarters. If Robin hadn't known better, he would have presumed she could ride.

Seven

Lady had wanted to cling to Robin, and it would have been so easy. But she fought her emotions because logically, something seemed amiss, even ominous. Since Robin had been so furious with her and Flea, it made no sense that he had insisted they remain together. So until Lady knew his reasons, she couldn't trust him. And instead of cozying up to him and finding solace in his warmth and strength, she held herself rigid during this last leg of their journey. The price she paid was stiff limbs and a sore back from the effort of keeping her distance.

Yet Lady didn't regret her caution, as Robin began showing another, more damning, side of himself. Casually—ruthlessly—he left Flea after turning his mount off the main road. She felt sure Robin understood Flea could not survive without them. The lad was quick in the streets of London, but alone in a forest? Lady doubted her friend could make it though more than a pair of nights. And if he succumbed to the dangers of the wild or exposure to the cold, it would be Robin who'd have killed him.

Her anger rising and her qualms unabated, Lady promptly slid off the gelding's rump without any assistance the moment Robin halted the beast before a modest stone-and-timber dwelling nestled in a grassy clearing. While she scanned the barely discernible path they had taken deep into the forest, praying to catch a glimpse of Flea trailing behind them, Robin also dismounted. Lady heard him muttering, more to himself than to her.

" 'Tisn't as I remembered it," he said. "Smaller by half, but it shall do."

She watched him walk up to the portal, use an iron key to unlock it, and push the door open while the rusty iron hinges squawked in protest. "Come inside," he beckoned her.

Another furtive, backward glance revealed to Lady nothing but foliage, which had closed in behind them like water flooding a gorge. With a shiver of misgiving, she knew she had no choice but to obey Robin's order.

Lady did not speak. She stood in the center of the darkened room, tensely awaiting Robin's next move.

He ignored her and began unlatching the window shutters, flinging them open. They banged against the walls, and she flinched at every sound. Now that the windows were uncovered, though, they allowed in shafts of orange late-day sunshine. Dust swirled, and Lady sneezed.

"Bless you," Robin said offhandedly, surprising Lady with his benediction as he strode across the wooden floor and sent up even more dust. "I fear this place hasn't been cleaned for ages."

The cottage certainly needed housekeeping, but it was merely neglected, not in ruin. The room in which they stood was ample, and the furnishings looked sturdy and comfortable.

Lady did not voice her observations. She wondered if the worst, for her, was presently to come. She couldn't imagine what the worst might be. After all, if Robin had intended to kill her, he wouldn't have saved her from the gaol; if he'd intended to force himself on her, he could have done that any night along the road. But except for the briefest of moments, Lady had never before found herself alone with Robin. Their proximity, their seclusion, filled her with anxiety. She knew a woman alone with a man could only be vulnerable and often the victim of masculine rage.

Robin, however, continued to ignore Lady as he focused his attention on two doors that led to other rooms. He entered the second of them, and while he disappeared from sight, Lady peered outside, hoping to see Flea and the pack-laden palfrey.

She didn't.

"Damn!"

The exclamation followed a loud crash that made Lady jump. Curious and dreadful, she peeked into the chamber where Robin had gone.

Under other circumstances, she would have giggled. Robin sat spread-legged on a tilting mattress. The large bed frame beneath it had collapsed at the foot, sending him sliding nearly to the floor and leaving him looking rather silly.

"Are you . . . all right?"

Robin eased himself off the listing bed and confessed, "I'm fine. The bed itself looked fine as well, a moment ago. No holes in the mattress or nests in the straw. I never considered the legs would give way. Let's see how the others fare."

Robin strode past Lady with barely a glance and entered the remaining bedchamber. Again, she followed and watched him as he examined three narrow cots. Yanking the mattress off one, he cursed as straw fluttered out a gaping rent in its underside. When he repeated the effort with the next bed, mold, like brown smoke, billowed out. Lady sneezed and retreated, leaving Robin to his continued inspection as she sought unadulterated air and some explanation for his innocuous behavior.

Standing before a plank table positioned near the cold hearth, Lady used her fingers to collect a wispy spider web fluttering from the candelabra that sat atop it. She could hear Robin's boots pounding heavily and objects thumping and scraping across the bedchamber floor. Had the man merely been hiding his temper? Had he begun to give vent to it? When he returned to this room, would she feel the wrath those unfortunate but unfeeling objects in the far chamber were now enduring? If only Flea were here! Lady knew she would not feel so uneasy if he were. Despite her friend's slight stature, since they'd met that sad day he had found her weeping on a Cheapside corner, he had always protected her.

"Lady."

Startled by Robin's voice so nearby, she whirled to find him returned to the main room again. When she fluttered her lashes, he repeated her name more gruffly. "Lady."

Unable to control herself, she jumped backward at what she deemed his threatening tone and hit the edge of the table with the small of her back. The candleholder rocked; impulsively, she spun around to catch it. When she set it aright, she turned, apprehensively, to face Robin again.

Seeing Lady tremble did, in truth, renew Robin's annoyance with her. "Dear God!" he barked, coming forward. "What have I done to make you quake in my presence? You act as though I'm the villain here, as though I'd been busy snatching goods from unsuspecting merchants. I paid good English money for our provisions. I stole naught!"

"That's true. Flea and I are the cony-catchers, not you."

Robin arched an eyebrow as he stepped closer to the girl. "Then, why?

"Why—what?"

"There. That!" he complained when he reached out a hand and Lady leaned back over the table. "Why are you suddenly fearful of me?"

"I'm not," she lied, hoping if she said so, it would be true.

"You are," he insisted, coming as close to her as he was able—his shins pressed against hers. The contact made his loins quicken, but he ignored her ability to arouse him so easily.

Lady lay angled above the plank table with her head against the candleholder. "If I am," she told him, " 'tis with reason."

"What reason?" Robin demanded, looming over her and peering down into her face. She had the sweetest damned face. No rouge or powder, yet a flawless complexion and rosy lips nonetheless.

Lady determinedly returned Robin's gaze. "I may be a street mort," she dared inform him, "but I'm not so dull-witted to think you bought my freedom and took me hundreds of miles across England for no purpose. Yet I can think of no purpose that would be to my liking. Besides, today Flea and I gave you good cause to be done with us. Yet you kept us—at least, you have kept me." She swallowed, noting how scratchy her throat felt. "Flea, you deserted in the forest because we disobeyed you and went to the fair to shave a few things. Since you abandoned him for that small crime, I can only wonder what you intend for me, since I can't easily get away from you!"

Robin's eyes narrowed as he braced his hands on either side of Lady's shoulders. She sidled backward, her rump on the table now and her feet up off the floor. Robin insinuated himself between her knees and felt an urge to press his weight into her cushioning curves. "Do you wish to get away from me?" he inquired in a low voice.

Lady knew she should. Without her begging, he'd done for her what she had prayed for: gotten her out of the gaol and then out of the city. Since he had demanded no payment in any sort of tender, she owed him naught. So Lady should have wanted to be free of his company.

Yet his presence wasn't odious, by any means. Even now, with him looming threateningly above her, Lady felt less frightened by his virility than comforted by the safe haven in the shadow of his brawn. She also sensed something else altogether, something warm, tingling, and quite indefinable, blossoming in the pit of her own belly.

"Only—" she managed to mutter before swallowing hard again. "Only if you intend me harm."

"Harm?" Robin frowned. "Do you think I'm going to beat you?"

"You might." Lady blinked. "You've no doubt been thinking of it, savoring the anticipation of it, all the way from Briarwick to here. Why else did you bring me all the way to this isolated cottage instead of leaving me behind in the woods with Flea? Beating women is what most men are wont to do, especially when the woman's the cause of his distress. Some even do it when they're feeling fine. They do it for sport."

Robin's frown creased his brow more deeply. "What

sort of men do you know, Lady? I certainly take no pleasure in hurting the fairer sex."

"But you feel you've the right to hurt them, eh?" she asked, sure his last remark had implied that he did. The moment the words left her lips, she flinched, also sure her bold inquiry had invited a demonstration.

The candleholder toppled and fell to the floor with a startling clang. Seeing Lady cringe and collapse full against the table in an effort to avoid him, Robin felt an urge to hit something, though not the wench herself.

"Nay!" he countered loudly. "I've ne'er hit a woman or a child, nor even kicked a hound! Men don't prove their manhood by beating those smaller and weaker than themselves."

He thought how men did prove their manhood; he saw that they were in a position for him try prove it well. Robin tamped down the burgeoning urge to take his ease with the female sprawled beneath him.

"So you say," Lady returned. "But I don't know that for certain. I know naught about you, not even your surname."

Ignoring her subtle inquiry, he lifted one hand. Though Lady steeled herself for a blow, he gently stroked her cheek with his knuckles until, despite herself, she leaned into his hand. "Nor do I know yours," he reminded her softly.

That gave her pause. That, and his tender touching, and the flecks of gold in Robin's dark brown eyes.

"Lady's the only name . . . I've been called for a long while," she admitted.

"Robin's the only name I've heard on anyone's lips for a long while, too."

His own lips were full and moist and pink. Lady noticed that, now that they nearly skimmed her own. She didn't notice the purring quality to his voice or how near his face had come to hers, until he kissed her.

Lady did not kiss him back; she did not know how. But she didn't resist, either. It felt pleasant, his kiss . . . oh, so pleasant. She had never imagined a man's kiss could be thus. He opened his mouth a bit, and she soon felt his tongue tracing the outline of her mouth. That tingling sensation in her belly flared, hot as a sparking ember glowing orange in a grate.

The energy, the connection between them felt palpable. Yet Robin could not be sure of the girl. Though she seemed receptive to his advances, she returned naught. Lady, he reasoned, might still—unfoundedly—be fearful of him. Or she might, as the lad had claimed so vehemently, not be a bawd at all.

He decided to err on the side of caution and proceed slowly, attempting to interpret her unspoken signals.

Then Lady blasted Robin with a mute, but very definite, cue. Shoving him back, she sat upright.

"What about Flea?" Lady cried, determined not to be seduced or waylaid from her logic, which was born of experience and nurtured by her present unease. "You've all but killed him, Robin, by leaving him to wander in the forest! Why? Why would you do that to anyone, let alone a young cove who obviously admires you?"

Caught off guard by the force of her thrust, the vehemence of her accusation, and the apparent overriding concern for her friend, it took Robin a moment to recover. Yet he did, and just in time. "A young cove like the one out there?" he asked evenly.

Robin canted his head toward the open doorway. Curiously, Lady slipped off the table and stepped toward the threshold, peering outside again. For a moment, she felt hopeful. But then she suspected Robin toyed with her, for she spied no one beyond, not even a stranger.

"What cove?" she demanded, glancing back at him.

"That one." He stood beside her, nodding toward the trees.

With a huff, Lady looked once more into the grassy clearing surrounding the cottage and the woods that ringed the yard. Only Robin's horse stood there, munching his supper as he cropped the wild grass. Yet the underbrush in the forest crackled. Lady heard the sound despite the wind sloughing through the branches, and the noise drew her eye. In a moment, another horse became visible as the beast broke the tree line. There he was! Flea walked alongside the mare. Obviously, he'd discerned the overgrown path and found his way to the cottage!

"You're here!" Lady shouted, buoyant with relief as she raced to her friend.

"Don't slobber on me, Lady. I'm not a little lad," Flea groused when she hugged him.

"That's debatable," Robin commented from the cottage doorway.

Flea straightened his narrow shoulders when Lady released him. "I'm sorry," he apologized to Robin. "I just couldn't walk as fast as your steed. But I be here now, m'lord."

"There's no need to call me 'lord,' " Robin said sternly.

"Aye. Robin."

"Unburden that palfrey, and haul the sacks of supplies inside."

"Straight away, sir. Uh—Robin."

With a nod, Robin walked directly to his stallion and began unsaddling the beast, offering Flea no assistance as the youth untied the bulky bundles lashed to the palfrey's back. Lady saw that it was a difficult reach for him. She also saw that Flea limped and suspected his feet were badly blistered. Finding her own hands empty, she took it upon herself to help her friend.

When they had all the provisions inside the house, Flea opened a bag and began sorting the contents.

"Let me do that," Lady ordered. "You sit, catch your breath. As soon as I can manage it, I'll get you some water to soak your poor feet."

"My feet are fine," Flea insisted, not even pausing to look up at her. "Besides, I don't want Robin t' catch me idlin' about."

"You've a right to rest! You've been walking hard miles on the road and in the forest! The twigs and stones you trod upon could have done naught for the soles of your feet."

"What matter? Lady, that gentry cove's angry with us. With me, anyway. An' though I deserve it, I don't want him t' be. So let me do what I must."

"He's not well-pleased with me, either," Lady said, though she no longer was sure how Robin felt. Men struck women in anger; she'd witnessed that often enough in the streets, in the stew. But did they kiss them in anger?

"Then it would behoove us t' get on his good side." Flea paused in his task long enough to give her a meaningful look. "You don't know who he is!"

"Do you?" She pounced, grabbing his arm. "If you do, Flea, tell me. Who is he, and what does he want of us?"

"I don't think he wants anything of us. He did you a service, takin' you out o' the city so that you could mend. He did me one, too, allowin' me t' come with you. Besides that, he's a cove what coulda' put me into prison an, didn't. He's a cove what got you out o' prison, when none else could. Leave it at that, Lady. Let me do this, now."

Before she could argue further, Flea exclaimed, "Will you look at this?" He held up a pair of serviceable shoes he'd found in his sack. "They look t' fit me!"

"They should," Robin announced as he paused in the doorway. "I had to guess, but they seemed about right for you."

"Thank you, Robin! I know I don't deserve them, but I surely can use them." Eagerly, Flea began exchanging his worn footwear for the new pair.

"Can you use this?" Robin asked Lady. He pulled a fine cambric smock, newly made and edged with lace, from the other bag. "Or these?" He handed her a pair of stockings along with the smock before passing a pair of boy's leggings over to Flea.

"Damnation! Aye, I can!" the lad responded with a grin.

Lady fingered the smock, knowing Robin's eyes were on her. But by the time she worked herself up to muttering thanks, he'd gone back to rummaging in his sack again.

"There was no need to pinch clothes for yourselves to spare me the expense," he explained. "I'd already picked up a few things for you. Picked them up *and* paid for them."

Lady blushed and finally blurted, "Thank you. We didn't know."

"No matter," Robin assured her as he placed a long, flat wooden box on one windowsill.

The sill wasn't quite wide enough. The box toppled

the moment he removed his hand, falling onto the floor and springing open.

Flea whistled. Lady gasped. On a satin lining lay two fine pistols.

Eight

Robin cursed himself. Why had he been so careless to let them see the guns? He was an experienced agent, a damned spy, for heaven's sake! He knew better than to be so negligent.

As he dragged his dark thoughts with him through the damp grass and into the woods this cool, brisk evening, Robin regretted many things. Foremost at the moment, he regretted not taking his mantle. Such was just another example of his thoughtlessness. Why were his wits so addled? Surely it could not be the young wench who confused him!

Sighing heavily, Robin put out an arm and hugged a gnarled old tree. In the years he'd been employed by the Privy Council, he had always kept to himself, never making close friends, seldom seeing his kin, and avoiding entanglements with either demanding or cloying women. Thus, he had been able to function unhindered, traveling hither and yon, acting out roles the likes of which would never be performed on stage. He could wear disguises and walk darkened alleyways, ferreting out traitors and unraveling treasonous plots—all without longings or worries diverting him from his purpose.

Not so any longer.

Robin slid down the tree trunk and sat upon a nest of tangled roots. From his position, he could see the lodge well enough. The windows in the main room were lighted, and he knew Lady sat by the hearth, waiting for the water he had toted inside to be warm enough for bathing in an old tub she'd discovered. Flea slept in a smaller, darkened chamber. This meant, of course, that Robin could be alone with Lady while she bathed. Yet instead of taking advantage of that opportunity, he'd charged—fled!—out the door without even his cape.

Such was not the behavior of a man intent on having his way with a woman. But then Robin's determination had waned despite his continued interest in the wench. It had been Lady's awkward kiss that restrained him from acting on the inclination that he take what he felt she owed. Despite the connection that had crackled between them, like the sizzling air before a summer's storm, Lady had kissed like a novice, like—dare he even think it?—a virgin.

Damnation! Robin had first presumed, and then subsequently hoped, she would prove to be what the evidence decreed—a beautiful but experienced bawd. Were he confident she was a practiced whore, Robin knew he would only feel lust in his loins. But he doubted her credentials, and instead he felt something else—in his heart. And a man like he could ill afford to feel even a pinch of emotion so tender, so significant, so unnerving.

"Damn!" Robin mumbled in frustration. Then he snorted. If he felt frustrated now, how would he feel after living in close quarters with that blond-haired, blue-eyed "lady" for weeks, without ever once touching her? Yet he knew he shouldn't touch her, not if she were chaste, and not if she made him fret over her whenever he was gone.

"Damn," he growled, pushing himself to his feet and purposefully striding back to the cottage. He intended to go to bed immediately, alone, so that sleep would prevent him from pondering overlong. Robin forgot that Lady had planned a bath—until, as he pushed the door open wide, he heard her squeal. Too late, or perhaps quite conveniently, Robin found Lady soaking in the worn wooden tub. At least he presumed it was she in the soapy water, though all he spied were a pair of glistening knees jutting above the surface like two islands surrounded by a murky sea.

He waited, and shortly Lady's head popped up, her enormous eyes blinking as water coursed down her face. "I—I didn't expect you back!" she choked.

"Where would I go?"

"I—I didn't mean I never expected you back. Just not so soon."

Lady clutched her breasts in her hands as though they were ripe apples she intended to shine. Robin supposed she meant to cover her nakedness, but it appeared as though she were presenting her attributes to him. He struggled to quell his instinct to accept her offering greedily.

Latching the door behind him, Robin changed his mind about going off to bed alone. He strolled to the fireplace and looked into the pot where the remains of Flea's "upright man's stew" sat upon warm embers. He retrieved a bowl and spoon and said, "I confess I'm still hungry even after all I ate at supper. I hadn't suspected Flea was any kind of a cook."

"Nor did I. I've never seen him do it before. He must have wished to make amends. Still, I expect the stew is the only recipe he knows."

Robin glanced over his shoulder at the hapless mermaid and nodded. Then he ladled some of the broth and vegetables into his bowl and sat down at the table to eat.

"Ummm," he murmured, licking his lips. "Quite good, I say. Quite good. Did you think so, too?"

He looked at Lady again and found her scowling. "Aye." She glanced at the blanket she'd left beyond her reach.

Robin rose, not to retrieve the blanket but to grab a flagon and pour some wine into his mug. Returning to his stool, he resumed eating.

"Flea's sleeping, I take it?" he asked between mouthfuls.

"Aye. Are you . . . planning to retire soon yourself?"

"Me? Nay, I'm not weary yet. And this food is so tasty, I may finish the remains."

"Oh."

Robin hadn't meant to torture the girl, but now that he'd begun, he found himself enjoying it, sharing the misery. He chuckled softly when Lady scowled at her bath water as though it were slimed with scum. He suspected both she and the water had grown chilly.

"We have bread somewhere, don't we?" he asked.

"Aye. Over there." Lady raised one hand to point, realized she'd exposed a rosy, pert-nippled breast, and grabbed herself again as she slumped down into the water.

God. What a breast. Robin thanked the saints he'd glimpsed only one. If he'd seen both of them, he might have been unable to keep himself from rushing to her, yanking her from the tub, and tumbling her before she was even dry.

He wasn't supposed to be thinking such thoughts. He'd been determined not to. Well, at least he had determined not to act on them. And he wasn't . . . yet.

Robin picked up the bread and returned to the table.

Breaking a sizeable hunk off the round loaf, he used it to sop up the gravy in his bowl.

"I think Flea's becoming a better horseman than he was," he said, chewing. "After today's hike, he'll probably prefer to be in a saddle next time out. Do you agree?"

"What? Oh, aye."

"Do you ride, Lady? That is, can you sit a saddle on your own?"

"Aye—can't, Robin. Nay, I cannot. Never had the opportunity in London, as you might expect." She shivered, leaned forward, and crossed her arms over her chest so that she could clutch her shoulders.

She was indeed cold. Robin knew he was wicked, forcing her to sit in the tub of tepid water. Yet he wondered how long she could endure before standing up to grab that blanket. He decided to wait and see, however long it took.

"You seem to be taking quite well to the country," he observed casually, scraping the pot with a wooden spoon. He'd given her his back again as he leaned over the fire. "Are you?" he asked, righting himself and spinning around to catch Lady if she'd made a grab for the blanket.

Her hand retreated with a jerk as she resumed her modest pose. "I don't know," she told him as he resumed his seat at the table. "I suppose."

"Ever been out of London before?"

"I . . . don't recall." She looked around the room, not at him.

"We should speak, Lady. There are some things I wish to know."

"What?" She frowned at him. "Now?"

"What better time? It's quiet. We're alone."

" 'Tis quiet," she agreed softly. "And we are alone."

"Will you answer my questions, then?"

"I would, if—"

"If what?" He popped a final bit of balled bread into his mouth and waited for her reply.

"If—nothing. What is it you wish to ask me? Is it about the man, the little man, Flea tried to rob? Because I know naught about him. Flea knows more, I suppose. But then, he's surely told you all he knows. The other bawds, too."

"Ah, yes. The bawds at Fanny's vaulting house." Refilling his cup, Robin took it with him as he pulled his stool away from the table and nearer to Lady's tub. Hunching forward when he sat, he sipped his wine. "Vaulting is an interesting profession. 'Doing the deed,' which most do for simple pleasure, yet getting paid for one's participation. I don't know why so many look down on whoring. 'Tis a clever idea, combining pleasure and work. Whoever thought of it first was certainly clever. As a livelihood, it's been with us forever. I doubt 'twill ever go away."

Lady squirmed. The devil in Robin meant her to. He was behaving horribly, yet he couldn't stop himself anymore than he could stop the fleeting images dancing in his brain as he spoke of debauchery.

"I suppose you're right on that score," she agreed, rubbing her hands up and down her arms, from shoulder to elbow and back again.

The friction didn't soothe the gooseflesh. She remained chilly and growing colder, Robin suspected.

"I don't think it's a very clever trade," she continued. "Most of the bawds I've known aren't too quick. Fanny always takes most of what they earn, and they don't get much for—for entertaining. There are the awful cuffins, too." She crinkled her pert little nose.

"Men neither too fine nor too handsome, eh?"

"Those who visit Fanny's, aye."

"Why did you stay there?"

"Flea arranged it. He never told you? I did the stew's laundry in return for a room and meals."

She spoke forthrightly, further convincing Robin of her untarnished virtue. It rankled him. And the irony did not escape him that he, a man who favored willing ladies over whores, found himself so thoroughly vexed that this particular wench was not a tart trading sex for money.

"Flea did tell me as much," he admitted with a shrug.

"Did he? Did he tell you anything more?"

"I can't recall, precisely. He may have told me you had a beau or two," Robin lied, hoping to discover that she had at least been bedded before. That would make all the difference.

"What!" Lady exclaimed. "If Flea said such, he's lying. I never—"

"Never what?"

Lady looked down at her knees and exhaled loudly. "Never had a beau. 'Tisn't likely, is it, with me living in a stew?"

"Ah," he sighed thoughtfully. "I see the dilemma."

"Flea's told me naught about you." Her gaze met his levelly.

"And you wish to know more about me?"

"Aye. Will you tell me?"

"Nay."

She scowled and shivered. The poor stubborn wench was chilled to the bone. Even Robin couldn't stand to see her suffer any longer. "Get up," he ordered as he stood.

"What!"

"Get up. You're freezing. You need to dry off."

"I shan't!"

"You'd rather catch your death than let me see you naked?"

"Aye! That I would!"

"Then catch your death." He sat down again.

Lady's face pinkened. "Why are you doing this to me? Why can't you leave the room or simply turn 'round?"

"Mayhap I wish to see you naked." Robin smiled.

"Oooohhhh!" Glowering, she studied the rim of the tub. Robin hoped Lady would do it, that she would grab hold of it and stand. But she remained in position, hiding herself modestly.

Oh, the hell with it, he thought. She had been tortured enough—he had been tortured enough! With a shake of his head, Robin resolved to behave gallantly. Grabbing the blanket, he held it in front of Lady, making a curtain.

"Close your eyes," she demanded.

"You're telling me what to do?"

"Only for a moment!"

"Very well."

He closed his eyes. He heard her splashing about as she came to her feet. Then the blanket flew from his fingers. Opening his eyes again, he saw Lady had wrapped herself up thoroughly.

She raised one leg with the intention of stepping out of the tub. But the edge was too high to manage without support, without someone's hand to hold or a free hand to grip the rim. Lady slipped, staggered and—

Robin grabbed her about her waist and hoisted her out of the water. When she stood before him, dripping onto his boots, he rubbed her briskly, buffing her body with the coarse blanket.

"You little chit," he chided her gently. "You'd have caught your death rather than get out of the water whilst I sat here talking to you."

Her teeth chattered so that she could not easily reply. But she nodded her head.

"Why?"

"Because I—I'm not one of F-f-fanny's b-b-bawds. A gentlewoman doesn't p-p-prance naked before strange men."

"You're a gentlewoman, are you?"

"Of course not. I d-don't even pretend to be. But—'tis better to emulate those above you than—than those beneath you."

Having a sudden and erotic image of Lady beneath him, Robin grumbled, "Prudishness is no virtue, especially if it puts your health at risk."

"A bit of chilly water wouldn't kill me if the Hole didn't."

He stopped rubbing her back and reached a hand up to Lady's chin. When he had her gazing right at him, he said, "The Hole would have killed you, if I hadn't managed to free you when I did."

"Yes. I suppose." Her eyes explored his. "Robin, why did you save me and bring me here? Does it have to do with those pistols?"

"Nay! Good lord, not at all."

"Then what? You must want something of me, at least some recompense for the trouble you've gone to on my behalf."

"I do not," he insisted, wishing he spoke true. " 'Tis possible that men sometimes rescue maidens without expecting a reward."

"Except for a kiss." She made a face, quirking her mouth to one side.

"Aye, except for a kiss."

Lady looked so damnably delectable eyeing him warily

through her damp, clotted lashes, he could have eaten her up. And here she was, all but asking for another kiss!

He had to be cruel now, for his sake as well as for hers. Robin took a step back and declared, "Skinny, naked wenches do not inspire me to offer kisses."

Lady flushed darkly. "I'm not skinny. Or naked!"

"You're not?"

A devilish impulse compelled Robin to wrench her blanket away, and both of them subsequently went rigid. Shocked, Lady didn't even try to hide herself; stunned, Robin stared at her splendid female form. Damnation, but the woman no longer looked like the waif he'd found sick and starving in the Hole!

"I stand corrected," he managed to say, straining to appear aloof and unmoved by her voluptuous beauty. "You are not skinny. Not anymore."

God in heaven, she was not. She displayed a package of ripe curves, from her breasts to her hips to her buttocks. Robin longed to stroke the outline of each with the palms of his hands. Possibly, too, with the tip of his tongue.

She found her tongue at last. Shivering again, she stuttered, "Y-y-you b-b-beast!"

"I'm no beast, and you know it."

If he'd been a beast, he'd be tumbling her on the floor already. Instead, he wrapped the towel around Lady once again. Before she could squirm free, he picked her up and carried her nearer the fire. On the way, he grabbed the smock he had purchased for her and then hooked a stool with the toe of his boot, which he dragged before the hearth.

"Nay!" Lady cried when he sat down, keeping her pinned in his lap. "Nay!" she shrieked more loudly when he began to pull the blanket off her shoulders.

"I only want to slip this smock over your head. Can't rightly do it if you're wrapped in a blanket." Once she was in her shift, he hoped Lady wouldn't affect him so strongly.

"V-v-very w-w-well."

Her teeth chattered, but she let the blanket fall away long enough to raise her arms and slip them into the garment Robin offered. Her pert, firm breasts strained high—he was relieved that they disappeared quickly as the smock settled over her body.

Lady put her toes on the floor and her weight on her feet, raising her bottom off Robin's thighs. He assumed she merely intended to get the smock all the way down and under her rump. But she surprised him by attempting to bolt.

He caught her arm and yanked her back into his lap. "You don't think you're going somewhere?"

"Aye. To bed."

It would have been wiser if he'd let her go—the damned smock wasn't coarse enough to hide her body from his keen perusal. Lady's damp flesh kept the fabric clinging to her in a most erotic way. But he couldn't do it.

"Nay," he countered. "You're still shivering, and your hair is all wet. I'll help you dry it."

"I'll dry it myself!"

"You shan't. You'll sit right here by the fire and let me assist you."

Pouting unhappily, Lady remained seated, her feet off the floor now. Taking the blanket, Robin used it to towel her damp hair.

She jiggled. It was his doing and not her fault. But, Lord! The motion of her bottom against his shaft was wildly exciting. So, too, was the vision of her vibrating breasts with their dusky aureoles visible beneath the linen that draped them.

"Robin, please. I'm going to fall."

He ceased his brisk ministrations, but Lady slipped one hand behind his neck and rolled her bottom against his thighs in an effort to better anchor herself in his lap. The motion nearly undid him.

He stopped working on her hair. Lady's luminous eyes locked on his, and he felt a lump in his throat the size of the lump in his braies.

"Robin," she said in a voice that could make stronger men crumble, "I need to understand. What am I to you?"

She was naught to him. Really. Truly. Nothing at all. Rather like a kitten he might have rescued from a flooding sewer. Clean it up a bit, feed it, send it on its way. Aye, a hapless kitten, that's what Lady was to him. Nothing more.

"Robin, I'm very confused, for I don't know what you expect of me. Tell me, please. What am I to you?" she asked again.

"A pain in the arse!" he replied abruptly, leaping to his feet.

Lady nearly fell on *her* arse as she tumbled out of his lap. Her expression went from startled to furious. Scrambling to catch her footing, she stomped across the room and wrenched open a door. Behind it were three narrow beds, two of which Robin had earlier repaired and one of which Flea had already claimed. Storming inside, she slammed the door behind her.

Alone, Robin told himself the dell was indeed a pain in the arse. But, by damn, she was more, much more.

Nine

Robin hid among the trees lining the road that wound its way toward Scotland, which lay beyond the not-so-distant border. He'd arrived shortly after dawn and intended to remain until nearly dark. Today he planned merely to observe, to make certain his presumptions were correct. What he presumed was that no coach would pass 'til late afternoon if its occupants expected to spend the night at The Sutter's Sword, several miles south of this spot. If so, the site he'd picked to lie in wait for his quarry would prove to be near the end of the travelers' daily journey, not in the middle of it.

While he waited, lying on the ground, munching the cheese and sipping the wine he'd brought with him for sustenance, he forced himself to think only of the conspiracy, the queen's vulnerability, and the mission at hand. He would have been successful, too, if he hadn't left the lodge so early in the morn, thereby giving him endless idle hours. Though determined not to think of Lady, her image became more insistent.

What he needed was some physical work so that he couldn't think so much about anything, especially about her. But he hadn't brought an axe with him, so chopping down trees and splitting wood proved no option.

A distant noise drew his attention. Glad for the distraction, he strained to recognize the sounds. Then he did: rumbling wheels and pounding horse hooves. His pulse quickening, Robin jumped to his feet and leapt into his steed's saddle so that he had a better vantage, a better view. Yet looking north, he spied no southbound coach. So he turned in the opposite direction, and there, coming around a slight bend in the roadway, he spied a conveyance moving toward him at a fairly brisk pace.

His heartbeat quickened. As though he had heard a battle cry, Robin spurred his mount into a gallop, and they tore out of the trees and into the center of the road. Cape fluttering behind him in the wind as he brandished a loaded arquebus, he charged toward the approaching coach as though he intended to meet it head on.

The team pulling the conveyance began to falter, all of the horses trying to veer off to one side or the other but unable to do anything but remain in their braces. Nickers turned to whinnies as the beasts began to skid, their forelegs leaping high, their big heads twisting, turning.

"Ho!" the driver shouted, sparing Robin little attention as he grappled with the reins. By the time he had his team halted, Robin had reined in beside him.

"Good day." Robin smiled, touching the narrow brim of his small cocked hat.

"Whatcha' doin'? You nearly got us all killed!"

Robin waggled his pistol before the man's eyes. "I may still, if you displease me."

"I'll be damned! You're a padder! A friggin' footpad!"

"Call me what you will," Robin returned with a polite smile, "but do as I tell you."

"Aye. Aye, m'lord, I shall." The coachman sat as still as he was able while still controlling the straps.

"You! In the coach! Come out!" Robin ordered.

A door opened; timidly, two men and a woman stepped down.

"Nay, nay, nay!" Robin warned when one of the gentlemen, one not much older than himself, dared to put a hand on the hilt of his sword. He nodded toward his own rapier, sheathed against his leg. "I'm quite handy with that weapon myself, and I've the advantage at this height. You don't want to lose your head now, do you? Better to lose it over a comely maid." He winked and waggled his pistol at the three people.

"I won't harm you," he promised the woman, who cowered beside the other man. "Just, ah . . ." He thought for a moment. "Give me your money. I shan't take your jewels. Merely hand over your purses and empty your pockets. Aye, that's right."

Leaning down, he accepted in his free hand what they offered up to him. Once he had it, Robin was at a loss what to do with the booty. He hadn't intended to stop any coach today. He'd gone a touch mad since last evening, when he baited Lady and tortured himself. Or he'd lost his senses even earlier, when he'd determined to take the wench and Flea with him on this assignment.

Robin blinked, focusing on the situation before him. He dropped the lucre into the pouch in which he'd carried his meal. Then, arquebus still aimed at his hapless victims, he slid one leg over his saddle and slipped to the ground.

"Papers," he said, advancing on the younger man. He might as well get in some practice for when he waylaid a coach heading down from Scotland instead of toward it.

The fellow responded to Robin's request with a belligerent, sullen expression. "I have no papers," he insisted.

"Methinks you do," Robin countered. "Good woman, would you please search his person? Confine your hands to his pockets, if you would."

She blushed as red as a ripe strawberry but hurriedly turned away from Robin to explore the man's mantle and doublet. From the inside of his doublet, her fingers emerged clutching a sealed fold of parchment.

"Well done!" Robin complimented her, taking the script and stuffing it inside his own plain jerkin.

"That's of no interest to you!" the man cried. "Give it back! I'll give you my ring instead!"

He tried wrenching a fat sapphire off his finger, but his knuckle thwarted the ring's removal.

"Never mind that," Robin told him, shaking his head. "I told you, I've no need of your jewels. Get back inside."

When he motioned with his gun, the woman and her companion hustled back into the coach. More reluctantly, the other fellow followed.

"Carry on, driver!" Robin called to the coachman as he climbed back onto his stallion. "Godspeed!"

At the crack of a whip, the team of horses lurched forward, cantering nervously up the road.

Damn, but that was fun! And not so difficult at all. He'd got a practice session in and been paid for his efforts. What else had he got?

Robin trotted some miles before veering back into the forest. He halted only when well hidden by the trees again and slipped his pistol into his leather belt. Curious to see what his stolen letter contained, he scanned the page.

"Damnation!" he swore, his eyes flicking to the top of the paper. He read the letter a second time. But nothing had changed, and Robin felt certain he'd intercepted a message intended for the conspirators in Edinburgh, not those in London.

Few would have realized what he'd stumbled upon. Written in Gaelic, the missive appeared innocent enough, except that it bore neither a destination on the outside of the page nor a signature inside. What it did say was disjointed, so that none but the intended recipient could make very much sense of it. The letter referenced imported goods and glittering displays—the writer might have been a merchant discussing new wares he intended to show in his shop window. But no innocent merchant had penned these words. Robin knew it even before he'd read the last two words on the page: *Dilis Ridireacht*—Loyal Knighthood.

He spurred his mount toward the footpath, his pulse racing. Were his three Scots from St. Paul's part of the Loyal Knighthood intent on seeking retribution for their queen's execution? He couldn't prove it yet, but his instincts assured him it was so.

In the distance, he heard another coach rumbling past. Robin ignored it, sure there would be no one aboard carrying a message to London. Not yet.

They were clever, that lot, more clever than Walsingham would have guessed. None of them rode furtively from one country into the other, no clandestine meetings were held under cover of dark, no secret knocks tapped out on locked alley doors. The Loyal Knighthood managed everything in the open, conveying critical news via messengers riding public coaches and plotting details among the noisy populace of St. Paul's Church. Nothing they did would raise anyone's suspicions, were it not for that short Scotsman who couldn't hang on to his clothes while he docked a painted-up whore at Fat Fanny's.

His luck was turning, Robin could feel it. Every doubt

and frustration that had recently plagued him seemed to have disappeared, like night mist dissipating in the morning sun. Mayhap Lady was his charm!

"Won't Robin be surprised," Flea chirped, "that I bagged a hare all on me own?"

Crouched before the fire, he carefully turned the spitted rabbit that he had snared. *The animal must have had a broken foot,* Lady thought with a wry smile. It was such a small thing, they'd be lucky each to get a taste. Still, Flea was right to be proud of his accomplishment.

She stepped outside. Having dusted, swept and aired the little cottage, having even laundered their hose and their shirts, she had nothing much left to occupy her time. In years past, when she never needed to consider doing the wash, the cooking or cleaning with her own hands, Lady still had seldom known an idle moment. Then, she'd had her widowed father to care for, and the rest of her time was spent with friends and suitors. But her sire had died, and the others deserted her even before his demise. Now, leisure proved an odd, almost unwelcome respite, for thoughts of Robin promptly filled her head. She consoled herself that none of them were good or pleasant thoughts. After all, he had treated her abominably last eve. Though she still did not know who or what he was, she did know what he wasn't: a gentleman.

"Forget him," she ordered aloud. But she could not forget how he'd made her feel when he'd rubbed her body dry, when he'd held her in his lap, when he'd dressed her in her smock. If she hadn't been so cold and damp that she had been shivering, Lady knew she might have melted under the smoldering look in Robin's molten eyes and the scorching heat of his very touch. Goodness! She had *felt* things, unfamiliar stirrings and heat, in her breasts, her belly, and between her legs. Worse, when Robin had held her fast in his lap, the bulge in his leggings nudging her naked bottom had made her want to press hard against it.

Lady understood his manhood had made that hard bulge. She was also aware that a man's staff had something to do with the business of coupling. She didn't know what, for certain, or how, but last night she knew that in some way or manner she wanted Robin's shaft.

What a thing! What a thing to want! Lady blushed, embarrassed by her lewd cravings, and held her face in her hands. Her fingers touched skin hot and flushed with humiliation.

After a time, she looked up again. Lady found it very pleasant here—the woods, the little house. Even knowing that Flea, flick-turned-hunter, was cooking up his day's catch, proved a comforting notion. Lady thought she could live here forever, quite happily, just herself, Flea and . . .

"Waiting on me, were you?"

She straightened with a start, never having heard Robin ride into the clearing. Then she gave him a look to let him know he was dreaming.

Leaping off his tall horse, Robin strode toward Lady and grabbed her arm, spinning her into his embrace, where he kissed her soundly. She was so surprised that, when he released her, she gaped at him soundlessly.

"Took your breath away, did I, m'lady?" He winked broadly. "Well, I've had a fine day. And seeing you first thing upon my return only makes it better."

Robin slipped his arm about her waist and led Lady into the cottage. Flustered, she forgot to be angry with him. His good cheer seemed infectious.

"What's the fine smell that's making my stomach growl?" he asked as they entered.

"A hare I'm roastin'." Flea looked up. "I caught it me own self. I'm not such a city lad anymore, am I?"

"Apparently not."

"What you been up to, Robin?"

Removing his hat with the peregrine feather, Robin's eyes danced between Flea and Lady. "No harm in telling you, I suppose," he said with a shrug. "We're all thieves here, are we not?"

Now Flea joined Lady in her befuddled look. They shared a glance before she asked doubtfully, "Are we all?"

"Aye." Robin sat on a stool near the table. "You two foist and cut purses. I practice highway law."

Their astonishment seemed to amuse him, though Lady grappled with her shock. She couldn't have been more surprised if he'd announced he was the queen's bastard son.

"You're a highwayman, Robin?" Flea asked in a squeaky voice. "You rob coaches?"

Grinning cockily, he nodded confirmation.

Lady sank onto a stool of her own. She could hardly credit what she'd heard. She'd had no idea, had never suspected. Yet now that she thought on it, Robin's being a footpad made a peculiar sort of sense. He probably excelled at his profession, which would make him quite wealthy and enable him to buy her way out of prison. And despite his being disturbed by her and Flea's petty thievery at the Briarwick Fair, he had not forced them to return their pickings.

But what of Olivia Crane? Lady knew she was Robin's lover. She had no personal experience with men, but she'd lived in a house with women who made men their occupation, so Lady understood intuitively that Olivia and Robin shared certain intimacies. But would a wealthy, beautiful widow who'd been married young to a handsome, successful wine merchant take a criminal as her lover? That hardly seemed likely, Lady mused, until her glance settled again on Robin's handsome face. Of course it seemed likely, she amended. Any woman would be attracted to his muscled body, his thick dark hair, his flashing eyes. That he was a dashing rogue surely served to make him even more appealing to a woman of Olivia's station. How delightfully wicked for a proper, dignified gentlewoman to have her rascal lover sneaking into her bedchamber at night!

A surge of jealousy flashed hot through Lady's limbs and singed her bosom. It wasn't fair! If Robin was an outlaw and she an outcast, they belonged together, not he and Olivia. The widow Crane could have her rich, mayhap even titled, gentlemen. Lady wanted this upright man for her very own!

The vehemence of her desire surprised Lady. But in all her time as a street mort, a cutpurse, a laundress in a stew, she had never met a man she found attractive, intelligent, appealing—except for Robin. And she might never again. Now that she knew who and what he was, and that they came from like worlds, Lady could allow herself to trust him. She could even allow herself to love him.

So she would definitely have him.

"Go to bed, Flea," Lady ordered. The three of them sat around the table, though their evening meal was long since finished. She did not mean to be so blunt, but she did not intend to be put off from her purpose, should Flea cajole Robin into playing a game of dice or cards.

Robin himself knew the boy would sit up all night if he and Lady could think of any more compliments to bestow upon him for his hunting skills. But he had run out of them, and the only person whose attributes compelled him to think in glowing terms were Lady's. He supposed he had best make for a solitary bed the moment Flea did.

"It's barely darkmans!" the lad complained.

"But it is darkmans, isn't it?" Lady pointed out, gesturing to the window. "And the best time for hunting is early morn, so you had best get your sleep now if you're going to catch us a few more rabbits on the morrow. Mayhap"—she slanted her gaze toward Robin so that his innards seized—"Robin might teach you how to use a bow?"

"Would you?" Flea asked eagerly.

"I believe I could," he agreed, purposely settling his gaze on the boy.

"That'd be kind o' you, Robin. Mayhap I could learn t' be a poacher, if we stay here in the country any length o' time."

"Aye. Perhaps."

Robin watched Flea's eyes dance between himself and Lady. A smirk marked his freckled face as he stood up, stretched his arms, and yawned. "Methinks I am a bit tired. I'll be off then, t' me own cot."

Lady fought a blush that determinedly crept up her throat. Flea was no fool, he knew what she intended. Though his obvious insight embarrassed her, she kept her eyes on Robin and said dismissively, "Good night then, Flea."

Meeting her gaze again, inwardly Robin groaned. He

wanted to consume the wench, beginning by nibbling her toes. Instead, as desperate to be away from Lady as he was to be near her, he made to stand and announced, "I should be off to bed as well, if Flea's going to have me up before dawn."

"Nay!"

The vigor of Lady's protest halted Robin before he had fully straightened. Before he knew what was happening, the wench had come around the table and flung herself at him.

Bemused but not at all displeased, he sank down again, catching her nubile figure in his arms. Questions formed in his mind, but he asked none of them. Robin was far too distracted, delightfully so, by the open-mouthed kisses Lady pressed on him with her moist tongue darting between his own parted lips.

Unsure she was doing it right—Lady's only experience with kissing had been with Robin, and that experience was woefully limited—she persevered. Since he did not push her off, she determined to lose none of the ground she'd gained until finally, desperate for air, she pulled back and gasped his name. "Robin," she whispered, sounding as incredulous and giddy as she felt. "Oh, Robin!"

The tone of her voice sent a shudder through him, and his staff sprang to life. Robin's brain went numb, but fortunately his fingers had minds of their own, apparently, for they began undoing Lady's hooks and ties. Then he discovered his hand on her breast, her bare breast, and Robin resumed his determination to get to bed—not alone, now, but in the company of this delectable wench. If, of course, he could make it that far. Perhaps, he considered frantically, he might at least get Lady on the floor.

Or just to her feet with her back to the wall and her skirt raised to her hips.

Aware that Robin intended to disrobe her, fairly sure he also needed to be similarly unencumbered in order to do the deed that would obliterate Olivia Crane's claim and mark him, instead, as her own, Lady reciprocated. She grappled with his clothes, tugging them free here, tearing them loose there.

That she had initiated this interlude surprised Robin. That she was no longer timorous but keen on seeing their amorous foreplay speedily through to its fated conclusion made him wary. Abruptly, he held her off, hoping he could maintain his control long enough to ask, "Lady, what are you doing? I am convinced you were never one of Fanny's bawds, and you've assured me you have never even had a serious beau."

Panicked by his sudden stillness and restraint, Lady panted, "I wasn't. I haven't." And she punctuated her breathless assertion by plugging Robin's mouth again with her tongue.

Her lusty aggression was proving too much for Robin's raging passions. Yet he managed to say between kisses, "Yestereve, you tried desperately to keep me from seeing you in your bath. What's changed, Lady? What's made you so bold?"

She took a ragged breath that made her breasts rise. Her heaving bosom made Robin's sex strain against his braies. It took all his willpower to be patient, yet he waited for Lady to explain. No matter how much he ached for what she offered, he had no wish to pay dearly if continuing along this path might prove an unwise indiscretion.

"You," Lady dared to admit.

"Me?" He peered at her with raised eyebrows.

"Aye. Before," she told him, "I'd no idea who you were, Robin. I could not fathom why you spent good coin on the likes of me and escorted me out of the city. But now I do. Everything's changed, since I've learnt who you are."

"You know who I am?" he demanded with a start, thinking he would strangle Flea before the boy ever wakened.

"Aye." Lady smiled and licked her lips. If her tongue had been on his maleness, Robin couldn't have felt more desire than he did at that moment. "You're a thief, like me. Bolder and better, no doubt. But we're the same, you and I."

The same. He almost laughed, except she wasn't jesting. And Robin realized that Lady, quite curiously, was completely correct. For the moment, they were in truth both thieves. Why, he asked himself, shouldn't she be his doxy and he her "upright man"? God knew, it would eliminate the strain he had been suffering while they continued to live together. Later, when they all returned to London and resumed their separate, disparate lives, neither he nor Lady would be harmed for having enjoyed this time together.

Robin took Lady's face in both his hands. "I adore you, dearling," he confessed. "But you know what this means, do you not? Henceforth, you are mine."

"Aye," Lady whispered against his neck when he scooped her into his arms and carried her into the unoccupied bedchamber. After he had kicked the door closed with his heel, she repeated, "You are mine."

He placed her on the wide bed, the one he had been sleeping in alone, tore off his jerkin, and tugged off his boots. In his hose and full-sleeved undershirt, he sat beside her on the mattress, kissing Lady as he removed her loosened clothing. Last evening had been hell; this evening would be heaven.

"You're exquisite," he said admiringly when he saw her naked. Then he did what he'd been longing to do—he captured one pink nipple with his lips.

Lady moaned and clutched at Robin's long hair. Raising his head to smile at her, he teased, "For such an innocent, you're a randy wench."

She did not know if his comment should be considered flattery or an insult. "I am?"

"You are."

"Is that good?"

"Hell, yes. 'Tis damned good."

Relieved, she grinned. Chuckling, Robin slipped an arm behind her shoulders and settled a leg across Lady's thighs. When she lay pinned against him, Robin couldn't recall another female fitting him quite so well.

"Touch me," he whispered.

"I am."

"Here." Guiding her hand, Robin slipped it inside his braies. Under his silent tutelage, she wrapped her fingers around his shaft and stroked it gently. Losing himself to her surprisingly skillful ministrations, he closed his eyes.

Lady had no idea what she was doing, but her efforts seemed to please Robin, and that pleased her. The appendage in her hand, though, felt nothing like she imagined it might—if, indeed, she had ever imagined the texture of a man's staff. Curious as to what Robin's sex looked like, especially now that it had grown stiffer and longer, she dared to examine it.

Robin's eyes sprang open again when he felt Lady tugging on his undergarment and hose. "I should like to see," she informed him in answer to his questioning gaze. "'Tis all right for me to see, isn't it?"

All this, and heaven, too. Robin gave himself up fully to the amorous virgin in his bed. With a smile and a sigh, he helped Lady strip off the garments that had covered his lower half. " 'Tis all right, indeed," he assured her, gazing at Lady from beneath drooping eyelids.

Having gained Robin's permission and cooperation, not only did she study his turgid member, she touched it. Naked herself, her breasts swinging freely, her round, alabaster bottom jutting out enticingly, she fingered him lightly, as though it were midnight and she were compelled to feel her way blindly through the dark. Lady's exploration aroused Robin more than her rhythmic stroking had done.

It aroused her as well. For some little while, she'd been feeling liquid and molten inside. Now, Lady felt an itch between her thighs, and though she did not yet understand the particulars, instinctively she knew what would ease her craving.

"I want it," she announced.

In all his life, Robin had never heard any woman make such a declaration. That it came from the lips of this inexperienced wench made him laugh aloud. And he'd presumed virgins were frightened, stiff, unsatisfying creatures not worth a vigorous man's efforts! If they were all like Lady, guileless and eager, honest and curious, he'd been missing much.

"Then you shall have it," he assured her, sitting up, forcing Lady down, and climbing between her legs.

In moments he had her squirming, hips writhing, though he had only plunged half the length of his member into the warm folds of her female flesh. Robin needed to thrust the whole of himself into her, but despite Lady's enthusiasm and her natural exuberance, he hated to hurt her.

"Dearling, I must warn you there'll be some pain at first. I'm told it subsides quickly, though, and when the pleasure resumes, you'll forget."

"You're . . . told?" Lady blinked up at him. "You don't know?"

He grinned crookedly. "Nay, I don't. We're neither one experts here."

This was news. Lady couldn't fathom it. Yet Robin's admission pleasured her nearly as much as his expert touching and tongueing. "Then we'll learn together?" she suggested. "Just you"—she bucked her hips, engulfing more of his manhood—"and I." She strained against him.

Lady's sheath felt so wet and warm, the velvet tunnel sucked him in as though it were oiled with liquid pearls.

"Christ!" Robin thrust downward, closing the gap. "I'm sorry," he rasped as he breached her maidenhead, only a flimsy curtain of flesh easily rent by the full force of his thrust.

The pain, startling even though she had been forewarned, made Lady gasp and her eyes snap wide open. Robin went still for some long moments, imitating the girl. When she resumed her undulations after only a brief interval, he continued to follow her lead.

"Robin," she breathed.

"Lady. Oh, Lady," he moaned in response, burying his face in the wealth of her hair.

He increased the tempo of his gentle assault, the intense downward thrusts and the slow outward retreats. She milked him, following his retreats, absorbing his thrusts. It was over too soon for Robin, yet when he spilt his seed, the explosion had him reeling. Beneath him, Lady spasmed with her own release, her first sexual climax. Watching her, Robin felt ridiculously pleased and proud, to be her first lover and to have provided Lady's initial erotic thrill. She rewarded him with a slow, satisfied smile and a sultry, azure-eyed gaze brimming with promise. Then she clutched him to her, twining her arms and legs tightly about his neck and waist.

Exhaustion. Robin had never known such exhaustion, not even on the training field wielding sword and shield, certainly not after making love to a woman. But Lady had exhausted him. Having no choice, he reluctantly disentangled himself and lay beside her lest he crush her small frame beneath his bulk.

"Did I hurt you badly?" he asked softly.

"Nay. The pain ebbed quickly, as you said it would, to make room for the pleasure, I think."

He chuckled and slanted an eye toward her, satisfied to find her smiling. "You are amazing, and I adore you," he told her again as he rolled onto his side to better see her. "Was it good for you?"

The moment he inquired, Robin realized he had never before asked a woman that question. In the past, he'd been confident of his lovemaking skills. But with Lady, he'd been unable to think well enough to allow for her pleasure, so consumed had he been with his own. Though at first he'd surmised he had done well by her, now he felt a niggling fear that he'd left her wanting.

"Aye, 'twas good," Lady assured him. "Truthfully, I'd no idea what the fuss was about. I never understood how women the likes of Fanny and her bawds could make a business of it. Now that you've shown me, Robin, I finally understand. Oh, my, I do understand!"

Robin's chest swelled like a strutting rooster's, and he grinned like a fool. But then he noticed the crimson smears staining Lady's thighs, and he forced himself to roll out of bed.

"Where are you going?"

"To fetch a rag and water. We both need a bit of washing."

"You're coming back directly?" Lady looked drowsy but content, the way a woman ought to look.

Robin said, "Of course I shall come back directly. Is there anywhere else better to be than your bed?"

" 'Tis your bed."

"Now it's ours." *For a while.*

Robin headed out the door on surprisingly wobbly legs, hoping that this *while* would prove good and long.

Ten

Robin knew by her look that he and Lady were going to have a tiff this morning. In not much more than a week, she'd gone from being his adoring lover to a shrew. Nay, not that. But a witch. Not that, either. A wife, that's what she'd become. A damned wife!

Last night, instead of making love with him 'til they both succumbed to sleep, she had wanted to talk. Talk! And after only doing it the one time. He didn't want to talk, not at all. Besides, he knew what Lady wanted to talk about before she even broached the topic—'twas the same topic about which she'd been dropping heavy hints for several days: going with him to the main road when he robbed coaches.

Flea went with him, she would say. Flea, who couldn't manage a horse on his own but instead had to ride behind Robin's saddle. Robin would point out that Flea kept him company while he waited for a coach to come along. Lady would say she could keep him company just as well, even better. He would say she'd divert his attentions too well; he couldn't chance being distracted and missing the blasted coach!

Then he would cajole her into showing him just how well she could occupy his mind, hands, and other appendages, and soon enough she'd surrender so thoroughly to his loving, Lady would give up her complaint.

But inevitably the wench renewed it again. This morning she would bring it up because Flea couldn't keep his mouth shut, kept prattering on about yesterday's heist of a private coach. (Robin had never intended to rob private coaches, but he'd recognized the crest on the side, disliked the old fart who owned it, and took the toady baron for a heavy purse simply for the hell of it.) The way Flea recounted the incident—which grew better with every telling—Robin had all but fought a duel with Lord Cunningham. In fact, the gout-ridden old coot had refused to climb down from his conveyance and had casually tossed out a bag containing the equivalent of Robin's usual monthly wages before ordering his driver on.

"I'm not suggesting you leave Flea behind," Lady announced, as though they'd been discussing the possibility of her accompanying Robin for some time already, when in fact neither he nor she had as yet said a word. " 'Tis only that I'd like to come, too."

"Nay." He slammed down his mug of perry, which he drank to slake his morning thirst because it was unfermented and allowed his wits to remain keen.

Lady glowered at him. Robin was simply impossible! He only paid attention to her at night, in bed. He wished she'd disappear during the day. But she wasn't a sprite, she couldn't disappear, and there was naught for her to do to keep herself occupied.

" 'Tis boring by half when you two are both gone!" she complained.

"Well, busy yourself doing wife—ah, womanly things. What did you used to do before we came here?"

"I did the laundry in a bawdy house," she reminded him dryly, crossing her arms over her bosom.

"Then do our laundry."

"I've done the wash!"

"Do whatever else it was you used to do."

"I used to rob people—that's what I'm asking to do again, with you!"

"You used to pick pockets, not rob coaches. And I'll be damned if you're going to start robbing coaches now!" Robin slammed his feathered hat onto his head and grabbed his mantle, swinging it over one shoulder.

Lady backed out of his way, or she would have been slapped by a corner of the flying cape.

"Robin, I'm quite bored here all day. What shall I do, if I can't come with you?"

"Damnation, Lady, I don't care! But you're not coming with us." Robin secured his sword at his side and lifted a gun from its box.

"I could stay home today," Flea offered a trifle belatedly. "I could practice me huntin' with the bow an' arrow."

"Aye, you could," Robin agreed, nodding at him. "But you're not going to, because I said you may accompany me. 'Tis the wench, here, who'll be staying behind."

Lady wanted to kick him in his backside. Instead she ground her teeth before declaring, "I may not be going with you, but don't expect me to be here when you return."

"Threatening me, are you?" Robin cocked one black eyebrow as he glared at her angrily. "I'd think better of it, were I you. I can do quite well on my own, but you can't do very well without me. Remember the gaol," he threw at her before stomping outside and striding to his saddled horse.

"I'll stay home with you tomorrow, Lady!" Flea volunteered as he hurried after Robin.

She refused to watch them go. Standing in the center room of the cottage, Lady breathed raggedly until she heard the stallion trot off into the woods. Then she slammed the door and kicked a stool, not once, but twice.

"Damn him!" she cried, tears burning her eyes. "If he could, he'd put me in a cupboard for the time he has no use for me! I'm like a child's toy, a plaything. If I'm not giving him pleasure, I might just as well not exist!"

To punctuate her solitary outburst, Lady grabbed a metal mug off the table and threw it at the stone wall above the fireplace. It bounced off with a clang and landed, bent, upon the floor.

Though her frustration remained, her anger was momentarily spent. Lady retrieved the battered cup and returned it to the table. Then she noticed the wooden box. It was not empty as it usually was. One of the guns remained.

Curiously, she lifted the arquebus from its satin bed. It was long, but not as heavy as she expected. She could . . . Nay, she could not. With resolve, she returned the pistol to its proper place, closed the lid, and began putting the box back where Robin stored it.

She never set the box down. His powder case and bag of balls were still there. Always, Robin took his ammunition with him. Perhaps he had not even loaded the pistol he had taken!

Lady knew how to load a gun. She had watched idly when Robin cleaned the weapons and explained the matchlock mechanism to Flea. She had not been very interested. But there was little to do between the time their supper ended and the time Flea went to bed, so that she and Robin could go to bed, too. Thus, she knew how to load the powder and lead, how to set the cock, how to squeeze the sear lever.

Sitting down at the table, Lady reopened the gun case and took out the arquebus. Carefully she spilled a trace of powder into the pan and more into the barrel, using the ramrod to pack it down with a bit of paper. Last she added the lead ball, ramming it home as well. She did not cock the weapon. Carefully, she returned the loaded gun to the box.

Then she hoisted the mare's saddle from where Robin kept it, standing on its front end near the door. She had carried the heavy thing all the way to the hobbled horse before recalling she needed both a blanket and the bridle. Dashing back inside, she recovered those articles and threw the saddle onto the palfrey.

She was good at it, though she shouldn't have been. It had been years since she'd ridden for pleasure, yet, as with the guns, she had learned because she'd once had idle time. Now that knowledge stood her in good stead.

Back inside the cottage, Lady picked up the pistol and opted to carry it tied to a piece of hemp rope, which she secured about her waist. Sticking the barrel of the gun inside her makeshift belt, she threw on her new cloak, ran outside, pulled herself onto the mare, and headed off along the path that led to the highway.

Knowing Robin would neither keep himself visible on the main road or do his business anywhere near the path that could lead disgruntled victims to the lodge, Lady rode along the edge of the forest, seeking her man. By chance she headed north, and after traveling a few miles in that direction, she was just about to turn back when she heard voices. Conversation. Robin and Flea. They spoke so softly, she nearly rode them down before overhearing them. Fortunately, she was able to dismount and lead her mare away as quietly as possible, before Robin became aware of her.

Lady didn't intend to let Robin know she'd followed him. She would wait, watch how he did his business, and perhaps be of some assistance. 'Til then, she tethered her palfrey, leaned her back against a tree trunk, and waited. After a time, a distinctly civilized sound made her senses sing: wheels in the dirt and horses' hooves!

Her heart began pounding as she scrambled up and untied the mare. By the time she sat in the saddle, the carriage had rumbled directly past her.

Immediately she urged the palfrey out to the edge of the trees so that she could spy the activity farther down the road, where Robin waited. No sooner had she craned her neck to look in that direction than he appeared alone on his steed, galloping toward the carriage pulled by a team of four. His stallion seemed to have taken wing and so, too, did he. In shades of tan and gray, the peregrine feather fluttering atop his hat, his mantle flying out behind him like a great bird's wings, Robin looked like a falcon made into man, a man made into a falcon.

He reined in his horse just as the coachman drew his team to a halt. Cautiously, keeping close to the trees at her side, Lady continued toward them, confident no one would notice her as she approached from the rear of the conveyance.

"Out!" Robin ordered the occupants of the coach. "One and all, I would see you now."

The door opened, the coach bobbed, and three people exited. Two women, one man.

"Where do you hail from?" he inquired conversationally.

"S-S-Scotland," one woman replied.

"Edinburgh," the man announced, rolling his r's with a thick, Scottish brogue.

"A pleasant city," Robin returned, mimicking the fellow's accent. "Now, give me yer valuables, would ya' be so kind?"

"I've none!" the second woman cried.

"I do." The other handed Robin a small leather purse.

"Sir?" Robin said to the gentleman.

He balked, and Robin aimed his pistol at the man's head. Lady was thinking Robin would never shoot him when, from her unique vantage point, she spied another figure still remaining in the coach.

She was very near, now. If any of the people in the road had turned their heads, they would have seen her. But none did. Robin's eyes were on his gulls, and their eyes were all on him.

The coach bobbed. Lady could see it wasn't the driver moving his weight to make it sway, so she knew the remaining passenger was moving about inside the conveyance.

"Robin!" she cried in warning.

He turned and saw her then, though she wished he hadn't. A hand and a pistol emerged through the coach window. There was a sharp report and a puff of smoke, and Robin jerked backward in his saddle as a ball slammed into his shoulder.

He didn't lose his seat, however, and he managed to get off a wild shot with his own gun. Lady herself was already bearing down on those in the road. Without even thinking about it, she pulled the arquebus from her rope belt and cocked it.

Just as she reined in on the far side of the coach, the man inside replaced the gun he had been wielding with a fresh, loaded one. But he had no chance to fire it, for Lady shouted, "Don't move, m' lord! I've a pistol aimed at your head."

She had him as her target through the other window, the one his back faced. Slowly, he turned to confirm the reality of her threat.

"Put your weapon down on the seat very slowly," she ordered, kneeing her palfrey close to the coach. From that vantage, she could see the man obeyed. Then she hailed Robin, taking care not to use his name, lest someone remember it. "Falcon!"

Robin came alongside the coach. "You're addressing me?" he asked with a cocky smile, though he had a hand pressed to his wounded shoulder, which bled copiously.

"Yes, I am. Was there anything you were wanting from the cove who shot you?"

"Aye. I've a fondness for reading. See if he has any papers on him."

Still astride the mare with her gun aimed through the window, Lady wrenched open the door and held out her free hand. "Papers?"

"I haven't any."

"Then give me your money." While she waited for him to hand over his purse, she slipped off the palfrey and leaned into the coach. Removing the man's loaded weapon from the seat, she handed it up to Robin. When she had the traveler's moneybag, she tossed that up to Robin as well.

"Remove your doublet," she ordered.

"I shall not!"

"You shall, or I'll shoot you."

The man appraised Lady's weapon as though it had a mind of its own. Then he unfastened his fine jacket with its slashed sleeves and opened it to display the lack of hidden pockets.

"Your ruff."

Giving Lady a contemptible glare, he undid the ruff about his neck and threw it at her.

She picked it up from the floor of the coach, shook it out, and flung it back at him. "Your hose."

"I won't do it," he grumbled.

"I'd wager that if I aim this pistol right there"—she pointed the business end of the weapon at his crotch—"your hose would fly off almost of their own accord. What do you think?" She raised her gaze to meet the man's and smiled sweetly.

Cursing venomously beneath his breath, he lifted his bottom off the seat and pushed the padded trunk hose down to his ankles and off of his feet. With a sneer, he kicked them to Lady, who inspected them by squeezing the stuffing that made them puff out roundly.

Something crackled. "Falcon!" she called, tossing the garment to Robin. "There's something in the wadding. You might want to cut these trunk hose open and see what's inside."

"Got it, dearling," he replied after a rending sound had reached all ears. When Robin returned the garment to Lady, it was ruined beyond all wearing.

"You may go now," she told the man who had shot her lover. She flung the trunk hose into his lap.

"I—I can't wear these!"

"Then you'll be stuck wearing your braies and gartered stockings, I suppose. I must say, your knees aren't half bad, for a cuffin."

"Bitch!"

Lady's eyes narrowed. "I haven't killed you for shooting my man. But you insult me again, and I'll shoot you for that."

Withdrawing, she slammed the carriage door closed. Robin informed the others they were free to resume their journey. After they scrabbled aboard and the coachman whipped the team into a furious pace that churned up a cloud of dust in the coach's wake, Lady angled her gun skyward and fired off a round.

The pistol's kick made her stumble and her mare rear up. If she hadn't been holding the horse's reins, the palfrey would have bolted. But she recovered herself and calmed the animal, and then looked with concern up at Robin.

He chuckled. "By God! That blasted thing was loaded?"

"I didn't expect to shoot anyone, but I thought to be prepared."

"Lady! Lady!" Flea cried as he stumbled out of the woods, carrying a dead bird by its neck. "Damnation, but you killed a goose!"

For a moment, Lady couldn't quite credit what Flea said, but Robin burst out laughing—before he swayed in his saddle.

"Get down from there before you fall," she ordered, reaching up to him, frightened by the pallor in his usually swarthy face.

"I'm fine," he insisted. "Fine enough to return to the cottage before we tend my injury."

"You're not fine enough. Get down!"

"You're as overbearing as you are disobedient," Robin complained, though he did dismount and lead his horse into the woods.

"Be glad I am. If I hadn't been here today, you'd have been killed."

"I never suspected you could be such a help," he admitted, tossing the gelding's reins to Flea before sitting down on the leaf-littered ground to prop himself against a sturdy tree. "How did you know to use a weapon like that? And when did you learn to ride? I thought you told me you didn't know how to ride."

"I lied," she confessed distractedly as she opened Robin's jerkin and examined his bleeding shoulder. She wasn't so distracted that she would explain how a London street mort might have acquired a skill usually exclusive to the wealthy upper classes. "You're lucky. The ball went clean through. We only need to staunch the bleeding." Lady raised her skirt and put the hem of her smock between her teeth.

"Don't do that!" Flea cried. "Don't tear your shift! Use me shirt. It's not new. In truth, it's so worn, it'll rip much more easily."

Yanking off his own jerkin, Flea removed his undershirt and tore off a wide strip. Lady folded the cloth and pressed it hard against Robin's shoulder.

He sat quietly, but he unsealed the paper he had taken off the traveler and held it up, squinting at the page. "Blast!" he muttered.

"What's the matter?" Lady asked. "What is your interest in some stranger's private letter? And why did he have it secreted on his person in the first place?"

"That, I couldn't say. But I confess that hidden communiques are most interesting to read. Unfortunately, my eyes are not focusing very well."

She snatched the script from him. "I'll read it to you.

"*You'll* read it to me?" Robin's brow furrowed.

Lady flinched. Obviously, fretting over Robin's injury had her feeling more anxious and distraught than she had presumed. She'd been careless, nearly allowing him to know she had the ability to read and write. That he knew she was an equestrian was one matter; if he knew she had an education, it would be quite another.

Tossing the page back into his lap, Lady said, "Very well, I can't read. But I do know my letters and I thought, whilst you rested, I could pick them out for you, and you could determine the words. Better, I suppose, you read the missive later when your head is clearer."

Robin continued to frown, but he said, “Aye. ’Tis a small pleasure reading stolen messages myself.” He stuffed the paper into a pocket and then snatched away the bandage Lady had been pressing to his wound. After considering the crimson stain, he announced, “I’m not bleeding overmuch. Let’s go home.”

Eleven

Robin and Lady rode together regularly—the wench had proved herself handy enough—while Flea stayed near the lodge, setting his traps and attempting to hit moving targets with Robin's bow and arrow. Today the pair rode a good many miles north on the main road. Robin planned to intercept the coach from Scotland before those riding inside expected a highwayman's attack. It had rained heavily during the night, and when they encountered a huge ditch filled with water, one that would force any coach to slow before negotiating it, Robin decided to lie in wait at that spot. Under cover of forest, he and Lady had a decent view of the highway without risk of being seen.

"You shouldn't have accompanied me today, Lady," Robin said reproachfully as the wind shook droplets from the branches above down onto both of them. "The weather's too cold and dank."

"But I love coming with you, Robin. Besides, you need me to cover your back."

He nodded, for it was, indeed, true. He felt safer knowing she rode behind him, wielding the loaded arquebus she had taken from the Scotsman who'd shot him in the shoulder. For ten of his score and seven years, though, Robin had managed quite well without anyone guarding his back. How had it come to be that he found comfort with this wench watching over him?

"Besides," Lady continued, "I simply enjoy being outdoors. After the stinking lanes in Southwark, and worse, the Counter's Hole, this open space suits me fine. Being able to breathe sweet, fresh air, even if it is damp and blustery . . . well, 'tis like heaven to me." She gave him a little smile and admitted, "I'd like never to return to London."

Robin felt a quick pain in his chest. He turned away and grumbled, "We have to return, Lady."

"Why? We're doing quite well here. Flea's tramping the woods near the cottage today, determined to bring down a deer. I cannot credit it! That rogue cove, who's known naught his entire life but the streets of London, determined to be a great hunter! 'Tis as if I'd determined to become one of Queen Elizabeth's ladies-in-waiting."

"It's an adventure for him. He's more a lad than a man yet, so he takes to anything new. But he'd tire of it soon enough, if this were all he had."

"I'm not so sure. I know I haven't tired of keeping house in the forest and robbing wealthy gentlefolk of their purses." She smiled devilishly.

Robin scowled. "Not yet, you haven't. But you will soon."

"Shall we make a wager?"

"Nay, we shan't. Because there'll be no time to see who wins. Lady, we must—"

He broke off as the sounds of wooden wheels churning up mud and shod hooves slapping the muck descended on his ears. Lady heard it too. Leaning forward in her saddle, she peered through the branches at the road.

"Wait here," Robin ordered.

There was no need for him to rush the coach today.

The ditch did the hard work of stopping the conveyance. So he spurred his gelding and lunged from the cover of trees just as the coach slowed. "Halt!" he ordered, aiming one of his two pistols at the driver.

"I know, I know," the man replied, raising his hand in a compliant gesture. "We met before, Sir Falcon."

"Then you realize no harm shall come to you, providing you cooperate."

"Aye." The driver rapped on the roof of the coach. "Out, all o' you! A gentleman wants t' have a word!"

Robin chuckled at the coachman's seasoned cooperation. While he watched, the door opened and three men wearing outraged glowers emerged. So, too, did a lady who appeared stricken at having to ruin her shoes in the mud.

"Tell him from whence you hail," the coachman instructed.

"Glasgow," one man said. "Ma wife, too."

"Lockerbie," said another.

"Edinburgh." The third man met Robin's narrowed gaze and held it.

"On your way to London, are you?" Robin inquired.

No one answered. Then the man who kept staring at him said, "Nay. I wasn't planning to go that far."

"Eh? Well, no matter. You can give me your purses now. And any papers you're carrying."

"That's an outrage!" the married man declared. "I'm travelin' on business. Ya canna' have mah papers."

"Can't I?" Robin waggled his pistol threateningly.

Huffing noisily, the fellow retrieved a tied bundle of letters from inside his cape and handed them up to Robin, who tucked them away.

"Now, your money."

The man and the woman shared a look. Then the man

handed over his purse. It was light, very light, and Robin presumed that in anticipation of robbery, they'd concealed most of their funds elsewhere.

"You?" He looked at the lady.

"I—I have no purse on me."

"Shall I search you?"

Her eyes widened, and her jaw dropped. "Nay! That is, ya could, but you'd find naught, I assure ya."

"Very well. You?" He pointed his pistol at the second fellow. That man handed over an equally light purse.

Robin thought that if he were truly a highway robber, he would have had to change his location to another byway. His reputation now preceded him.

"And you?" He settled his gaze again on the third man. There was something about him, something that tickled the back of his mind.

"You shan't get anything from me."

"I shan't, eh?"

Robin hadn't expected this sort of resistance, so he was actually surprised when the traveler drew his sword. But he responded reflexively, aiming his cocked gun more surely at the gentleman's head. "I've no time for blustering displays."

" 'Tisn't blustering. I know you could shoot me if you wished. But aren't highway lawyers supposed to be gentlemen of sorts? A gentleman fights fairly."

"Were we fighting?"

"I am."

Damnation, but this fellow rankled Robin. He thought he knew him somehow, but he hadn't the time to figure how.

Impulsively, he swung a leg over his steed's neck and slipped to the ground. "Dearling!" he called, and Lady came out of hiding, halting her palfrey beside his mount. "Hold this for me. Use it, if you must."

He gave her the pistol he'd been brandishing and removed his rapier from its sheath. From the corner of his eye, he saw the other passengers backing up against the coach and the coachman settling back to watch the entertainment. Then he whipped his sword in a circle so that it stirred the air with a sound like the drone of humming bees and braced himself for the duel.

The other fellow was good. Damned good. Too good. And though he never drew blood with the tip of his sword, he did manage to maneuver Robin farther and farther from the watery ditch, the coach, and their spectators. They were near the side of the road where the trees came up to meet it when he lunged, forcing his sword down the length of Robin's so that the blades crossed just above their respective hilts.

" 'Tis I, Dekker!" he hissed.

Robin blinked, and they both sprang away from each other, though they continued to thrust and parry.

"Good God! I felt that I knew you; I didn't know how. Why are you here?"

"Came to find you," Dekker said as they danced around, their swords slicing the air. By now, it was all for show.

"Why?"

"I've news. We must talk. When and where?"

"The Sutter's Sword. Next inn you'll come to. I'll be there—as soon—as I can." Robin clicked his sword against Dekker's—*clang! clang! clang!*—and leapt away.

"Good."

"I must wound you. 'Twouldn't look good for the Falcon to be defeated in swordplay."

"Very well. Just don't ruin my mantle. 'Tis a recent purchase."

"Fling it over your shoulder, then. That's it. I'll score your doublet."

"Damn," Dekker swore, but he nodded.

With the tip of his rapier, Robin cut the wine-colored velvet. Dekker dramatically flung his sword down, and Robin stretched out his arm, laying the point against Dekker's throat.

"Here's a warning to you all!" he shouted. "Cooperate with the Falcon, and you'll remain unharmed! Do battle with him, and you die!"

"Don't kill him!" Lady pleaded. Her request startled Robin, but her timing was perfect.

"For you, my pet, I'll spare the cur." He sheathed his sword again. "Give me your purse, man, and then be on your way."

"What!" Dekker looked affronted.

"I'll return it," Robin vowed under his breath, and Dekker complied.

As soon as the other passengers returned to the coach, and the driver had whipped his team through the ditch, Robin climbed back onto his steed.

"Oh, Robin!" Lady cried. "I was so afraid he'd run you through!"

"Why? I told you to use the gun if you had to. I expected you to save me before it came to that."

"You did?"

"Aye." He smiled gently. "Didn't you remind me a short while ago I needed you to cover my back?"

She smiled, too. "Aye, I did. But you shouldn't trust me so well. My aim's not very good, especially when two of you are moving about as you were."

"What do you mean, your aim's not so good? You once shot a blasted goose out of the sky!"

In the taproom of The Sutter's Sword, Robin discovered Dekker sitting alone, nursing an ale, his hat pushed far back on his fair head as he ignored the females who kept stealing glances at his handsome young face. Robin ordered an ale, too, and sat down at his table.

"Methinks your days as a highwayman are numbered, Moreton. Word's spread among the coachmen, and they're warning their passengers. Someone's going to blow your head off the moment you order them to halt, if you're not careful."

"I planned to return soon to London. I've been having little luck intercepting messages of late." He slapped a packet of letters onto the table between him and Dekker. "See that these are returned to your fellow passenger. They're of no interest to either you or me."

Dekker nodded. "Did you nip any of the missives they've been sending by coach to and from London?"

"Aye. Two, written by those calling themselves *Dilis Ridireacht.* I can't be certain, but I believe they are planning some sort of a 'glittering' display. Distraction, more likely. Or, mayhap, that was a reference to the Accession Day festivities."

Dekker nodded. "What else?"

"I couldn't make much of the second missive. I have it here. Read it for yourself."

Dekker took the letter Robin offered him. After a moment, he said, "It appears to me as though they're promising the London contingent that the assassin will be sent to them from Scotland."

"Aye." Robin nodded. "That's what I thought, too."

"Well, it's all the news you'll get, Moreton," Dekker announced, handing the parchment back to him. "They've stopped sending messages, at least by couriers in public coaches. When you took this letter out of the conspirator's hose, they determined you were after them directly."

"You'd heard I'd done that?" Robin asked, and Dekker nodded. "Blast! I should have killed the cove outright, but I worried that such a move might create more problems than it solved."

"It doesn't matter now."

"Why were you on the coach?" Robin asked.

"I told you. I wanted to find you. I knew you were playing the footpad this side of the border, but I'd no idea where. I took a chance you'd stop the coach I was riding in. 'Twas no chance, really. You stop every coach headed down from Scotland."

"Now you've found me. What is it that I need to know?"

"The assassin. He's a MacKinney. Fiercest of the clan. Angus, by name. Seems he took Queen Mary's death quite personally. Heard a tale that he loved the woman from afar since before she married Darnley. He's rumored to have been involved in every plot there has ever been to free her."

"This vengeful scheme, then, is more a matter of the heart than mere loyalty to queen and country. Damnation. 'Tis the worst it can be!"

"Aye, it is," Dekker agreed, sipping his ale.

"Do you know how he'll attempt to kill Elizabeth?"

"He's a warrior, Angus is. Dagger, sword, pistol, crossbow, mace—he can wield them all with precision, so I'd rule out poison."

"Damnation, Dekker! If they plan to carry out this

murder on the queen's Accession Day, he certainly intends to utilize a weapon he can use from afar. An arrow or bolt or, more likely, a gun." Robin scowled. "Still, what weapon MacKinney plans to use should be of little concern to us. We know who he is. All we need do is waylay him at the last possible moment."

"That shan't prove as easy as you make it sound."

"Why not?"

"Because I've no idea where he is, or even what he looks like."

Robin's scowl deepened. "You've been in Scotland awhile. Why couldn't you find him?"

"Because the man's a frigging legend! He's almost mythical. Everyone claims to know him, but I suspect they only know of him, for no one supplies the same description. He has red hair or dark, blue eyes or black. He has a fine, manly figure or he's built like a bull. He's fair of feature or battle-scarred—damnation! I almost suspect Angus MacKinney exists not at all."

Robin stayed silent for a moment before asking, "What did you learn of his history?"

"Only the tall tales, and those from men drinking heavily. When I heard about MacKinney, I set out to learn more. I tell you, Moreton, the stories I heard about this warrior were as diverse as pebbles on the shore! The only constant is that the man seems to see himself as Queen Mary's champion. As well, he feels he personally failed her by not managing her escape before her execution. But who he is, where he is, I don't know. Angus doesn't reside in Edinburgh or any populated town. Or if he does, he lives under a false identity."

Robin exhaled noisily. Glancing at his mug, he saw that he'd barely touched his ale. "Are you going back?

Will you try to find him and follow when he leaves Scotland for England?"

"Nay." Dekker faced Robin directly. "I came too close to being found out. Those who plot mayhem become skittish if they see the same face too often. And I had no other sources to investigate than the few I uncovered in Edinburgh.

"I thought, after advising you of what I know, to continue on to London and speak with Walsingham. Mayhap you should do so as well, Robert. As I said before, your days as a highwayman are finished."

Robin nodded. Dekker was right, though he wished it weren't so. "Are you staying with the coach?"

"Aye. May as well. I haven't a horse of my own at the moment. What about you?"

"I'll be along directly."

"Why don't you come with me?"

"Dekker, I can't. My situation's . . . complicated. I have a woman with me, and a youth."

"That comely wench who accompanied you today?"

"Aye."

Dekker winked. "She's a piece, isn't she?"

Offended, Robin managed not to convey his ire. "Aye. She's an exceptional female."

"Well, she'll keep 'til you decide to return, if ever you do. Won't she?"

Robin shrugged. He had no wish to explain that Lady wasn't a local girl.

"Burghley sent me here," he told Dekker. "Walsingham has been unwell. If I were you, I'd contact Burghley as soon as you reach London. I'll join you as soon as I'm able."

Standing, Robin gestured with his chin to the pack of

letters. "Make sure that fellow gets his property back. I hate stealing when it isn't necessary."

"Do you? I wouldn't mind an excuse to lift a few purses. They hardly pay us well enough to justify risking our lives."

"How often do we truly risk our lives?"

"Often enough to expect an increase in our pay?" Dekker asked before laughing. "See you in London, Moreton."

Robin did not know how to tell Flea and Lady that their sojourn in the north country had ended, not without disappointing the lad, not without hurting Lady. So he simply blurted it out, curtly, without preamble or explanations, the moment he returned to the lodge.

Flea looked at him hard for a long, silent moment. Then the youth shrugged and muttered resignedly, "That's that, then."

"What do you mean, 'that's that?' " Lady demanded, glancing briefly at Flea before returning her gaze to Robin. She felt as though he had put a leg out and tripped her; mentally, she scrambled to regain her footing.

"Lady, we spoke of this earlier, did we not?" Robin reminded her gently. "Our time here has to end."

"Why? Why now?" She hoped her voice hadn't truly risen to the mewling pitch it seemed to have.

"Because my business here is ended."

"Business! What business?" She took a step toward him. "You rob coaches to make your living. There's an endless stream of coaches. Your business has no end!"

Deciding to give her a bit of truth, Robin explained, "They know me. The purses I took today were light. Travelers are prepared for my coming and take precautions now. Today there was a sword fight; on the morrow, someone may well shoot me with a lead ball before I've time to halt the coach." Seeing her pale, he pressed, "If you don't mind risking my life, Lady, I do mind risking yours or Flea's."

"I don't want you dead! I want . . ." *You always.* "If the road we've been working has become too dangerous," she suggested, "we can hide alongside other roads and waylay other coaches!"

"Nay," he insisted calmly.

"Why not!" she shouted back.

"Because it isn't just that my efforts as a padder in this area will continue to prove less and less profitable, Lady. We must leave here because I need to return to London. I work there as well, you know."

"Lady." Flea spoke softly and attempted to comfort her by grabbing her wrist gently. "Lady, you know Robin resides in the city, that he's not always a padder on the north country roads. As well, you've always known that we'd go home one day."

She had indeed known it, but she had put it from her mind. That had been a good place for that knowledge, out of mind. She did not like even speaking of their departure from this, the most pleasant place, the sweetest interlude, of her life. She couldn't bear to anticipate actually going back.

Tears burned her eyes, but Lady knew crying would be a feminine, even childish, thing to do. Despite the fact he'd never used the word, Lady knew Robin loved her. She understood, too, he had only come to love her when she proved herself forceful, reliant, and a helpmeet to him. She refused to show her weakness now, or to reveal her vulnerability, so she forced the tears back. It seemed she swallowed them, hot and salty, for her throat burned.

"Very well," she managed to say stiltedly. "If you sometimes work abroad in the country, and sometimes work in London town, then there'll come a time soon when we'll return, aye?"

Robin had heard people bemoan and poets describe their broken hearts, but he had never understood that keen emotion. When Lady looked to him so beseechingly, he felt a twisted pain in his chest and suspected that now, at last, he knew. He also suspected that though she spoke to him about residences, Lady was really asking for commitment, for a future together with him.

He could not give it to her, so Robin refused to pledge it. He would not even hint it might be so, just to ease the strain until the three of them were again within the city walls of London, and Flea could lead Lady out of Robin's life. The wench deserved better than a lie, after all she'd given him.

Glancing at Flea, who nodded as though he understood, Robin settled his gaze on Lady's pale, pinched face. "I think not," he said evenly. "You have both been a boon to me during this sojourn; I'd not expected either of you to be of such assistance. But I work alone, Lady. These weeks have been an exception, but I shall work alone again. 'Tis how my work is best accomplished."

"But—but I saved your life!" she sputtered.

"And I yours. Not only did I see you freed from prison, I brought you with me, to this place, so that you might regain your health, your strength. You have, Lady. You know you have. Now, it is time we return home."

She had no home. The house in which she'd grown up had long been occupied by strangers. Lady did not even have the squalid little room at Fat Fanny's anymore.

Did Robin know he was condemning her to life in the streets? she wondered. She decided he did. So despite how much she loved him, she hated him.

"We'll do fine, Lady," Flea assured her.

"And you'll have a good deal of white money," Robin added, "for I intend to share my booty with you both."

He intends to pay me! Lady wrenched her arm free from Flea's grasp and laid her hand over her heart, as though to shelter it. Never had she once believed she'd be reduced to whoring, no matter what befell her. But if Robin paid her, that's what she would be: a bawd, a tart, a whore.

Lady wanted to tell him he could keep all his damned money, but she knew she couldn't speak, not coherently. She managed only to stare at him, though she had no desire to look at Robin's handsome face ever again. His features were already burned into her memory.

He braced himself for her condemning stare and steeled himself for the slam of the door when Lady dashed off to the room Flea usually slept in alone.

None of them ate supper that night. Not another word was spoken. Later, Robin slept solitary in the big bed he usually shared with Lady. His sleep proved fitful, so he attempted to convince himself he didn't care about Lady, not the way she wanted him to care. The wench may have deluded herself about the depth of their feelings for each other, but he had always known their affair was naught but casual, born of convenience. Certainly, when she was gone, he would not miss her.

But already, though she remained nearby, he did.

Twelve

The ride north had seemed interminable. The ride south flew by as though their horses had winged hooves. The journey up to Briarwick had been ripe with possibilities; the journey down to London was rife with grim certainties.

Robin wished he were free to tell Lady everything: who he truly was, what he had, in fact, to do, and why they were not suited to each other. But Lady suited him quite perfectly, that was the damnable thing. Her body, her mind, everything about her complemented him. Except, of course, that he was an educated gentleman, a knight serving Queen Elizabeth's Privy Council, and she was a low-class thief from London's dirtiest streets. Now that they'd left their fantasy world, they could not be a couple no matter how much he might wish it.

And he did wish it. Being near Lady without having her, not just in body but in mind, had forced Robin to admit to himself she had never been a casual tryst. He berated himself for allowing their mutual need to become mutual caring. But he would not compound the wrong he'd done her. He had to be stoic and set her free. If he never fully got over this street mort, she could at least get over him. Angry with him, hurt by him, Lady's heart would mend quickly, Robin hoped.

This particular evening was finally the last on the road

before entering the city's gates, the last spent sleeping under the stars. Before the trio made camp, Flea hunted with Robin, and they brought down enough game that their bellies were now, hours later, quite full of roasted meat. But Robin worried about his young charges, fretful that the warm victuals weren't enough to sustain them through the frigid night. Warm breath escaped in little clouds, and the earth had hardened with frost when the sun went down. Robin brooded that under these conditions, one or the other of his companions might fall ill.

Lady slept some distance away from him and the fire he tended, preferring discomfort to seeking Robin's warmth. Flea, however, could have easily singed his shoes, he'd tucked himself so close to the flames. Every so often, Robin nudged the boy's feet away from the stones containing the fire to prevent just that. Flea snuffled but didn't rouse. Farther away, Lady lay perfectly still. She also seemed to be slumbering deeply, but Robin worried that she might, instead, be succumbing to the cold.

After adding another pile of deadwood to the flames, Robin approached Lady's inert form. To his dismay, he found she wasn't as still as she'd appeared from a distance. She was shivering violently despite the blanket she clutched tightly around her like a thin cocoon.

"Damnation!"

Grabbing his own blanket, Robin lay down beside her and spread his mantle over them both, as though he were a great bird tucking Lady under his wing. Pressing his chest and thighs to her back and rump, he hugged her close.

Lady made a little, incoherent sound. She was sleeping, after all, but freezing while she dozed. Foolish wench.

Removing his gauntlets, Robin placed a bare hand over hers. Massaging her gloved fingers, he nuzzled her neck. Beneath the scent of cold and pine clinging to her skin, Lady issued her own distinct perfume, a fragrance that drew him to kiss her.

"Mmmmm," she murmured softly and rolled toward Robin, insinuating herself against him, now with her bosom pressed to his chest, her belly pressed to his groin.

He hardened and hugged her closer still. "Lady."

Her blue eyes fluttered open, though only to drowsy slits. Robin kissed her lashes, her nose, and finally her mouth.

"Unnnhhhh." Another sound was her only verbal response, but Lady returned the kiss. Beneath their covers of blankets and capes, she slid one arm over his waist, anchoring herself firmly.

Robin neither spoke again nor made any sounds. He nibbled Lady's lower lip and stroked her body through her clothes. She palmed his sex through his leggings and braies, squeezing, rubbing. Her eyes remained barely open, as though she drifted someplace between wakefulness and sleep. But her fingers were busy, deftly skilled now after weeks of ardent tutoring. Robin could not have fought the response she gained from him even if he'd had a mind to.

He had no mind to. He had no mind at all.

Working his own hands nimbly, he drew up the skirt of her dress and the smock beneath it. His fingertips skimmed Lady's stockings and garters, and her naked thighs. Then they found the curls at their juncture and the cleft hidden between.

Her heat made him hotter. Lady explored his neck with her lips and her tongue. She also unfastened his clothing and dipped her hand into his garments, searching for his rigid maleness.

She found it, and his entire body stiffened when her fingers wrapped about his member. Delirious with pleasure, Robin feared he might spend himself like a stripling youth. But he managed to control the sweet agony Lady forced him to endure until she was undulating against his fingers and beckoning him with that age-old dance.

Her eyes fully open now, she wore an expression of awe and amazement. But if full consciousness had just come upon Lady, she failed to cease her gyrations or protest in any way. And when Robin climbed above her, so hot now he would have thrown off all their covers were he not mindful of his lover's needs, she took him readily.

Having gone so many days without her loving, Robin nearly climaxed immediately upon entering Lady's tight sheath. But he drew on his old control and plowed her slowly enough that she finally cried out her release. The wait, the teeth-clenching strain, proved worthwhile, for her inner muscles milked him so thoroughly, Robin saw colors flash behind his eyes when he exploded.

Lying atop her, he crushed Lady to him until their breathing slowed. When he rolled onto his side, he clutched her close. "Are you still cold?" he asked, tugging her skirts down and settling the cloaks and blankets over them once more.

"Nay. I'm almost over-warm."

"I should be sorry, but I'm not. Are you?"

"Nay. I'll regret it on the morrow, though, when you leave me."

"I'm not going to leave you."

Lady stiffened in his embrace, but her silence allowed him to recover from his impulsive vow. By the time she relaxed and her whisper, competing with the wintry wind, drifted to him, he knew no regrets.

"What do you mean?" Lady asked.

"I find I rather like you in my life." Robin drew her closer against him. "I'd prefer not to be parted from you."

Her expression brightened hopefully. "Then we'll go back to the cottage? You'll return to the highways to earn your living?"

"Nay, I cannot. I have obligations—work, you know—in London." He hated to see the light in her eyes dim when he quashed her dreams.

"What sort of work?"

He responded with a regretful shake of his head, and her lashes feathered against her cheek as she looked down, away from him. But abruptly she raised her eyes again, and she met Robin's gaze. "I suppose it doesn't matter. I trust you, Robin. And I'll have you, in London or anywhere at all." She punctuated her declaration with a smile.

Robin's heart soared. He felt ridiculously happy. He imagined the house he would let for Lady. Flea could live with her there, in the walled city, not in Southwark. And she would be waiting for him, always, whenever he returned from traveling. Mayhap she might even bear him a child. . . .

"I'm afraid my London accommodations aren't appropriate for a—for you," he explained hurriedly. "I shall have to find a house. That may take a bit of time, since I have those commitments I mentioned, which I must first attend to. But I think . . . I think I know somewhere you can stay temporarily, since I shan't have you returning to Fat Fanny's under any circumstances."

"Flea? Can Flea stay with me?"

"Once I've acquired a new place, aye, of course. And if he wishes to stay in my current apartments, he may."

"Oh, Robin!" Lady exclaimed, hugging him. "I am so happy. I thought you intended to put me back on the streets again. Flea thought those were your plans. I can't wait to tell him our news."

Robin glanced at the slight sleeping figure. "Why don't you wait until morning? He's dead to the world, and whilst he's asleep, that gives us our privacy. . . ."

After entering London through Moorgate, Robin deposited Lady and Flea at a public house. He bought them each a plowman's luncheon with a mug of ale, and then, advising Lady he intended to see about her accommodations, he left them together.

"What's goin' on?" Flea demanded. "You an' Robin haven't been speakin' since before we headed home. Now you're both smilin' like cats who've got at the cream."

Lady couldn't help grinning. "Flea," she announced, "we're going to be married."

"What!" The boy nearly choked on his ale. Ignoring the foam covering his upper lip, he set his heavy mug aside. "Robin asked you t' be his wife?"

She nodded. "He has business to attend to in the city, so we must wait a bit. But he's going to find a house for us, and then all of us—you too, Flea—can live together!"

Flea frowned instead of joining Lady in a giddy grin. "Have you tol' him, then, about yourself?"

His question effectively erased Lady's own smile. "Of course not! Flea, he's an upright man, a highway robber, and who knows what business he gets up to in the city.

He can't know all about me, or he'd never want me, then."

The youth looked down at his platter of bread and cheddar cheese. "Tell me this. Has he told you all there is about himself?"

Lady exhaled a loud puff of air. "Nay. He hasn't. But I trust him," she added, meeting Flea's gaze. "Besides, since I have a secret or two, he's entitled to some of his own."

"Lady, are you certain he asked you to marry him, to be his legal wife?" Flea pressed, reaching across the table to take Lady's hand.

The gesture surprised her, distressed her, but she ignored it. "I told you he did. Why do you doubt it? Do you think I'm not good enough for him?"

"Nay, Lady, nay! O' course you're good enough. Mayhap you're too good."

"I don't think so. Flea, I never thought to have a man of my own, a husband, mayhap even a family, not since . . . I'd lost any chance of that, I believed, once reduced to living by my wits in the streets and sleeping at night in a ramshackle stew. And when I was in the Counter . . . ! But then you brought Robin into my life, he rescued me from the gaol, and everything changed. It's only going to be better now, I promise."

Flea nodded, but he remained scowling. He said nothing more, and barely managed to eat his lunch.

Robin hoped Olivia was home from Paris. He could not recall if she'd advised him of when she planned to return, but it had been awhile. If he were lucky, she'd be back in London now. She had to be, for she was critical to his plan. Without her assistance, Robin didn't know what he would do. First, though, he had to declare the end to their liaison *and* persuade her to help. He did not look forward to that encounter. Thus, dread and desperation compelled him to get it all behind him.

"Sir Moreton," the manservant greeted him, responding to Robin's knock at the front door.

"Is Mistress Crane in? Has she returned?"

"Aye, m'lord. I shall announce you."

"Is she alone?"

"Aye, she is. Upstairs."

"I'll announce myself," Robin declared, pushing past the fellow and taking the stairs two at a time.

"Robin!" Olivia gasped when he appeared in the doorway of her bedchamber. "Is something wrong? Or are you merely that anxious to see me?"

"I am, of course, always pleased to see you." He hugged her briefly, stiffly, feeling guilty for even that demonstration of tenderness. "Olivia, there are some matters of import I must discuss with you immediately."

"And I with you."

"Olivia—"

"Let me speak first, Robin." She put her shoulders back and raised her chin a notch. "I hope this doesn't hurt you overmuch, but in Paris, I met a man."

"Oh?" He hadn't expected this, but he was not displeased. "Someone special?"

"I find him special, yes. He is a count, the Count Luc D'Arcy." Olivia blinked slowly and raised both her eyebrows before forging straight ahead. "Robin, he's asked me to marry him, and I've accepted."

"Oh!" he said again, surprised and very pleased. Yet he dared not allow his relief to show. With a scowl, he offered, "I'm happy for you, then. For both of you. Do you love him, Olivia?"

She smiled thoughtfully. "Aye, Robin, I believe I do." Stepping forward, she reached out and touched him. "I'm sorry for telling you so abruptly, but I thought 'twas best to get it done with, since—since we won't be going on as we were before."

"Of course," Robin agreed.

"You knew there was no future for us?" she inquired softly. "I'm not any more the sort of woman you'd wish to take to wife than you are the sort of man I'd choose as a husband. We were best as lovers, and only that."

"Quite right, Olivia. Though I must admit, your finding someone so unexpectedly, so quickly, comes as a bit of a surprise."

"You'll get over it," she assured him with a grin. Then, taking Robin's hand, she led him to a seat beneath her window. "Now, tell me what it is you find so urgent."

Sitting beside her, Robin asked, "Do you recall the young woman I brought here just before you departed for Paris? The one called Lady?"

"Oh, aye. How could I forget the thin, bedraggled, dirty wench? What's become of her?"

"I've had her with me whilst I was out of the city. Now we've returned, and I wondered if you could take her in for a time. I've serious business I must see to—the queen's life may be at stake—so I can't look after her properly myself."

"Why are you looking after her at all, Robin? I thought she was part of this matter you're investigating. Surely you don't usually shelter either villains or witnesses."

"She's neither a villain nor a witness. But—" Robin left off, unable to explain more. So far things with Olivia were proceeding smoothly, yet he dared not risk offending her by explaining that Lady would be replacing her in his life. No matter that Olivia had become betrothed to another man, she'd most likely receive the news as an insult.

"Robin, you care for her!" she suddenly exclaimed. When he did not deny it, she went on. "You were going to tell me we were through because your heart is set on that wench these days!"

He dared neither confirm nor deny her supposition, so Robin remained silent. And then Olivia chuckled. "I believe Ben Jonson should write a play about us. But at least we each found someone new at precisely the same moment. Still"—she shook her head and frowned—"I wouldn't think a 'street mort,' as she called herself, would prove a suitable mistress for you."

"She's quite suitable, Olivia. Except . . ."

"Except what?"

"She is a bit rough," Robin admitted. "She speaks better than most of her sort, but she needs some polishing. Everything from how a gentlewoman should eat at a fine table to, perhaps, learning how to read. She knows her letters, she tells me, but 'twould suit me better if she could read and write a bit. Could you . . . ?" He looked at Olivia hopefully.

"You're asking me to not only shelter her, but tutor her?"

"If you would, Olivia. You're the only one I dare ask."

"Very well, Robin," she consented with a sigh. "And be sure you're the only one I would do it for."

"Thank you, dearest!" Gratefully, Robin hugged her again, and then they stood. "I don't expect great gains, you understand. But if you could get Lady started. I should be done with my assignment, in one fashion or another, in a fortnight or less. Hopefully, I will be able to find suitable quarters during that time. Then I'll come for her, take her off your hands, and tutor her myself."

Smiling crookedly, Olivia shook her head. "I doubt you'll be teaching her to read, Robin. More likely, you'll be improving her bedroom skills."

Smiling ruefully, Robin accompanied Olivia down the stairs. "There is something more I should tell you," he admitted.

"Oh, dear. What's that?"

"Lady doesn't know who I am, what I do. She knows me only as Robin and thinks I'm a highwayman. I should like to keep it that way."

"A highwayman? A footpad?" She covered her heart with her hand. "Sir Robert Moreton, you must be jesting!"

"Nay, I am not. Therefore, I shouldn't like you confiding in her or even mentioning in passing anything to do with my heritage or occupation. I'll tell Lady in due time."

"Very well."

They paused at the front door. "Robin, don't take umbrage at what I am about to ask, but . . . do you think the girl is worth it? Any number of better bred females, gentlewomen, ladies, would be glad to be your mistress. Why bother trying to polish a pebble into a gem?"

"She's already a gem, Olivia."

Robin pecked her on the cheek, and with that gesture of farewell, left his former lover to hurry back to Lady.

Thirteen

Robin collected his "wards" and deposited Lady with Olivia. The two eyed each other prudently, as though each took the other's measure. The slight tension between them made him uneasy, but rather than explore it and seek some resolution, he chose not to put himself between a pair of women, both of whom he had bedded. Instead, he assured himself Lady would be safe in Olivia's care, and departed immediately with Flea in tow.

Standing with the youth in the street outside Olivia's, Robin sensed Flea seemed less than happy, too.

"What's on your mind, lad?" he asked him gruffly.

"I . . . shouldn't say, m'lord."

"Why not?"

"I've no right."

"Forget about rights. Tell me what's troubling you."

Flea scuffed the toe of one shoe with the sole of the other and studied his handiwork with a scowl. "I don't understand what you're doin' with Lady."

Robin sighed. "She cannot stay with me at Whitehall, so this arrangement with Mistress Crane is a temporary measure."

"I don't mean that. I was referrin' to your plans to marry Lady."

"Marry her?" Robin felt as though he'd been struck from behind. "Who told you I intended to marry her?"

"Lady did." Flea looked up at Robin. "Are you sayin' you didn't propose marriage to her?"

Dear God. So that's what she'd taken his offer to mean! How would he ever explain to the wench that he could only take her as his mistress, since that would prove difficult enough?

"Nay, Flea. I did not suggest marriage. But I see now that Lady could have misunderstood."

"You're a knight, m'lord. Titled. You have rooms in the palace. You're the sort o' man who might take a mistress," Flea surmised. "But you've not told Lady any o' this, have you? She believes you're a highway robber. She thinks you're one of us, not another cony we like t' cut purses from. Am I right, m' lord?"

"You are," Robin said grimly. Then he added, "I intend to tell her when the time is right. For the moment, I see no need to complicate matters."

Flea shook his head. "You think she'll be pleased, don'cha? You think Lady'll be happy, bein' kept by a nobleman. But I'm doubtin' it, meself."

Robin's brow furrowed as he wondered if the lad understood Lady better than he. "Why? Because she thinks she's involved with an upright man?"

"Nay. Because she's too good for what yer really offerin' her."

Robin wanted this discussion no more than he wanted to be privy to any conversations Olivia and Lady were currently engaged in. With a dismissive wave of his hand, he climbed onto his horse and waited for Flea to climb onto the palfrey.

"Where are we goin'?" the boy asked presently.

"To my apartments. I told Lady you could stay with me 'til I've found a house for the three of us."

"Nay. I'm headin' back t' Southwark."

"Why? What's there for you?"

"What's there for me this side o' the Thames?"

"Employment."

"What?" Flea pulled a face as he turned to Robin, riding slowly beside him.

"Let me explain a bit more about myself to you," Robin offered. "I am a knight, aye, but I'm employed by the Privy Council. My job is to see Queen Elizabeth is protected from harm. Presently, we've some serious concern that a group of Scots are planning to slay Her Majesty in retaliation for Queen Mary's execution."

"Scots? Like that cuffin whose clothes I took?"

"Precisely. I wasn't merely waylaying coaches up north because I enjoyed it, but to intercept messages coming down to London from Edinburgh. Now, my work's brought me back to the city. I could use you to keep watch on the activities of a few suspicious coves—one in particular named Gowan. And perhaps you might encounter and identify the man who visited Fat Fanny's. I'd pay you a steady stipend for your efforts. Are you interested?"

"A steady stipend? How much?"

Robin suggested an amount, and Flea negotiated a higher wage. Then he grinned. "All right, then. I'll be your spy for a bit."

"And you'll sleep on my chamber floor?"

"Only if me auntie's barred me from my room at her stew."

Robin reported directly to the Lord Treasurer's office and found Burghley in. With him were Sir Francis Walsingham and James Dekker.

"Been waiting on you, Robert," Walsingham announced.

He noticed the secretary had lost weight since he'd last seen him. "You knew I'd returned?" he inquired, a bit surprised.

Walsingham nodded, and Robin glanced at Dekker seated in a chair beside him. "You explained all we know?"

"I did," Dekker confirmed with a nod.

"And we've concluded 'tis far from enough. A phantom warrior who may or may not be in Scotland!" Burghley scoffed. "And displays. What blasted displays? At least we're certain they intend to make their move against the queen on her Accession Day, most likely at the height of the festivities."

"But that's little more than a fortnight away," Walsingham pointed out. "We don't know enough to waylay the assassin, whoever Angus MacKinney might be."

"You know of him, do you not?" Robin inquired.

"Aye. Rumor has had him involved in every plot there ever was to free Queen Mary, even that Babington business. But he's never been caught at it, and anyone who knew him on sight died without describing him. So I thought to plead with Elizabeth herself, urging her to make herself scarce on the anniversary of her Accession. Make only an appearance, I suggested."

Robin studied Burghley's expression. "But she refused?"

"Damned if she didn't, the stubborn woman!"

"Then we must find this Angus person," Dekker declared.

"And determine what havoc his colleagues have in mind as diversions," Robin added.

"Yes." Burghley looked at the two young men. "Can you do it?" he asked them.

"We will do it," Robin said with determination, "because we must."

Dekker and Robin sat at a shadowy corner table in the taproom on the ground floor of the inn where Dekker kept a room. The Fox and Hare was a large inn, able to accommodate nearly a hundred lodgers with ease. This evening, it seemed to the pair, most of the guests were downstairs drinking.

The two young men shared a pitcher of beer that had already been refilled a couple of times over. Their expressions were dour, and neither spoke much.

"You like it here?" Robin inquired abruptly. "It must be terribly noisy. Hard to sleep."

"'Tisn't bad. Besides, I'm almost never in London. The Fox and Hare's only a place to stow my belongings."

"You wouldn't prefer Whitehall?"

"Damnation, no!" Dekker made a face and shook his head. "Too much intrigue at court, toes you must keep yourself from stepping on and all that."

Robin nodded. "I live there because, methinks, Walsingham hoped to maneuver me into a spot where I'd catch the queen's eye. Thought I had a chance of becoming one of her favorites."

"Be grateful you're not. She's a fine enough lady, a grand queen—I'd lay down my life for her. But—she's frigging old, Moreton! Hair's falling out and teeth gone yellow. Yet that damned Raleigh keeps tickling her ribs and whispering in her ear, as though Elizabeth were a blushing virgin! Supposedly she remains a virgin, but the bloom's long off that rose."

Robin nodded. He had a rose still in bloom, a flower fair. And he hadn't seen her, let alone made love to her, in over a week. That thought made him decidedly more miserable than he had been all evening, and he'd been feeling damnably miserable.

"I intend to leave soon, make my home elsewhere." He drank and wiped his lips of foam.

"Taking a wife or a mistress?" Dekker inquired, and Robin replied with a shrug. "Is it that wench from up near the border, the 'Falcon's' doxy?"

"Aye. But she's a Londoner, same as we." He gave Dekker a look. "You're not that good a sleuth after all, are you?"

"As if you are!" He reached out and swatted a serving maid's derriere. She squealed, slapped Dekker's hand away and moved on. When Dekker turned back to Robin, propping his elbows on the table, he said, "We're sitting here getting cup-shot, Moreton, because today we're no nearer the bottom of this conspiracy than we were a week ago. And now, 'tis less than another week 'til the queen's Accession Day!"

"Don't remind me," Robin snarled into his beer. "Even the lad, the boy I took under my wing, has learned naught. I thought he might—he's small and clever. The perfect criminal or the perfect spy."

"He's not out foisting, do you think?"

"Nay. Flea's an honorable fellow, in his own way. Besides, how could I expect him to uncover anything when we can't?" Gazing across the table at Dekker, Robin raised his black eyebrows questioningly. Abruptly, he slammed his fist on the boards. "I just cannot frigging believe it!"

"What?" Dekker blinked.

"That it all dried up. Those blasted Scots are surely

still communicating. But despite all we've done—everyone spying for Burghley and Walsingham—we've come up empty-handed. 'Tis worse now than before I went north and you to Edinburgh! No missives being passed, not even any meetings amongst Gowan and his friends at St. Paul's. I could have stayed in bed with Lady all this time, considering the little I've accomplished away from her."

Mentioning Lady and bed in the same breath caused blood to rush to his loins. Robin grimaced, raised his mug, discovered it empty again, and refilled it from the pitcher.

"Watch your voice, Moreton. You speak too loudly, someone will overhear us."

"Good! Then mayhap he'll come over and tell us something we need to know!" Robin belched. His head hurt; his eyelids were heavy.

"Did you ever consider," Dekker said, "that we're going about this all wrong? Skulking about in the shadows and under cover of night watching Fraser, Gowan and Murdoch? Oh, we know they're into it somehow, but they're clever and cautious. Mayhap we ought to look to those involved in previous conspiracies."

Squinting, Robin tried to follow his companion's words. But focusing his vision didn't clear his ears any. "I don't understand. Why would we want to do that?"

"Because Angus MacKinney is supposed to have participated in several efforts to free the Scottish queen. We're all but sure he's a part of this plot to assassinate Elizabeth. If he's involved again, mayhap others are involved again, too."

Robin's upper lip curled, and he shook his head. "You're referring to those who took part in the Babington Conspiracy? But Anthony Babington and the rest, far-flung as they were, are all gone. Escaped clean or beheaded."

"But they had kin, Moreton, and friends. Several of those Catholic conspirators on Throckmorton's list were Londoners. Damnation!" Dekker swore spiritedly, making Robin wince. "One of those involved was the son of the queen's own undertreasurer! I'm thinking, Robin, that we might dig up new leads to pursue if we went back and started sniffing 'round those who had associations with other guilty parties."

Resting his head in his hand, Robin mumbled, "Dekker, how can you come up with such a far-fetched scheme when you have, at the moment, less blood in your veins than beer? I'd be hard-pressed right now to recite all my sisters' names."

"Well, you've got too many blasted sisters, by half!"

"Piss off," Robin grumbled, quaffing his beer. "What about this son of the undertreasurer?"

Dekker told him what he recalled and added, "There was another, I think, a knight, an older fellow who came from a Catholic family."

"Most of our families once claimed to be Catholic."

"Bite your tongue," Dekker advised. "Let me think, now. Rose. Aye, that was his name. He may still be imprisoned."

As Robin watched, Dekker again reached out to grab the comely serving maid when she approached their table. This time he pulled her into his lap and slipped an arm around her waist. "Care to come upstairs with me, Colleen?"

Robin slumped forward against the table, held his head in his hands, and waited to see how Dekker fared. His good-looking companion's eyes looked bloodshot, and

Robin doubted that if he got the wench upstairs, he could get his staff up, too.

"I'm almost finished for the night," Colleen admitted. "I suppose I might slip away early."

"Then let's slip." Dekker nudged the girl off his lap and staggered to his feet. "Catch the bill, will you, Moreton? There's a good fellow. See you . . . on the morrow."

"It had better be early. We've work to do."

"Wake me," Dekker urged as he lurched off, leaning heavily on Colleen's shoulder.

Seeing the two depart made Robin ache for Lady. All week, he'd been quelling the desire to go to her. Now he needed her, craved her, simply had to have her.

Fumbling about for the coins to pay for their night's drinking, Robin splashed a handful of white money onto the table as he stood. Tossing his cloak over his shoulder, Robin slapped his hat onto his head and began making his way to the portal. To his chagrin, he discovered his legs weren't as sure as the floor boards, and he stumbled into several people before reaching the door. Once he hit the frosty night air, his head swam and his stomach churned.

"Damn." Dizzy, Robin leaned against the building, annoyed by The Fox and Hare sign creaking on its chains directly overhead. If he was this far gone that his temples pounded and his vision blurred, he thought it might be easier to head directly to his rooms at Whitehall. But, ah! If he could make love to Lady, if he could bury himself in her flesh, inhale her scent, cover himself with her hair . . . that would serve him even better. In the morn he could go forth and slay dragons. A few disgruntled, Scottish Papists would be unable to thwart him—he would step on them as though they were bugs!

Sure Lady was the only tonic to soothe his miseries,

Robin pushed off the wall behind him and imagined himself strolling surefootedly, shoulders squared, stance erect. In fact, he listed spinelessly and stumbled up the lane.

Lady sat with a scowl in Olivia's parlor. She felt like a trussed-up goose in her flat-bodiced dress with its starched, wired ruff, and worse, the damnable farthingale jutting out from her hips. Oh, how Lady longed for the simple clothes she used to wear after relinquishing her last fine gown and moving to Southwark. Wealthy women suffered for fashion; common wenches, as she'd become, did not. Their outmoded frocks not only revealed a bit of feminine flesh at the neckline but, more important, allowed a female to breathe. Yet for some reason Lady couldn't fathom, Olivia felt it necessary to garb Lady *as* a lady. She did not understand why, since they went nowhere and entertained no one.

Nor did she understand Olivia's compulsion to tutor her in manners and other fine ways. Though Lady knew Olivia was done with Robin, having betrothed herself to a Frenchman, she wasn't sure that Robin had confided his own intentions to Olivia. Yet even if he had mentioned his plans to marry Lady, why would Olivia think she needed to appear more refined? A rogue the likes of Robin would never wish it. Upright men needed helpmeets of the sort Lady had been in the north country, not pampered, powdered, perfumed gentlewomen. So Mistress Crane's motives remained beyond Lady's ken while the lessons themselves tested her endurance.

Today's reading lesson at last made her lose her patience. Though feigning ignorance was, in general, trying, what infuriated Lady now was not Olivia's tedious instruction but Reverend Goddington's tract. Olivia had provided the pamphlet, and Lady, skimming it quickly, discovered it to be a hateful piece of literature claiming the poor were ignorant by their own choosing and thus should not be pitied. Unable to keep silent, Lady interrupted Olivia's explanation of the pronunciation of the letter "k." Standing, she tossed the offending pages into Olivia's lap.

"What the Reverend Goddington says, there, is naught but cruel and thoughtless," she announced. "Ignorant by choice—what drivel!"

Olivia blinked up at her, and her jaw dropped. "You read it? You read the pamphlet?"

"Aye, I can read quite well, thank you. I also know how to dress myself and how to eat at a table set with silver plate and Venetian glass. Mistress Crane, just because I worked in a stew does not mean I'm completely lacking an education."

"You—you—" Olivia sputtered, coming to her feet and staring at Lady as though she'd never seen her before. "You worked in a stew?"

"Aye, and lived there as well. But 'twasn't as a bawd that I earned my keep, only as a laundress. Also," she added, since she'd decided to be honest, "I cut a few purses."

"I can't—can't—" Olivia shook her head in disbelief, still staring. "I knew you came from an . . . uncertain . . . background. But I can't understand why Robin would want—why he would be involved—why he would—"

"Desire a low-class thief the likes of me?" Lady finished for her. "Mayhap because he's also a thief, though of a higher order."

"Aye." Olivia nodded. "Robin the highwayman, I know."

"Since you're now aware you may suspend your vigilant instruction, may I ask you, Mistress Crane, why you think Robin wants me polished and refined? Because I don't feel he does. When we lived in the forest and robbed coaches together, he seemed only to care that I knew how to shoot my pistol and cover his back."

Olivia sat down again, hard, and clutched her heart. "You shot a pistol? You robbed coaches?"

When Lady nodded her affirmation, Olivia inhaled a deep breath. "Sit down," she urged, gesturing to the chair Lady had recently vacated. "There are some things about Robin I think you should know, some things he's neglected to tell you."

Curious but suddenly apprehensive, Lady sat and waited for Olivia to continue. The woman finally leaned toward her and confided, "Robin's not always a footpad. In London, he's something else. I don't think he'd like me to give you all the details—they're his to tell. But I can say he's a—a gentleman. He wears fine clothes, he mingles with a class of educated, wealthy, even noble people. He's quite educated himself, Lady. Though I can't imagine how you two lived when away from London, here in the city, Robin requires a woman who can appear at his side no matter what the occasion."

Lady exhaled a pent-up breath. Perplexing as this news was, it relieved her to know she could do this for Robin. It was nothing for her to behave like a lady—for that very reason, Flea had given her the name.

But then Olivia added, "It isn't as though Robin has a wife to take about town, so you shan't be the sort of mistress who stays at home awaiting his visits. Surely he'll expect you to accompany him to all manner of affairs."

For a moment, Lady stopped breathing all together. *Mistress!* Is that what Robin had proposed? She thought back to that last night outside of London. Robin had never mentioned marriage, she had only presumed. But Flea had been doubtful when she told him. Flea knew! Flea knew that Robin was a gentleman in fact, not a gentleman rogue, and that Robin thought her far beneath him. Why hadn't Flea warned her? Or had he?

Lady felt a headache coming on and stood abruptly. "Excuse me," she said. " 'Tis quite late, and I'm tired."

When she headed toward the staircase, Olivia followed. "Lady, I do hope you're not upset. I presumed a woman in your position would be—thrilled—to learn her lover is not—not always—an outlaw, but instead a gentleman. A female can only better herself through her associations with men of higher rank and class. Like the late Master Crane and I, and now, Count D'Arcy."

She knew Olivia was attempting to be consoling if not helpful, but Lady wanted only to be alone. With a nod, she dashed up the stairs to her room.

Taking out her confusion on her clothes, Lady tore off her ruff, her gown, her hoops, and her stockings—which was no easy feat without someone's assistance. Yet she had no desire to wear the latest fashions. She didn't want anything associated with London, or the places or faces that harbored dark memories for her. What Lady did want was to live in a little house in the forest, or perhaps on the moors, with her husband, "the Falcon."

Naked now, she climbed into bed. *Husband!* Robin did not want to be her husband, only her paramour. That realization tore at Lady's heart, until slowly she began to understand why he felt that way. Obviously, Robin didn't believe her capable of fitting in with his peers, and why should he? He had seen her only in the company of whores, thieves, and other prisoners in the gaol. Of course he would presume she could not be any better than those low-class felons she consorted with!

In any case, why did she feel the need to wed him? Lady had known only contentment in her role as his doxy. If she and Robin had remained there, in the country, living and working side by side on the wrong side of the law, she'd never have broached the topic of marriage. Why did she need marriage now?

Lady fell asleep mulling over all these things. Sometime during the night, Robin came to her—not in her dreams, but in reality. He woke her, stumbling around in the dark, fumbling with his clothes, until she helped him out of them. In bed, Robin held her, kissed her, tried to make love to her, and then, too drunk to perform, fell asleep snoring. Lady clucked and shook her head as she arranged the bedclothes over his nude body and kissed his brow.

But when she climbed into bed beside him again and snuggled against Robin, backside to backside, she knew why she wished to be his wife: In her head and her heart, he already was her husband.

Fourteen

Flea woke early. The sun had not yet risen, but he could no longer bear to linger in Robin's rooms. Whitehall wasn't part of his world, so though he appreciated Robin's generosity, he hated spending any time there. He always felt as though a guard might grab him by the scruff and heave him into a dungeon. Damn his Aunt Fanny for putting him out of her house!

Robin's bed remained in order, Flea saw with a passing glance. He felt relieved. He so very much wished to prove himself helpful to the cove—the knight—who had saved Lady and taken him on a great adventure where he learned to hunt and trap. But despite the hours he'd spent loitering at St. Paul's and the many questions he'd asked old copesmates who still worked as flicks and such, Flea had learned nothing Robin could connect to a Scottish Catholic conspiracy against the queen.

Still, Flea had set out to learn all he could about Gowan, the Scot who most interested Robin. Once, Flea had even picked the cove's pocket, hoping to find some correspondence of the sort Robin sought. Flea had come away excited when he'd discovered he'd filched a piece of script. But he was disappointed when Robin examined the paper and proclaimed it unimportant, nothing more than an order for wheaten flour and rye Gowan would use in his bakeshop. But then, a balding, squinty-eyed baker could not be expected to have anything more intriguing on his person than a flour-dusted apron or a recipe.

Murdoch was another suspect Flea shadowed. He owned a warehouse on the docks where imported goods were stored 'til the merchants came to take possession. A slender man, Murdoch rarely went down to the ships where the burly, muscled dockers toiled, but instead busied himself in private quarters somewhere within his wharfside building. He seemed as dull and predictable as any yeoman, arriving and departing the same hour every day.

Sometimes Flea wondered if Robin and the Privy Council weren't looking for trouble where none existed. Robin was so keen on these three immigrants, despite their unnoteworthy appearance. The trio claimed only one minor distinction, as far as Flea could tell: All had trades and worked for themselves, not for others.

The third man, Fraser, was a smith who, like his friends, toiled alone without even an apprentice to assist him. His smithy stood on the lower edge of town near the Thames, and Flea presumed he was not very skilled, for he seemed to have few customers. He had no wife, either, and probably no ambition. Such a man, Flea believed, could pose no threat to Queen Elizabeth.

Yet he now had Fraser's image in his mind, and thoughts of him drew the youth toward the river. Still dark, the eastern horizon glowed with a smoky iridescence that only hinted at sunrise. The air was cold and Flea's stomach rumbled. The bakeshops would be among the first to fling open their doors; when they did, he thought it would be clever to go to Gowan's shop and buy some buns. At least he could then tell Robin he remained ever vigilant, and he would not be lying.

As Flea neared the river, the water's familiar dank, musty smell tickled his nose. He turned a corner to put himself on the alley at whose end sat Fraser's smithy.

Piles of rags heaped against the back walls of buildings lining the narrow, dirt-packed passage shivered and snored—drunks and vagrants sleeping. Though Flea lived his life beyond the brink of gentle society, he had never been reduced to such mean comforts. He hoped he never would.

Clang! Clang! Clang! Metal pounding metal. Smithy sounds. The noise drew him on, and Flea quickened his pace.

Coming to a silent stop across from Fraser's enterprise, he backed into the narrow recess of a closed doorway. Flea glanced about, wondering if any other agents, possibly Robin himself, hid nearby, observing the Scot. But he didn't even see any beggars curled up on the ground.

Flea saw Fraser clearly, as no obstructions blocked his view. The structure that housed the smithy was only three-sided, two mean-looking mongrels serving as the fourth barrier. The fire the man used to fashion and mold his implements bathed the Scot's form in light.

Clang! Clang! Clang! Flea couldn't see what the cuffin was working on because his broad back remained between him and the anvil, the sledge. More thoughtful than curious, Flea watched and waited, wondering what Fraser toiled at so early in the morning.

Then the Scot moved, turning sideways, and lifted up a magnificent sword. Even though he'd never had the opportunity to own a rapier of his own, Flea recognized the quality of the beautiful weapon Fraser had crafted. The hilt was a swirl of stiff gold cord, thin as wire and so elaborate it encompassed Fraser's hand like a gauntlet.

The blade, blue steel, shone like a bolt of lightning in the firelight.

He made weapons. Fraser was an armorer.

Flea sucked in a breath and moved to one side, crunching some stones. Fraser failed to hear the gravel grinding beneath Flea's shoe, but the dogs did. They raised their heads off their huge paws and stared at him through the dim dawning light. To Flea, their eyes looked like four glowing coals.

His heart pounded, not so much in fear that he might be discovered, but because he knew something Robin surely did not: Fraser was not just a farrier but an armorer! And that meant, most likely, he knew how to wield those arms he made!

Holding his breath, Flea stepped out from his hiding spot and, keeping his back pressed to the wall, made his way along the narrow alley. As soon as he could manage it, he leapt into the middle of the lane and sprinted away.

Robin woke with a start in his own bed, in his own rooms. He had slipped out of Olivia's house much earlier that morning, without waking Lady. For some reason, their lovemaking had not renewed his spirits or his energy. Now his head throbbed, as though someone pounded at his door.

Hell and damnation, someone *was* pounding on his door! With a snarl, Robin dragged himself up and answered the knock.

"Why are you here at this hour?" he demanded of Dekker. "I would have thought you'd still be in bed with Colleen."

" 'Tis almost midday, Moreton. I left her hours ago. In the meanwhile, I've been working."

Robin shuffled away and Dekker followed him, closing the door.

"Moreton, do you recall what I said last night about past conspirators possibly being involved in this scheme?"

"Aye." He splashed water on his face and exchanged his dirty shirt for a fresh, full-sleeved one.

"I went to the Tower and inquired after Sir Leslie Rose. He was one of those supposedly involved with Babington."

"I remember you saying that, too." Robin shrugged on a leather jerkin and fastened it up the front.

"You won't believe this, but he's still confined there! He's been locked away for years now, has never been tried for his crime—I swear he's been quite forgotten."

"Did you speak with him?" Robin sat on the edge of his bed and pulled on his shoes.

"I did." Dekker nodded. "He seemed relieved to speak with anyone, 'tis been so long since he had a visitor."

" 'Tis a sad story, Dekker, but what has he to do with our current dilemma?"

"Nothing," he admitted. "Rose insists he is innocent, and I'm inclined to believe him. But he knows the Babington story as well as he knows his own life story: how they sneaked messages to Queen Mary whilst she was living in confinement, and how they planned to get her free, murder Elizabeth, and then set Mary on the English throne. What these others did cost him his freedom, so the man has their deeds memorized. Rose gave me names, Moreton, names of small players in that grand scheme. We should find these people, their families, and question them."

Robin secured his sword at his waist and put his hat on his head. Opening the door, he ushered Dekker into the corridor. "I suppose we may as well. At least we'll feel that we're doing something. But I fear this will all be for naught."

"Our only consolation is no one else is having better luck than we."

"That will be no consolation if our queen is slain!" Robin pointed out, and Dekker nodded.

"Here, take this." He handed Robin a small sheet of paper. "Their residences, if Rose had any idea, are noted beside each name. Mayhap we'll have some luck this day."

"I only hope it is good luck and not ill."

Flea meant to go straight to Whitehall and wait on Robin. But his belly growled, so he diverted to Gowan's bakeshop and bought himself some hot cross buns. A mort, the Scot's wife, Flea presumed, took his penny, and he only glimpsed Gowan through a doorway that separated the shop from the ovens.

Instead of leaving promptly, the youth lingered, sitting on a barrel in front of the shop. He felt badly that he had been so unsuccessful at the task Robin set before him. Even now, glimpsing the baker *baking.* What good was that? And though he'd been scared and certain Fraser was up to no good when he spied him fashioning that grand weapon, smithing and armoring were companion trades. In the end, Flea had come up with naught. He knew it, but he wasn't keen on Robin knowing it.

Chewing his doughy bun and licking the sticky icing from his fingers, Flea watched the activity bustling in this part of town at this early hour. Gentlemen and ladies, servants and laborers, and more than a few people Flea knew to be cony-catchers traversed the lane, going about their business. Flea's old friends were mostly curbing—lifting goods from shop windows with hooks—or simply picking pockets. He exchanged glances with them but they otherwise failed to greet each other.

"Flea!"

He almost jumped from his skin at the loud salutation. Southwark's upright man, the cove who had months ago helped Flea find Lady, halted before him. Octavian was not old, but he was not so young anymore, either. He had broad shoulders, arms knotted with muscles, and his hands always seemed to be clenched into fists, as though he were perpetually prepared to brawl with the next comer.

"Octavian. What're you doin' here?"

"I got business." The ruffler stroked his beard and considered Flea with a thoughtful gaze. "Whatever happened to the mort you had me find? She die in the Hole, or what?"

"Nay. We—I—got her out. She's fine now, she is."

"That's good. And you? Are you flush, lad? You're looking quite the gentry cove, in that fancy mantle you're wearing."

Flea considered his response. Despite the dismal results of his efforts, Robin kept him in coin. But a fellow could never have too much money. Besides, Octavian wasn't the sort of man one refused, if he offered you a job.

"I'm doin' all right. Why? Did you have somethin' for me t' do?"

"Mayhap. You're a bit of a runt, you are. But I'm lookin' for a few hands I can trust." Octavian glanced over his shoulder at three fellows loitering across the dirt lane. "You interested in joining us?"

Flea nodded.

"Wait here a bit. I'll be back directly."

Octavian strode into Gowan's shop. Through the open doorway, Flea saw that he bought neither buns nor bread. After a few words with Gowan's wife, Octavian ducked through the back door and disappeared.

Flea's heart pounded. Octavian had gone to speak with Gowan! Did this job have something to do with the baker?

He felt the urge to piss, but he wasn't about to miss the upright man returning. Besides, the other coves on the opposite side of the street watched him with narrowed eyes. Well, he was as good as any of them; Octavian had recruited him, too. So Flea bounced up and down on the balls of his feet, telling himself it was because of the strain on his bladder, not because of excitement or, worse, trepidation.

"Damnation, Flea!" Octavian exclaimed when he reappeared a bit later. "When my children were small, they didn't fidget as much as you. You're wont to wet yourself, if you don't do something quickly."

"You have children?" Flea couldn't imagine it, and he had to ask as they rounded the side of a building together before stopping in its shadow. The other coves sticking close to the ruffler had fallen into step behind them the moment Flea and Octavian strolled away from the bakeshop. Though they seemed to be paying him no mind, their presence greatly confounded Flea's task of relieving himself. It took him a little time before he managed to water the weeds.

"Aye. You have a mum and da?" Octavian asked gruffly.

"Nay."

The upright man and his cohorts waited silently as Flea put himself back together. His intimate conversation with Octavian abruptly ceased. Wordlessly, the pair headed off together, leading the trio who trailed.

"What sort o' job d' you have for me?" Flea asked casually, wishing instead he could inquire about the ruffler's business with that Scot.

"Can't say."

"Then what—"

"You'll just do as you're told, if you want to earn half a crown." Octavian fixed Flea with a stern eye.

In their world, Octavian reigned as supreme master. Flea nodded obediently and assured him, "I can do that."

The scraggly parade continued along in silence as the ruffler headed toward the docks. Flea dared not hope their next stop might be Murdoch's warehouse. It would be too grand if he learned something about all three of those Scots Robin claimed were traitors, and all in a single day.

"Eddie! Been looking for you," Octavian called out to a thin young man Flea knew by reputation. Eddie crouched near the ground, out of the way of traffic, with several others who looked to be mean laborers. Eddie was a cozener who cheated his gulls by using fullams—weighted dice—in the games he organized. "Come join me and Flea, here."

"My brother, Paulie's, comin' with me," Eddie announced, and Flea saw a cuffin, slightly younger than himself, tagging along behind Eddie.

"Good." Octavian gave them both a brief nod and continued his stroll.

The upright man was definitely leading his party to the docks. Flea found himself fighting giddiness, not only because suddenly he had good reason to be hanging about where the Scots plied their trades, but because Octavian seemed to have taken a special interest in him.

They walked side by side; Flea didn't follow the ruffler like a duck in a row, as the others were doing. Damn, but Flea felt proud!

By the time they reached the wharf, their heels clicking loudly on the wooden planks beneath their shoes, Flea's heart was thumping in noisy counterpoint.

Octavian halted within sight of Murdoch's building, but nowhere near the warehouse's oversized door which, at this hour, stood wide open. Workers bustled in and out, but Flea noticed their hands were always empty going in. The workmen only carried kegs and crates when they exited, and they loaded those containers onto wagons.

"Gather 'round." Octavian turned to his underworld minions, and they formed a close group. "You're a privileged lot, you are, because I been asked to choose some men what would help with the queen's Accession Day celebration, and I chose you. Imagine that!" He smiled. "Cuffins like you, assisting to honor our queen."

The scruffy young men nodded at each other, and Flea found himself, like them, straightening his shoulders.

" 'Tis here we'll be meeting, lads, directly after Bow Bell sounds two nights hence."

"Methinks that's a day early," one of the coves observed.

"If you must know, our job is to start the city's celebration," Octavian announced.

"Doin' what, exactly?" another asked.

"The less you know, the less likely you'll spill your guts over a pint of ale in a boozing ken. 'Tis a surprise, not just for Her Majesty, but for all of London." Octavian nodded, emphasizing the importance of their task.

"How much are you payin'?" Eddie inquired. He sounded too eager, Flea thought, and purposely tamped down his own high emotions. Though Flea had never worked with Octavian before, he'd heard that the upright man liked coves who showed no nerves. No interest, either. With a sigh, Flea put a bored expression on his face.

"Whatever I think you're worth," Octavian growled, "which, at the moment, 'tisn't much. Eddie, I'll remind you but once: This job is as secret as the heavy sides of your dice. If'n I hear you been spouting off about your business here, you won't have a mouth to talk from when I get through with you. Understand?"

Eddie nodded his head with a quick, tight motion and backed up half a step. So did his brother, Paulie, though the lad had not uttered a word.

"Now, none of you had dare forget the time or the place, or find yourselves delayed. This is important, what we're to do here. 'Tisn't about shaving goods or stealing purses, 'tis about *honoring the queen,*" Octavian said in a stage whisper. "As well, since everything we'll be doing is all quite legal, you can flash your earnings without fear of the sheriff pinching you. Should you fail me, though, I'll pinch you myself."

The others shared knowing, uneasy looks before nodding at Octavian.

"Be gone, now, the lot of you. Don't open your traps, and don't show your faces 'round here again 'til the appointed hour."

Everyone scattered like windblown leaves except Octavian and Flea. Flea had expected some nefarious scheme and had hoped it might have something to do with Gowan and Murdoch. But this proved good, too. Being thick with Octavian could only improve his career opportunities.

"I'm heading back across the river," the ruffler announced. "Have some gulls lined up for card play at a gaming house there, and I need a 'barnacle' to wander in once the action's begun, to help me with the cony-catching. You up to it, Flea?"

The boy's pulse raced. Octavian, king of all the outlaws in Southwark, was asking him, Flea, to be part of a card game scheme to fleece some witless players. It was more than an opportunity, it was an honor—one Flea couldn't refuse.

"Aye. Be glad to, Octavian. I know I can do it."

"I know you can, too, lad, or I'd not have suggested it. Let's go. Can't leave those conies waiting."

They headed off together again, the burly ruffler and the pint-sized flick, as though they were frequent comrades. Flea squared his shoulders and walked as tall as his limited height allowed him. He thought passingly of Robin and recalled his intention to alert Lady's love about Fraser the smith. But there was nothing to that, he told himself. And besides, he had already devoted many fruitless days attempting to spy for Robin. If, after all this time, he'd found nothing, Flea decided, then there was nothing to be found. But with Octavian, there were sacks of money to be made.

Fifteen

Olivia had gone out with friends for the evening; except for the servants, now sleeping, Lady found herself alone. Her first thought was that she could now remove her constricting, high-fashion garments, but she reconsidered. Robin would be coming to see her soon. Whether he knew it or not, he hadn't got what he'd come for the other night. Whether he knew it or not, he needed her, and not as some careless mistress to be tucked away for his convenience, but as his wife to share his life with in every way.

So Lady remained gowned, coiffed, and waiting. She wasn't disappointed.

Robin dismounted before Olivia's house and tethered his horse to a post. He'd had a horrible time of late, tracking down cold leads that led nowhere but to a long-solved conspiracy, not the immediate threat. And Burghley chastising him and Dekker for running off in all directions while curious activities occurred in the spot where they should have been: at Murdoch's warehouse on the docks. Other agents had reported the building being vacated, so the treasurer now believed the Scot was cleaning house and closing doors. There seemed no reason for him to, unless Murdoch planned to depart London immediately. These developments did not bode well, not with Accession Day on the morrow.

But worse, for Robin, was that Flea had gone missing. The lad hadn't slept in Robin's rooms for a couple of nights now. He worried the little flick had stumbled into something and got himself caught, or worse. He regretted ever taking the lad into his confidence, let alone sending him out on the streets like a seasoned sleuth. The Scottish conspirators could be naught but desperate men; they would never let a young street thief interfere with their plans for Elizabeth.

At the door, Robin knocked, expecting Olivia's manservant to respond. But when the door opened, he was shocked to find Lady standing there. Shocked not because Lady answered, but shocked to see her put out like a princess.

"Lady?"

" 'Tis what I'm called, aye." She stepped aside to allow Robin access.

"My God, you look beautiful! That is, you always look beautiful, but tonight you look even more so. I never—"

"Thought I could pass for my namesake?" she finished for him, raising both her eyebrows.

"Nay. Aye! Forgive me, I don't know what I'm saying. My work has been frustrating, and I've had little sleep . . ."

Doffing his cap, Robin stepped closer to Lady, rubbing his cheek against hers and blowing softly in her ear.

Lady intended to point out he'd slept very well in her bed, last time he visited. But his breath tickled her neck, and Robin smelled so good, felt so good. When she backed up, he came forward, allowing no distance between them. Shortly, she discovered her back against a wall, imprisoned there by Robin's masculine bulk, and she did not at all mind.

He heard her sigh and felt her melt against him, even as a part of him grew rigid. This was what he wanted, Lady, quivering in his arms. This was what he needed, Lady's softness to renew his strength.

"Where's Olivia?"

"Out for the evening."

"And the servants?"

"Gone to bed."

Robin pushed himself closer, insinuating the bulge of his maleness into the folds of Lady's skirt. Her lashes fluttered, and her breasts seemed to plump above the stiff, straight line of her bodice. He ran his fingertips over that swell of ivory flesh and lost himself in her eyes.

He overwhelmed Lady's senses. In an effort to free herself from the erotic net he'd cast over her, she glanced down. But her gaze went no lower than his lips, full and beckoning. He parted them, moistened them with his tongue, and then kissed her, deep and plundering.

She had no choice. She'd missed him, she desired him. So she slipped her hands behind his neck and did nothing to thwart him when he raised the hem of her gown, ran his hand down her stockinged calf, and guided her slippered foot to the back of his waist. "Robin!" was all she managed, and that as little more than a sigh.

Lady fell silent again because Robin occupied her mouth with more delicious pleasures even as his hand sought her heat and new thrills ignited between her parted thighs.

"God, I've missed you," he confessed as he licked her throat and the plump curves of her breasts. "I need you."

His shaft suddenly replaced his fingers in the folds of her moist sex. The wall braced Lady's back, and his hands braced her bottom as he pushed himself full inside her. He thrust and retreated, she retreated and thrust. Their passions flared to a frenzy as each sought solace and satisfaction in the other.

They exploded with their climaxes at nearly the same time. When Lady called out with her release, Robin swallowed her cry by claiming her lips. When they both came back down, when she lowered her foot to the floor and he settled her skirt modestly around her, Robin held Lady to him as though she were the only thing keeping him anchored.

He thought perhaps she was, and admitted, "I wish I did not have to leave you."

"Have you looked for a house?"

"A house?" Robin pulled away, confusion wrinkling his brow. "Nay, Lady. I've had no time. My work—"

"What work, Robin?"

Shaking his head, he turned, moving away toward a chair.

"Robin, I should like to know what sort of work you do in London, work that's so different from your pursuits in the country."

" 'Tis . . . complicated."

Lady walked toward him and stood beside the chair where he had collapsed. "I understand that. Olivia told me—"

"What did she tell you?" He looked up sharply.

"That in town, you're ofttimes more a gentleman than a rogue. That explains the variety of clothing I've seen you wear. But it doesn't explain what you do and why it keeps us apart."

"Another time, Lady, when my current assignment is finished."

"Assignment? Are you employed by someone? I thought upright men were always their own masters."

"As you already understand, sweetling, I am not always a highwayman."

"But what are you?" she demanded.

His dark eyes met hers, and he smiled tiredly. "The man you love, I hope."

"The man I love doesn't love me. Not enough to marry me." Crossing her arms over her bosom, Lady walked away.

Inwardly, Robin cringed. He knew this conversation was inevitable, but he'd no wish to have it right now. "Lady, in time I shall explain, but now I've no time."

Whirling about, she countered, "Aye, you do! You owe me for sneaking into my bed and then passing out, reeking of beer."

Embarrassed, Robin rested his forehead against his hand. "Forgive me, sweetling. You know that wasn't my intent."

"Nor is it your intent to marry me."

"I would if I could!" He dropped his hand and stared at Lady.

"Yet you think you cannot. Why? You vowed you had no wife already."

"I don't."

"Then what is wrong with me? Do I not look every inch the lady?" She gestured with her arms to indicate her gown, her hair. "Mistress Crane will tell you I'm acquainted with all the courtly manners those of the upper classes deem appropriate. Surely I could not humiliate a robber who passes himself off as a noble or a wealthy merchant time to time, in pursuit of ill-gotten gains!"

Robin did not respond. Of course, Lady would never disgrace him, and she'd do very well as his mistress, even in public or among his friends, such as he had. But with his family? A wench with no true name, no surname, no parentage or heritage would never be accepted by his family. All five of his sisters would disapprove vocally and in other, more subtle ways, which could prove pure torture for Lady. And his frail, widowed father would harken to an early grave, perhaps disinheriting him beforehand, if Robin presented a woman with no bloodlines at all as the mother of the future Moreton line.

But he could not tell Lady any of this, not this eve, not ever. He would never purposely hurt this woman he cared for so intensely. An excuse was required, one Lady would accept. He wished he had more time to concoct one.

He stood and improvised. "Lady, my love, I cannot marry anyone. Not because I'm already wed, but because of my career. I know we did well together in the north country, robbing coaches. But I have other work here, in the city. I'd not make anyone a fit husband.

"Please, don't argue," he begged, grabbing her shoulders and looking pleadingly into her eyes. "There's more to it, and I'll discuss it with you in the future. But now, I must go. Will you give me a kiss to hold me?"

Robin took the kiss before she offered it, and Lady had no choice, once again, but to accede to his wishes. She was walking him to the front door when he asked, "Have you seen Flea?"

"Flea? Nay! I thought he was with you."

"He was, but he's gone missing."

She shook her head as she opened the door. "I wouldn't worry about him. He'll turn up. He's probably picking pockets at St. Paul's."

"You're certainly right," Robin agreed as he fitted his hat to his head. "Farewell, now. I'll see you soon."

Lady closed the door and leaned against it. There had to be something she could do to persuade Robin they made a good match, not just as lovers but as wedded mates. He should have just known it, the thick-headed fool! But as he didn't seem to, she felt compelled to make matters clear. He didn't need an occasional lover, a frivolous mistress who did naught but satisfy his lusts, a mere replacement for Olivia, who had moved on from her rogue to a French count. Robin required a helpmeet, which Lady had been when they practiced highway law together. Yet how could she aid and abet him in London when she knew nothing of how he earned—or stole—his money here in the city?

Olivia wouldn't tell her. She'd got all she was going to get from that woman. But perhaps Flea knew something. Lady had always suspected he did, and since the two rascals had been together of late . . .

But Robin had said Flea had gone. Well, her copesmate had better make an appearance soon. She had a few questions for him!

This was the life. Flea hadn't known it could be so fine, especially in Southwark. But at the gaming house, where food and beverage flowed as though from a spigot, and money drifted across the tables into his hands as though pushed by a gentle wind . . . well, it was as near to heaven as Flea expected to get.

He had been with Octavian for two days and nights. They went to bed late and rose even later, for card cheating wasn't the domain of early risers.

"Getting late," Octavian noted, leading Flea out of the gaming house into the lane with a hand on his shoulder. The pearl gray sky was fast growing darker.

"Not late for cards."

"This eve we'll not be playing cards. Have you forgot?"

"Nay!" he countered quickly, but he lied. Only now, with prompting, did Flea remember their work tonight, their work that had to do with the queen's annual celebration.

"I suppose we'd best go across the bridge before darkmans comes," Flea suggested. Octavian agreed, and they headed in that direction.

"Now can you tell me what it is we're goin' t' do?"

"Aye. I'll tell you, lad." Octavian dropped his voice low. "We're going to light fireworks along the river's banks."

"Fireworks!" Flea exclaimed.

The upright man gave him a look to hold him silent, but he nodded. "You've seen them before, on the queen's birthday, have you not?"

Indeed Flea had. He remembered the first time, a few years back. The booming blasts had nearly made him piss in his leggings. But the colored lights spinning and spraying out across the night sky made up for the noisy scare. Flea had thought the fireworks looked like exploding stars.

"An' we get t' do it? I thought some honored servants o' the queen's had that privilege."

"Not this time. Her Majesty doesn't even know about the display. 'Tis to be a surprise, a gift from the merchants of the city to Queen Elizabeth. They've planned the spectacle for this eve, the night before her Accession Day festivities, so it's truly unexpected."

Flea looked down at his shoes. He'd lived most of his life on instinct, and something nagged at him now. "I can understand that," he said. "But if this grand display is a tribute t' the queen, why wouldn't the merchants do it all themselves in order t' take all the credit? Why'd they want to hire us?"

"I asked that same question of the cove what hired me. He said—and I believe him, the stupid Scot, they're all bluster, no brains—that they're afraid of getting hurt. 'Tis a bit dangerous, lad, to light the squibs. Usually it's the Venetians and Romans who make the things what set them alight. But have you ever seen those foreigners?" Octavian gave Flea a curious glance as they stepped off the bridge on the opposite bank. "They're all missing arms or feet, or at least a couple o' fingers. They look as though they're seasoned warriors."

Scot. Octavian had said the man who'd hired him was a Scot. Gowan? Murdoch? Damn! Flea belatedly recalled his intent to inform Robin about Fraser crafting weapons early in the morn. He should go to the knight's rooms and immediately share what he'd learned. But if he did, Octavian would be angry. He'd never hire him again for any job, and Flea rather liked working the gaming house, so he couldn't risk earning the ruffler's ill will. Besides, fireworks couldn't hurt the queen, safe in her palace as she was. And there were far too many guards protecting Her Majesty for anyone, even Fraser, to get near enough to skewer her with a sword.

Confiding in Robin could wait, at least until after the display. But, oh, Flea wished Lady could see the fireworks up close.

"Octavian, it's still light. D' you mind if I run a quick errand before I join you at our meetin' place?"

The upright man frowned. "You won't be late now, will you? I warned the others about being tardy."

"Nay, I'll be there on time, I vow."

"Go on, then. Be quick about it!"

With a nod, Flea scampered off, breaking into a run as he headed to Robin's friend's house. To his relief, Lady herself opened the door. To his astonishment, she looked like a true lady. He had never seen her garbed like this, not even when she dressed to play the part when they worked the gulls at St. Paul's.

"Good Lord, Flea, where've you been? Robin came round, asking after you. He's worried."

Flea frowned, feeling guilty. He should speak with Robin straight away. But there was Octavian and the fireworks . . .

"I told him I figured you were curbing goods or cutting purses," Lady went on.

"I been with Octavian at a gamin' house. Lady, that's why I'm here. We got a job tonight, somethin' special. 'Tisn't even breakin' any laws. It's goin' t' be excitin', an' I want you t' come with me, t' see it."

"What is it?"

"Fireworks," Flea whispered.

"Really?" Lady looked intrigued at the prospect. "All right, I'll come, but I have to change first."

"We haven't time. I have to meet the upright man by the time the Bow Bell sounds." Flea grabbed Lady's hand and tugged, attempting to pull her out the door.

She held her ground. "Very well, I won't change my clothes. But I'm not leaving here 'til you answer some questions about Robin."

He had known this conversation would happen sooner or later, but it had to be later. "I'm late, Lady, for comin' t' get you."

"One thing, then. Just one for now," she insisted.

Puffing out his cheeks and exhaling a noisy sigh, Flea demanded, "What?"

"His name, Flea. I should like to know Robin's full name, if you have it."

Flea decided it would be prudent to leave out the "Sir" before confiding, "Robert Moreton. That's the cove's name. Are we finished here? Because we have t' hurry."

"Robert Moreton," she repeated, retrieving her cape before joining him on the stoop. "Robert Moreton."

Flea was grateful they had no time for conversation as they hurried down to the river at such a brisk pace, they nearly ran. Once they reached Murdoch's warehouse, Flea found a place for Lady to sit. One thing about a wharf, there were always crates, barrels and other objects to serve as makeshift stools. "Stay here," he told her. "It might be awhile yet, but don't come lookin' for me or headin' home. Just wait."

Lady nodded, and Flea hurried off. Just as the bell sounded, he joined Octavian and the other coves.

"Here's what we're about." Octavian explained to everyone what he'd already confided to Flea, and then told them what their individual tasks would be.

Footsteps approached from the warehouse. Octavian turned and announced, "Here be our benefactor now."

Murdoch, Flea surmised. He knew the building's owner was a man of modest height and build, so Flea presumed this cove was he. But as the fellow drew closer and his raised lantern lighted his face, Flea felt a start. This Scotsman wasn't Murdoch, but Alice's gull—the cove from the stew!

Oh, Flea regretted not having run to Robin earlier—days ago, in fact, after spying Fraser crafting that fantastic sword.

The little Scot conversed privately with Octavian, pointing to several crates near the river's edge. Then he handed the ruffler both a purse full of coins and the lantern, and departed more quickly than he'd arrived, disappearing into the darkness.

"Come on, lads," Octavian urged. When they congregated around the wooden crates, he opened one, revealing neat rows of cylinders all plugged with long, thick wicks.

"All of you but Flea grab half a score each," Octavian ordered as he opened the remaining containers. "Up and down the wharf you go," he continued, gesturing. "Stand the squibs on end. When all the projectiles are placed, return here for lighted candles to set them off. And be careful when you light the wicks, lads. Stand too close, you could end up losing a part of yourselves you'd rather keep."

"Don't you need me anymore?" Flea asked.

"Of course I do, lad. Saved you to assist me with more important work, I did. See that donkey cart over there?" Octavian pointed. "We're going to take that to Gowan's bakeshop and load it with sacks that've been left for us there."

"Sacks full o' what?" Flea wondered aloud.

"Magic powder, lad. This fireworks display shan't be like anything anyone's ever seen before. This exhibition will live in the city's memory for years to come, and Queen Elizabeth will know 'twas the flicks and foins of London who helped present it to her, not any Popish foreigners from Rome."

Sixteen

"Blast and damnation!" Robin swore, glancing at Dekker. "What are they doing over there?"

"Can't hardly see," Dekker admitted, turning away from the window. They were hiding in a building near Murdoch's warehouse.

"It's like trying to follow rats in a cellar, only those men's eyes don't glow red in the dark."

"Let's go." Dekker swung onto a ladder propped between the main floor and the loft, where he and Robin had been holding vigil. "We need to move closer."

"Does Burghley have others in place on the docks?"

"I've no idea. The Lord High Treasurer doesn't confide much in me."

"I didn't expect this," Robin admitted, following Dekker between buildings and piles of rope, nets and rigging.

"Mayhap it's naught to do with the 'Loyal Knighthood' and the queen. She's safe in her palace, protected by courtiers and guards alike."

"Aye," Robin said. But he didn't agree. Whitehall was near enough to the water. Besides, a feeling in his belly warned him trouble loomed.

"Here!" Dekker whispered, sliding behind a crate tall enough to hide both himself and Robin. "Do you recognize the fellow with the lantern?"

"Damnation!"

"What is it?"

"Methinks . . . aye, he's a little runt, that one is."

"Your foundling, is it? The boy you took in?"

"Flea? Nay, 'tisn't Flea. I think, though, it's the Scot who first put Walsingham onto the conspiracy. The puny fellow who, whilst vaulting at Fat Fanny's bawdy house, lost both his clothes and that incriminating message he'd left in his pocket."

"Where have the rest of the men gone, those we saw before?"

"If I knew that, Dekker, I wouldn't be hiding with you, freezing my arse off and trying to see through the murky haze. Blast it all, but it's damp!"

"We're on the friggin' river, and 'tis the middle of November. What do you expect?"

"Ho! What's coming?"

Though both men had been looking around the sides of the crate that provided them cover, they now stood. Stooping their shoulders, they peered over the top.

"A donkey cart," Dekker supplied as the conveyance made its creaking way through the wharf area. The driver appeared to be heading directly to Murdoch's warehouse.

"I wish there were some light!" Robin groused.

"Activity on the docks after nightfall is usually the sort best done under cover of darkness. These traitors aren't about to light a lot of torches so we may better see them!"

"Be still," Robin ordered. "Good God!"

"What is it?"

He didn't answer Dekker's question. The first man of diminutive stature had not been Flea. But this other one riding in the cart surely was. What in hell was the lad doing here? And who was that with him, hauling sacks from the cart? Flea's companion resembled none of the three Scottish suspects Robin had been tailing these past months. Yet that did not mean he wasn't a member of their ranks. Flea, though! He couldn't be. He'd never join with traitors. The boy had to be working for him, trying to get the information Robin had asked him to gather. What lengths would the foolish lad go to now? Flea might well be in real danger!

"What is it?" Dekker repeated.

"That cart, those sacks. Do you think they're the ones Gowan took receipt of? The flour sacks that surely contain something other than flour?"

" 'Tis a good guess, Moreton, though I confess I understand none of this," Dekker said with a shake of his head. "The Accession Day festivities are not 'til the morrow. Besides, the queen isn't likely to stumble into these ruffians here on the wharf."

"The displays," Robin muttered. "Remember, Dekker, in the correspondence I took off one of the couriers riding by coach? Reference was made to displays. Mayhap that implied diversions. They may be attempting to concoct one."

"Damnation." Dekker made a sour face as he looked at Robin. "We should alert Burghley. More men may be required down here."

"Too late." Robin began to move out, and Dekker followed.

Lady was growing impatient. Flea had said to wait, not to leave the spot where he'd left her. But it had been a long while since she'd seen him, and dark had descended completely. A mist swirled in off the river now so that even in her cloak she shivered. She also heard rats scuttling about, and her legs were growing tired as she kept her booted feet raised off the ground so no rodents would scurry over her toes.

Hundreds of seagoing ships were docked quayside, and though many were lighted from within, there seemed to be few pedestrians on the wharf itself. The dockers would arrive before dawn, queuing up to be hired on for the day. But for now, the only people in the vicinity trod softly and kept to the shadows.

She felt uneasy. She'd gone soft, Lady realized, living in the comfort of Olivia Crane's fine house. When she had called Southwark her home, this rough area of the city wouldn't have disturbed her so much, not even in the dark of night. Now she longed for a footman, an escort, or better still, *the Falcon* to protect her.

Footsteps drew near. Lady looked through the dark toward the sound. She sucked in a breath and held her body very still.

The footsteps ceased and a familiar voice called, "Lady!"

"Flea?" She leapt off her perch and made her way to him. The youth looked a parody of a Christmas angel as he stood in the darkness holding a small burning candle beneath his chin. "Where've you been? I've seen nothing thrilling or otherwise."

" 'Twill all begin soon enough." He grinned and held up a half-filled sack he carried in his other hand. "I've been given a special task. Come on."

Glad for his companionship, Lady accompanied Flea to the edge of a dock. Boats rocked in the river's current, but those nearest to them were dark, uninhabited.

"Paulie, you here?" Flea whispered.

"Aye. Who's that?"

"Flea. I've a friend with me, Lady."

"You brought a damned woman down here?"

"Aye, he did," Lady confirmed. "Is that a problem for you?"

"Nay." Reaching out for the squat, greasy candle Flea held, Paulie asked, "Is that for me?"

"It's mine. I'm going t' light the first squib."

"The hell you are," he argued, making another grab for the flame.

Flea danced out of his reach. "Not yet, you witless cuffin! Soon as we hear the whistle—that's the signal. One at a time we're to set them alight, and they'll fly upwards, brightenin' the whole night sky. But there's somethin' special I have t' do."

"What?" Paulie demanded, sounding suspicious.

"You got ten o' these here things ready t' go, do you not? Before the last one's lit, I'm t' pour a pile o' sand from this sack an' stick the squib in the center o' the mound. When it goes off, 'twill be as big as the sun explodin'. An' a thousand colors, too."

"Who told you that?" Lady asked. "Octavian?"

"Aye. An' he was told by the cove what hired us. We made the rounds, Octavian and me did, and everyone's got one squib stuck in a pile of sand, as the last of their batch to be lit. But I want to make an extra huge mound o' sand here, so ours is the greatest firework t' go off this eve." He grinned at Lady. "Queen Elizabeth shall be impressed, don't you think?"

She nodded, but she asked, "Who's paying for all this, Flea? Not Octavian."

"Nay. London merchants," he explained. But even in the darkness, Lady saw him frown before he turned away.

"What London merchants?"

"I don't know. The whole lot of them, I suppose! 'Tis only, I don't care for the cove who's paying us t' do the work. He's that foreigner, Lady. The one from the stew. The little Scot."

"Robin's friend?"

"He's no friend—hey!" Flea barked, distracted from his conversation with Lady by Paulie, who was tugging on Flea's sack, trying to free it from his grasp. "Let go!"

"Nay! This is me spot, me squibs, an' I want t' pour the sand that'll make all those extra colors!"

Flea handed his candle to Lady, and the boys struggled over the bag. Soon enough it tore open wide and spewed black sand.

Or something else.

"Flea, are you sure this stuff makes colors? It"—Lady grabbed a pinch between her finger and thumb; she sniffed it skeptically—"it smells like the gunpowder you use in an arquebus to make the ball explode from the barrel."

"Aye, it does, but it's nothin' o' the sort. The Scot explained it to Octavian, who explained it t' me. 'Tis potash an' sulphur, an' I don't know all what. Don't worry, Lady. This is goin' t' be thrillin', not dangerous."

He scowled at the planks beneath their feet. "Damnation, Paulie!" he complained, yelling as best he could while keeping his voice to a whisper. "You've spilt the friggin' sand all over!"

A sharp whistle rent the dank air. Lady felt a shiver of excitement, of trepidation.

"Now!" Flea said, and he reached for the candle she was holding. But Paulie grabbed it from Lady first, and with a sneering grin cast in Flea's direction, spun around to light the first device.

The wick sparked and the flame worked its way toward the cylinder. Instinctively, Lady stepped back. It shot off, *whoosh,* soaring into the sky. They could hear other such whistling sounds and then, of a sudden, the fireworks exploded, raining down small, sparkling stars, some of which blinked out, others of which hissed when they hit the water.

"Sweet Jesu!" Flea said reverently. But as more fireworks exploded, he grabbed the candle from Paulie and lit another wick. An awesome, flame-colored flower blossomed in the velvety blackness of the night sky.

From behind them as well as across the river, a murmur of voices reached their ears. People were stepping outdoors now, standing on balconies and in the lanes, to see the fireworks display. Lady wondered if the queen had come out, if she watched from the palace.

"They're mine to light!" Paulie shouted, drawing Lady's attention back to him and Flea. The two boys were presently struggling over ownership of the candle.

"Flea, give it to him, or you'll snuff the flame," she advised.

But Flea was determined to hold on. Dodging Paulie, he touched the burning candle to the cylinders, one after another, sending them flying upward and bursting outward with showers of colorful light.

"Damn you to hell!" Paulie cursed him. "I'm doin' the last, you cozener! You cheated me o' the rest, but I'm goin' t' light the big one."

"Nay." Flea held on tight to his candle. "We'll do it together."

Paulie appeared to have given in to Flea's demand, but Lady was distracted. The fireworks boomed when they exploded, yet she'd heard an earthbound boom. To her right, through the acrid cloud of sulfur that dimmed her view even more than the misty night, she saw flames. This was not the glitter of fireworks but a blaze burning high and wide upon the wharf.

"Flea! Paulie!"

Neither paid her heed. Their heads low as they bent over the last cylindrical tube, they watched the flame eat up the wick the way a mouser sucked up a rodent's tail. Sparks danced, and though suddenly the squib took off with a tearing sound, at that same instant the black sand ignited. Booming deafeningly, it tore off the end of the dock where they stood. As the length of the pier sagged, balls of flame arced onto the boats harbored nearby.

"Flea!" Lady shrieked, stumbling backward, attempting to stay ahead of the fire dancing toward her. "Flea!"

She heard a splash and wondered if he had fallen into the river. But no, there he was, rushing at her, pushing her back and down. Flea's soot-rimmed eyes gleamed emerald in the firelight; he looked like a madman.

"Oh, Christ, I'm sorry, Lady!" he cried, still rushing her.

She stumbled, fell, and lurched back up onto her feet. Still the crackling flames continued to bear down on her. Lady heard more explosions; she couldn't be sure if they were erupting in the sky, the Thames, or on land.

A stench worse than the sulphur and smoke made her cry. It smelled like scorched cloth and hair—

"For God's sake, Lady, lie down!" Flea screamed.

Lady couldn't. She had to get away. Why was Flea clawing at her, pulling at her? She couldn't understand. Did he want her to stay in the center of this conflagration?

Something, someone, grabbed her from behind and threw her down. The air fled Lady's lungs, yet she couldn't seem to inhale. Her face lay in the dirt; she couldn't see. Hands slapped at her, many hands, more than one pair. It hurt. She was suffocating. She was confused.

She was unconscious.

The flames were out that had gobbled her skirts. Robin picked Lady up and carried her to safety, as far away from the burning buildings on the wharf and the blazing ships at the docks as he could manage. Flea stumbled along beside them.

"I don't know why you're one of them," Robin snarled through gritted teeth. "But I truly can't understand why you'd convince Lady to join you on your deadly mission."

"Deadly mission?" Flea blinked and wiped his damp, dirty cheek with the back of his hand. "By all that's holy, Robin, I'd no idea this was a deadly mission! Somethin's gone awry!"

"Gone awry, has it? You mean nearly killing Lady when you set fire to the wharf?"

"I didn't set fire t' the wharf! We were hired t' set off fireworks for the queen. But the powder that makes the colors, it started explodin', catchin' afire!"

Robin looked around. They had lots of company down here now as the wharf suddenly teemed with frenzied people. They ran and they hollered, they pointed and they dashed in different directions. Some were forming bucket brigades, others stood looking dazed at the flames eating up the docks, the buildings, and even some of the boats.

"Who hired you?" he snapped at Flea, though he was tenderly stroking Lady's singed cheeks.

"Octavian, the upright man what helped me find Lady when she was in the gaol. He didn't know this would happen, Robin! We thought this was a gift for Her Majesty."

"A gift?" Robin snorted. "From whom?"

"The merchants o' the city"

"Any merchant in particular?"

Flea licked his parched lips. "I only saw him this very eve, Robin. I swear, or I'd have got word t' you. 'Twas that cove I stole the clothes from. The Scot."

"I saw him. Any others?"

"Nay." The boy inhaled raggedly as he shook his head, hatless now. "But the sand that exploded came from Gowan's bakeshop." Flea looked fretfully at Lady's limp form. "Is she all right? Will she survive?"

"She'd better, or you're dead." Robin grabbed Flea's cape and pulled him across Lady's prostrate form so that they were nose to nose, eye to eye. "What else do you know, Flea? What have you seen or heard in the time you've been absent?"

"Fraser, the smith. He's more than that, Robin. I saw him put the finishin' touches on a fine sword. He did it in the wee hours so no one would see him workin'. Fraser's an armorer, Robin. He makes weapons!"

Robin wanted to cuff the lad soundly, for surely he hadn't seen Fraser making a sword just today. Instead, he released Flea with a shove. "Damn," he grumbled, looking at Lady, wondering how he could care for her and protect the queen from Angus MacKinney, who'd been in London all along, working as a blacksmith.

"Lady! Lady, wake up!" Robin patted her face gingerly; it was raw and red where her cosmetics had melted away. But he had to try and rouse her.

Lady's lids fluttered before her eyes opened to slits. "Robin?"

"Aye, dearling, 'tis me. How do you feel?"

"Not . . . very well." She tried to sit up, and he helped her.

"Flea." Robin turned to the boy. "That donkey cart you and the ruffler brought to Murdoch's warehouse. Get it. Take Lady back to Olivia Crane's house. Do you hear me?"

Nodding, Flea pushed himself to his feet. He swayed a little, and Robin wondered what condition the boy was actually in.

"I depended on you before, Flea. You disappointed me. *Don't* disappoint me again." The boy nodded obediently. "You will also remain at Mistress Crane's residence 'til I come for you both. Tell her 'tis on my order you remain."

"Aye, Robin. I will." He ran off to collect the cart.

"Robin?" Lady murmured. "You're . . . not coming with us?"

"Nay, my sweet, I cannot."

Flea returned with the skittish beast and the rickety cart. Robin lifted Lady into the wagon, made certain the boy controlled the donkey, and then slapped the animal on the rear to get it moving again. He did not pause to say farewell. There was no time. He had to find Dekker, and they had to find Angus MacKinney.

Seventeen

Robin realized, as he pushed through the throngs, that the multitude had grown quickly while he was with Lady. It seemed as though most of London's population had descended on the docks, all of them in an assortment of dress and undress while they either gawked at the flames in horrified awe or tried to contain them. The noise was so great he tried blocking it out, tried keeping it to a din in his head. The air was so thick with smoke and bitter smells, he covered his nose with the edge of his cape so that he could breathe.

He couldn't find Dekker. Everyone in England was suddenly within arm's reach, but he couldn't find Dekker. Giving up his search, he made his way to Fraser's place—not the Scot's smithy, but his residence.

Robin would have had no more luck finding Fraser than he'd had finding Dekker if the Scotsman hadn't proved himself recklessly arrogant. Certainly the foreigner had never been imprudent in the past, or he'd have been caught with the other conspirators when plots against Queen Elizabeth unraveled. But this mission of his, this attempt to avenge his own queen's death, seemed a personal affair, a matter of pride. And this eve he used no caution.

Robin found the warrior easily, even amidst the chaos, because he proudly garbed himself in his tartan, the plaid of the clan MacKinney. Despite the smoke, the flames, and the press of people, mostly on foot but some on skittish horses, Angus MacKinney, self-anointed executioner, stood out like a beacon on the shore of a black sea, his crossbow slung behind his back.

The Scot reminded Robin of a lost goose flying north in autumn, as MacKinney launched himself against the onslaught of humanity heading south to the River Thames. Amidst the shouting and crying, he walked in ominous silence, with determined strides, shouldering away any who surged into his path. Robin knew where the man headed, though he fell into step some paces behind, taking advantage of the slim path MacKinney forged.

The Strand was lit as though by rays of sunset from the dockside fires' glow. MacKinney marched straight along the thoroughfare, turning only when he reached the road that connected the Strand with Whitehall Palace.

Robin slipped his hand beneath his mantle and felt for his pistol. Pulling it from his belt, he clutched the grip in his fingers. One shot, that's all he had.

His heartbeat quickened; sweat slicked his palms. How in hell did Fraser—MacKinney—expect to reach the queen? She was safe, she was guarded. Walsingham himself probably lay prostate over her, pinning her down, since the fireworks, explosions, and blazes had begun. Elizabeth would never present herself to make her royal personage a target. Neither the secretary of state nor the Lord Treasurer, Burghley, would allow it!

Robin's heart stopped for a moment. Like a galloping horse that collapsed in the heat, his racing pulse went still. There, above the crazed crowd on a magnificent, dappled white steed, rode the queen. Good God, she knew better! Yet she reigned as monarch of all England, beloved by most all her subjects, especially those in London. She had to suffer with them, struggle with them, feel their pain, know their joy. Even Robin's superiors could not restrain her. She had not headed to Whitehall's river landing, but instead appeared intent on making her way to the Thames's unsavory docks. Her purpose, surely, was to rally those who sought to protect the bridge from falling prey to the flames. Elizabeth was grand, she was great, she'd already given her name to the age. Now, she would give her life, if Robin alone did not protect her from the assassin's bolt.

His eyes flicked to where he'd last seen MacKinney, before the queen's noble presence deflected his attention. MacKinney was gone. Frantic, Robin scanned the people and the edges of the road.

There he was! The Scot had moved off the road as the crowds parted to make way for Elizabeth and her retinue of knights. He had made himself all but invisible behind the line of admiring subjects who paused in their frenzied scrambling to witness the queen's brief nods as she acknowledged them and their plight while trotting into the fray. But Robin saw him and, scurrying nearer, raised his arquebus and cocked it. Taking careful aim, he held his breath and squeezed the long sear lever.

Nothing happened. A click, but no fire. Damnation! He shoved the useless weapon back into his belt and unsheathed his sword. Robin never took his eyes off the Scot, who was raising his bow, seating the bolt, aiming . . .

Slipping up behind MacKinney, Robin gripped the haft of his sword in both hands, raised the blade high, and swung it in a downward arc that met his enemy just above the man's shoulder. It sliced through the grizzle and bone of his thick neck as though it were butter and clotted cream. For a weird, awful moment, after his head had rolled, MacKinney continued to stand, spurting blood from the stump of his neck. Then his knees buckled and his body fell forward, hitting the ground so near Robin, he jumped out of the way.

Some saw; some screamed. But few of Elizabeth's subjects realized what had happened. Only a couple of the royal guard kneed their horses out of line and converged on Robin.

"Sir Robert Moreton," he identified himself simply. "On Sir Francis Walsingham's staff. That," he explained, pointing at the decapitated corpse, "was an assassin attempting to slay Her Majesty, our queen."

The fires had been out since well before dawn, and considering their potential for damage, the carnage had been well-contained. London Bridge remained intact, and though much of the docks and dozens of ships had been damaged or lost, now that the sun was up, debris was being hauled away and the area made safe enough for normal work to resume.

Robin had reported to Burghley as soon as he'd been certain the queen was safe. They, the ailing Walsingham, and eventually several other agents, including Dekker, had been in meetings that lasted throughout the night. Dekker reported that Murdoch and the other unidentified Scot had escaped. But he'd caught Connor Gowan and arrested him. Already that Scottish baker was in the Tower and being interrogated. Other agents confirmed several deaths among those who'd been involved in lighting the fireworks. Though their suspicions, and Robin's, were not yet confirmed, it seemed the dead, in their own way, were innocents. Rogues from the streets they had been, petty thieves and the like, hired to light the squibs and, unsuspectingly, set off the fireballs that ate up the wharf and the quays. One agent, familiar with Southwark's upright man, confirmed that Octavian was among the deceased.

Flea hadn't been lying. The little flick and sometimes hunter had been duped, but he'd survived unscathed. It was Lady who'd been injured, burned by the flames that ate up the trail of gunpowder which had somehow been scattered along the pier. Robin wanted to go to her immediately, to make certain her injuries did not endanger her life.

"May I be excused, my lord?" he inquired of the treasurer as the discussion wound down. "Someone—close to me—was injured in the dock fires. I'd like to see to her."

"Go on," Burghley urged with a wave. "We've all had a long night. Though you, Moreton, and you, Dekker, worried me with your far-flung searches, you acquitted yourself well in the end. The queen's alive to oversee her revelry today because of you two—most especially you, Sir Robert."

"Thank you, my lord." With a courtly bow, he retreated, and Dekker joined him in the corridor.

"I told you interrogating those who remain from the Babington Conspiracy would come to naught," Robin muttered as they made their way downstairs and on outside. "We'd have spent our time better watching the docks."

"We didn't know that then," Dekker pointed out. "We were desperate for clues. And some good comes of minor misdirection."

"What do you mean?"

"That knight, Rose, do you remember him? The one who's languishing in the Tower? The one who gave me those conspirators' names. Well, I'm quite sure he's innocent of any crime. I think I may do a good deed and see to providing evidence that will get him released."

"That's kind of you, Dekker, it truly is. But the woman I love is injured, burnt in that blasted fire the Scots set. I must go to her now."

"Go then," Dekker urged, clapping Robin on the shoulder before they parted company in the street.

The woman he loved, the woman he loved . . . Robin had never allowed himself to think of Lady in those terms before. He cared for her, desired her, at times even needed her. But he'd never realized he loved her, heart and soul, until he'd thought he might lose her.

He still might lose her. God only knew the extent of her injuries.

Robin set out for Olivia's house at a run.

"Where is Lady? How does she fare?" he demanded, having burst through the front door and confronted Olivia without so much as a knock to announce his arrival.

She clutched his sleeve to keep him from bounding up the stairs. "Lady's resting, Robin. She's asleep. Come, have some wine, talk to me."

Reluctantly, he accompanied Olivia into her parlor and accepted a glass of Spanish red. "Is Flea here?"

"He's in her room. The boy is racked with guilt. He's told me little, but I gather he feels he failed you both and is responsible for Lady's injuries."

"I'll speak with him. He's not to blame."

"Robin, what happened? Last eve I was terrified to return home from an engagement only to find Lady missing. No sooner did I realize she was gone than the fireworks and the fires themselves began. If there had been a wind—" She broke off with a shudder. "It terrifies me even now to think what might have happened. All of London could have been lost!"

"So, too, the queen." Robin provided a brief account of the previous evening's events, but he felt distracted and kept glancing toward the stairs. "I must go up to her, Olivia. There are things I must tell Lady."

"Aye, you should."

"What does that mean?" He frowned at Olivia curiously.

"It means you should tell her who you really are, what you really do. I think then she might tell you the truth about herself."

"What truth is that?"

"I'm not certain." She shook her head. "But methinks you've both been keeping secrets from each other you oughtn't have."

"You speak in riddles, madam, and I've no time for that." Robin stood. "I will go see Lady, now."

In her bedchamber, Robin found Flea in a chair, scowling at Lady's sleeping form. Softly, Robin said, "You look angry, lad."

The boy leapt up, startled, and whispered back, "Aye, I'm angry with meself, Robin! I—I did everythin' wrong. I nearly got Lady killed. I nearly got us all killed an' burnt up the city doin' so!"

"You did nothing of the sort, Flea. 'Twas bigger than all of us, the events played out last night."

"I only wanted Lady t' share the fun. I thought 'twould be excitin', seein' them fireworks up close. I knew she'd be missin' you, m'lord. I thought t' distract her, an' I nearly made her dead."

" 'Twasn't you," Robin insisted, his eyes flitting between Flea and Lady as he sought to reassure himself she slept peacefully. " 'Twas the blasted Scot conspirators. They set you up, Octavian and the rest, so their assassin could get himself close to the queen."

Flea paled. "Did he? Oh, bloody Christ, did he?"

"Hush." Stepping nearer, Robin put his hand on the boy's shoulder. "Nay, he did not. 'Twas Fraser, you know. In truth, he was Angus MacKinney of the clan MacKinney who tried to slay Elizabeth with a well-aimed bolt. But after you told me about the sword you saw him crafting, I knew him as the assassin. I went to his lodgings and followed the cur, cutting off his head before he could harm Her Highness."

Flea blanched. Then he breathed, "Thank God! Thank you!"

"Rob . . . in?"

They both turned toward her at the sound of Lady's voice. Her lashes fluttered before her eyes opened, wide and blue as a sunlit ocean. Robin felt a wave of relief, a wash of love. "Aye, dearling, 'tis me."

"I—I'll be goin' now. Farewell," Flea muttered.

"You needn't."

"Aye, I must."

"Flea, no!" Lady pleaded weakly.

"Absolutely not," Robin added.

"But—how can either o' you stand t' look at me? I helped try t' burn down all London! If you'd died, either o' you, an' the queen as well, 'twould all have been me fault! I don't belong here. I'm headin' back t' where I do belong."

"Flea, you're like kin to us," Robin said, hoping to reassure him. "I told you before, when I find us a house, you can live there. You'll always have a place in our home."

"Nay, Robin." The youth shook his head.

"Aye!" Lady looked at him imploringly as she raised herself up, resting her back against her pillows.

"An' what would I do?" he asked truculently. "You're no padder, Robin, no thief at all. You couldn't have a flick livin' in your house. An' I can't go on workin' for you. I was no success in your employ before."

"What—what do you mean, Robin's no thief?" Lady inquired, speaking to Flea but looking directly up at Robin.

He hadn't wanted the truth to come out this way, but it was too late. "Flea, could you go downstairs for a bit? I don't want you running off where we can't find you, but I need some time alone with Lady. Would you . . . ?"

"O' course," he agreed. "I do have to go now. But I'll come 'round again to check on you." He nodded at Lady, and then quit the room.

Robin sat on the edge of the bed. It hurt him to look at her face, with her unnaturally pink cheeks glistening with unguent, same as her hands resting on the crisp linen folded over her coverlet.

"Tell me," she urged softly. "I know your name is Robert Moreton, and now I hear you're no footpad, despite the fact I myself assisted you in robbing coaches. What are you, Robin?"

"A knight. Sir Robert Moreton."

Lady blinked and repeated, "A knight? *Sir* Robert Moreton?"

"I'm sorry I couldn't tell you earlier, but—"

"I understand it all now," she interrupted. "You couldn't ask me to marry you because you believed I was naught but a street thief whilst you . . . were not. I can't say I blame you."

"Lady, it is far more complicated."

"My name's not really Lady," she admitted before Robin could continue and explain about his work, how it took him away so often, the dangerous aspect of it, everything. But because he'd been thinking of a way to broach the particulars, it took him a moment to comprehend what Lady had said.

" 'Tisn't?" He scowled, bemused, confused.

"Nay. 'Tis what Flea calls me because I *am* a lady. That is, I was raised to be a lady by my mother, Lady Winnifred, and my father, Sir Leslie." She smiled a small smile and peeked up at him through her lashes. "My Christian name is Caroline."

"Caroline." Shocked, Robin couldn't say more. Chagrined, he wondered how he hadn't realized it, for her looks and her speech both indicated she'd been higher born than he'd believed. Blast, she could even sit a horse! Yet Robin felt elated as it came to him that now he *could* marry her. His tribe of sisters couldn't fault her, nor would his father be heartbroken by his only son's choice in a wife. Sweet Jesu! Things had appeared so bleak only yesterday. Now, the queen was alive and safe, Lady was Lady Caroline, and he could marry his love after all! "How . . . ?"

"I'll tell you everything, Robin. But could I have a sip of water? My throat is parched."

"Certainly. Forgive me, dearling. I should have thought of it myself." He rose and poured her a cup of water, which he handed to her with great care. "Your hands," he said sadly, looking at her blisters.

"It looks worse than it is, according to Olivia's physician. Except for having to trim my singed hair, I should be myself again in a few days."

"You don't know how relieved I am." Taking the cup she returned to him, he dared to kiss her fingertips. "Now tell me what happened. Where are your parents? How did you find yourself living at Fat Fanny's?"

"My mother died of illness when I was ten and five," Lady explained. "An only child, I lived with my father, who worked in the Treasury until . . . until . . ."

"Until what, love?"

"Until that horrid Walsingham threw him in the Tower! The secretary accused him of being one of the conspirators who'd attempted to free the Scottish Queen Mary!" Lady's chest heaved and her eyes welled with tears. "He was innocent, completely innocent. He'd nothing to do with Throckmorton or the rest. He just had the bad luck to know the son of the undertreasurer, or some such, who was indeed involved in the Babington Conspiracy."

"Wasn't his innocence proved at trial?" Robin asked, panic rising like a tide in his chest. Christ! Could he marry the daughter of a Catholic conspirator, even one who claimed innocence—he, who toiled to keep the queen safe from such traitors?

"What trial?" Lady returned. "My father was never tried, and he died in his cell! That damned Walsingham, Puritan that he is, believed anyone who'd ever been Catholic was part of the plot, whether or not he had proof. He ordered my father arrested and forgot about him until it was too late." Her lower lip trembled with anger and imminent tears.

"Don't cry, Lady," Robin urged, checking himself before he reached out to flick a tear from her tender cheek. His mind raced, yet he managed to urge, "Tell me about you, dearling. What misfortune befell you?"

"I rather think my father's arrest and subsequent death was my misfortune," she declared. "I had no close relations other than he, and soon I found myself without friends. In short order, I also found myself without funds. Thrown out of our home by the landlord, I had naught but the clothes on my back. Fortunately"—she sniffed—"Flea found me standing on Cheapside and brought me home with him to Fanny's. He arranged for my lodging in exchange for me doing the stew's laundry, and he also taught me my trade. You know. Cony-catching."

Lady dropped her gaze as she strained for control. Robin's heart felt heavy as he imagined the horror of her circumstances. It was one thing to be born to the lower classes, another thing altogether to fall into such a mean life.

Leaning forward, Robin gingerly touched his lips to hers. "God, I wish I could hold you," he admitted as he drew away. "But I fear I'd hurt you if I took you in my arms."

"I could hardly feel worse," she said. "Please, Robin. Hold me."

Tentatively, he took her into his arms, and Lady rested her cheek on his shoulder. Robin wished he could weave a cocoon around her so that she'd always be safe. Failing that, he would protect her with his sword arm and his name. She'd be his wife, he determined, no matter who her father had been or what he'd been accused of. If Burghley or Walsingham took exception, he would find a new career. If his family objected, he'd spurn his inheritance and the two of them could strike out on their own.

"Would you like to move back to the north country?" Robin whispered into Lady's ear. "I rather enjoyed being a highwayman, especially when you rode with me. Care to make a life together as a footpad and his doxy?"

"Oh, Robin." She sighed. "You're teasing, but in truth I would love it. With Flea, too, hunting game in the forest. Truth be told, I don't care much for London. I never really noticed how dirty and foul-smelling it is until I moved from Westminster to Southwark."

Lady pulled back, and Robin released her gently. Her eyes met his as she said, "I understand you're a knight, but I know you once robbed coaches, and that I don't understand. Nor do I know how you happened to be at the docks yestereve so that you could save me from the flames. Robin, what is it you do?"

"I protect the queen."

"You're a palace guard?"

"Nay. All monarchs are frequently the target of disgruntled subjects and foreign enemies. Elizabeth is a target more often than most rulers, and she must be kept safe from harm. Lady, do you recall that when I first saw you outside Fanny's stew, I asked about the little man whose clothes were stolen? He was part of a plot to kill Her Majesty. And once, when we waylaid a coach together, you searched a fellow's trunk hose for hidden letters. What you found was a message going from Edinburgh to London, one to do with that same plot."

Robin searched Lady's impassive face. He could not tell what she was thinking, so he went on.

"Yestereve, I was watching the docks because of suspicious activity going on there. The fires that Flea and his cohorts inadvertently set were all arranged by this group of Scots to draw Elizabeth out of the palace. One of them attempted to slay her with a bolt."

He paused, waiting for Lady to say something, at least to murmur. But she stayed silent.

"After I sent you off with Flea, I followed the assassin and killed him before he could harm the queen."

Again, Robin paused. For a long moment, Lady said nothing. Then her eyes narrowed, and she shouted, "You work for Francis Walsingham! You're one of his hateful agents! *You* arrest those you think are traitors, even if they're not! You arrested my father! *You killed him!*"

"Nay, I did not." He grabbed Lady's wrists as she began to flail at him. "Lady, I've no wish to hurt you," he begged, worried that he was chafing her raw skin. "I want never to hurt you."

Abruptly, she went still and Robin released her. "You can't hurt me," she snarled, her voice low and grave. "Not anymore. Because of you and your kind, I've no life save for that in the streets or a stew. No income except what I can steal. No family, but for Flea." She swallowed hard. "Get out. I've no wish to ever see you again."

"Lady—"

"Get out!"

Robin stood and moved swiftly to the door. He wanted to say something to her, anything that might assuage her anger. But he could think of nothing.

Then, as he opened the door to depart silently, Lady wailed, "For the rest of your days, Sir Robert Moreton, know that you have the death of Sir Leslie Rose on your head!"

Sir Leslie Rose. Alone in the hallway, Robin stopped cold as that name reverberated in his head like a clanging bell. Sir Leslie Rose . . . Sir Leslie Rose . . . Sir Leslie Rose.

He had it, suddenly. Racing down the stairs, he again caught up with his former mistress and grabbed the woman's shoulders. "Olivia," he said, "keep Lady here.

If she tries to leave, tie her to the bed, sit on her if you must. But keep her here 'til I return."

"Robin, what's happened?"

"Nothing, yet. But a great wrong is about to be set right." Releasing Olivia, he strode to the front door. As he turned the latch, he turned back to her and said, "By the way, you might like to know that Lady's true name is Caroline Rose. And if all goes well, it shall soon be Lady Caroline Moreton."

Eighteen

Lady hated the world, except for Flea and for Olivia Crane who, she had to admit, had been extremely kind to take her in, not only when she'd been burned in the fire but earlier, when she had just been freed from prison. But Lady despised everyone else, from Fat Fanny, who had stolen her savings, to all the lords in the royal Privy Council who had arrested her father and let him die in the Tower, to Sir Robert Moreton, who had deceived her as no other ever had.

Though she had never dreamed she would entertain the notion, Lady wanted desperately to return to Southwark. Virtually everyone she'd ever known this side of the Thames had lied to her, shunned her, tricked her, abandoned her. So though the people who lived on the other side of the river were considered disreputable, at least there she knew where she stood, and she could stand tall.

This morning, Lady had managed to garb herself in the simple, dark green frock that Olivia Crane had given her upon her first visit. It revealed a bit of white smock where the ruffled edge skimmed her breasts, and it did not have tight sleeves that would chafe her sensitive skin. Despite the fact she'd had neither hooks nor ties at her back to deal with, dressing herself without assistance did not prove a simple task. But then, Lady was not so well yet. Under other circumstances, she might have stayed abed another day or two.

But two days already were enough, and Lady intended to leave Olivia's house this very morn. Flea had promised to come for her, and she planned to be waiting when he arrived.

"Lady?" a familiar, welcome voice called from beyond her door.

"Flea! Come in."

"How do you feel?" he asked as he entered. "You still sure you want t' go?"

"I'm sure. I'd go if I were half-dead."

"You can't go!" Olivia insisted, appearing in the doorway behind Flea. "Robin said—"

"I care naught what Robin said." Lady picked up her cape but then allowed Flea to take it from her and drape it gently over her shoulders. She took a step toward the woman, and her tone changed. "Olivia, I do appreciate your many kindnesses. I know I've been an imposition. But if ever there's something you think I can do for you, please let me know."

"How?" Olivia's expression looked pinched. "How would I find you, Caroline?"

"Send a servant to ask after me in Southwark. They know me there."

Lady stepped around Olivia and went down the stairs slowly, pressing her hand to the wall for support. Flea followed directly behind.

"Flea!" Olivia called after him. "You mustn't do this! Robin's your friend, is he not? You don't want to disappoint him."

"Lady was me friend long before I knew Robin," the boy pointed out. Then he added, "Mistress, don't fret that

Robin might be upset with you over Lady's leavin'. He'll understand."

"He shall not," she muttered, but Flea ignored her, escorting Lady out the front door.

Lady stopped abruptly at the street. A good-looking, fair-haired young man stood beside a simple wagon harnessed to a swaybacked old plow horse. He doffed his cap when she approached, and now he said, "At your service, my lady."

"What is this?" she demanded suspiciously, turning to Flea.

" 'Tis a surprise, Lady. A nice one, I hope. This is me friend, Dekker. He's agreed t' give us a ride t' where we're goin'."

"Southwark is just across the river. We can walk."

"Lady, you've been hurt, an' you still be unwell. Let Dekker take us."

"I promise not to hit too many ruts or bumps," Dekker vowed with a cajoling grin. Lady thought he probably made women swoon with that smile. But she'd had enough of that sort, and he couldn't affect her.

"Very well." She gave him her hand. "But only since Flea is so keen on it."

Seated on the bench between Dekker and Flea, Lady clutched her cloak closed as an indefinable wintry mix drifted down from the leaden November sky. It occurred to her that Flea had said Dekker would take them where they were going, but she didn't know where that would be. Back to Fat Fanny's stew? She doubted it.

"Flea—" Before she could inquire, she broke off abruptly. Then she exclaimed, "We're going the wrong way. We're headed toward Aldgate!"

"That we are, Lady. That we are," Flea agreed.

Suddenly, the youth had hold of her and so did Dekker.

If their hands on Lady's arms hadn't caused her major discomfort, she would have done what they seemed to expect her to do—climb over Flea and leap down to the muddy little road. But it hurt too much, so she begged, "Please, release me!" and they did.

"Lady, it's nothin' terrible," Flea promised. "We're just not headed t' Southwark. There's nothin' there for us now after all that's happened. We wouldn't want t' be livin' with me aunt, now, would we? Not anymore. An' even Octavian's gone, so there's no upright man keepin' order amongst the ordinary flicks, foins, an' cony-catchers. Nay, we have t' go elsewhere."

"But out of London?"

"Mayhap. We'll see. Lady," Flea urged, "let's have us a day in the country. We both liked the country, didn't we? An' after that, we'll decide what t' do. Will you agree with that?"

She glanced sidelong at Dekker. He seemed to have no interest in their discussion at all.

"Very well. But remember, Flea, I'm counting on you. If you've got some trick in your head you're thinking to play on me, I suggest you reconsider. Remember, I'm not a cony you can catch."

He nodded seriously and kept his eyes straight ahead. Lady watched the scenery herself, surprised at how fast they left the noise and dirt of the city behind them. It had been a long, long time since she and her father made excursions to outlying villages or even the heath at Hampstead. His life had been in London, and so had Lady's. After he was taken away, Lady had no life but that which she found in the teeming, narrow streets.

The wagon jogged along for nearly two hours, by which time Lady became suspicious again. What would

Flea know about this area? What cause could he have to lure her out here unless . . .

"Did Robin put you up to this? If he did, Flea, I swear by all that's holy, I'll never speak to you again!"

Dekker replied before the boy found a voice to go with his open mouth. "There is someone out this way who wishes to see you, my lady," he confirmed. "But it isn't Robert Moreton."

"You know him?"

"I know him, aye. And you know the person who wishes to visit with you."

"Who?" she demanded, glaring at Dekker's profile. "Who!"

"You'll see him in a moment," he announced as he urged his horse onto a path that led through a cultivated garden and up to a large, thatch-roofed, stone and timber house.

"Flea?" She snapped her head to the other side and glared at him as she waited for a more detailed explanation.

"Dekker's right," was all he said. "You'll see your— You'll see. In just a bit. Then, if you wish, we'll turn straight around an' head back t' London."

Flea jumped off the wagon as soon as Dekker halted it. But before Lady could jump as well, Dekker climbed down, reached up, slipped his hands beneath her mantle, and grabbed her around the waist. Effortlessly, he lifted her to the ground.

"Where?" she demanded of them both.

"Inside," Dekker answered.

"I'm not going in there alone."

"Nay, we'll be escorting you." Dekker smiled so disarmingly, she'd have fretted for the female population of London, if she'd cared about any of them at all.

"Whose home is this?" she asked, waiting for either fellow to reply.

"An aged scholar's," Flea supplied. "But 'tisn't he who wishes to see you. 'Tis—"

As Flea was speaking, the trio entered the front door, which opened onto a large room with tall mullion windows that caught a great deal of the morning light. Rising from a chair as they approached was one solitary figure, a man, someone Caroline Rose had never expected to see on this earth again.

"Father?" she asked, her voice strangled, strange. "Father, can it be you?"

"Aye, Caroline, 'tis me!" He opened his arms and strode forward, catching her up as both Flea and Dekker stood aside. "Dear God, I missed you and worried about you. But here you are, whole, and very nearly well."

As he loosened his hold on Lady, she stepped back and looked into his face, studying the familiar features. "You're aware I was injured in the fire?"

"Aye." He nodded. "I learnt a great deal about what's happened to you these last years. Oh, Caroline, forgive me. I am so sorry."

"You! You've naught to be sorry for!" Despite any discomfort, she hugged her father, Sir Leslie Rose, again. " 'Twas that despicable Francis Walsingham, and Burghley, and the others." Robin's face loomed among the guilty crowd she pictured in her mind. As she added to her imagery, fantasizing their heads on pikes at the end of London Bridge, one face came into better focus as the man who owned it stepped into the room.

"You!" she gasped, releasing her father.

Sir Leslie turned. Spying Robin, he nodded. "Aye, 'twas he and his friend here"—he glanced at Dekker—"who got me out of the Tower. I've been exonerated,

Caroline. They found the proof, took testimony from those who knew I was never a part of that Babington plot. The Lord High Treasurer himself secured my release."

"You did?" Lady's eyes met Robin's. He did not speak, merely nodded his head slightly. "But you were dead, Father!" she exclaimed next, gazing up at the older man beside her. "That's what I was told. Why? Why did I receive that news?"

" 'Twas my doing. When I realized I'd been forgotten after all the conspirators, even Queen Mary, were executed, I presumed I would rot there, in the Tower. Caroline, I did not want you living with that knowledge. I hoped you'd go on with your life, marry, create a family of your own. I'd no idea you'd become penniless, that you were forced into the streets."

Leslie began to weep, and Lady comforted him, urging him into a chair. She sat beside him and took both his hands in hers. "Father, it matters naught. I had to do things Mother never taught me, but I never did anything very wicked or truly evil. Just cut a few purses." Trying to make the moment lighter, she turned to flash a smile at Flea. Then she looked at her father again. "I survived, and now it is all in the past. You're free, we'll live together again as we used to."

"Nay." The older knight shook his head.

"Nay?"

"Caroline, you must move on with your life. I understand Sir Robert wants to wed you."

Lady's eyes leapt to Robin, still standing near the doorway where he had entered the room. She stood and addressed him.

"You spoke of this matter to my father? How dare

you! I told you I'd no wish to see you again. Do you think I'd marry you nonetheless?"

"I hoped you'd change your mind."

"I shan't."

"Caroline," Leslie interrupted, "Robert Moreton has done a great deal on my behalf. Without him and James Dekker, I'd still be languishing in prison. And you'd still be—"

"I care not! He's the one who put you in prison in the first place! I care not if he himself failed to clap you in chains. He's one of them, one of those damnable spies who toils for the Privy Council and casts blame upon innocents!"

"Caroline!" Her father appeared shocked by her language.

"Forgive me, but I am no longer the sweet innocent I was when Robin and his mates deemed you a traitor and arrested you. And I'd never spend my life with one of them, especially him. Not even you could coerce me."

"I wouldn't coerce you."

"But I would," Robin announced, stepping forward. He glanced beyond her, at Dekker and Flea, and when he spoke, he included Sir Leslie in his request. "May Lady—Caroline—and I have a few moments alone? 'Twould seem we have some serious matters to discuss."

"We do not," she countered, spinning away from him as she folded her arms over her chest.

"Certainly," the three men agreed, and Dekker ushered them out of the room into another.

"Lady." Robin came around her until he faced her squarely. "I love you."

The announcement made her blink in surprise. He had, she'd known he had. But he hadn't known that he was in love with her. He had never said so, only that he cared for her, desired her, relied upon her. It was nearly the same thing, but not quite. And besides, he'd been deceiving her at the time, making her think he was an honorable thief, not a dishonorable knight.

"If you think that will persuade me to abandon reason and become your wife, you're wrong still again." Lady turned her head away and raised her chin a notch.

Robin touched a finger to her chin, bringing her face toward his. "Would this persuade you better?" he asked before leaning down and kissing her until her breasts, her belly, even her toes tingled.

She wanted to kiss him back—perhaps she was already doing so, Lady couldn't be sure. But she kept her arms at her sides, refusing to cling to him. The result was that her legs felt wobbly and she wondered if, any moment, she'd begin to sway.

"No, it would not," she insisted, already fairly sure she was lying.

"What, then? What must I do or say to make you want to be my wife?"

Taking a deep breath, Lady took a few steps away from Robin. "How long did you know about my father? All the while we were together?"

"Absolutely not. 'Twasn't until you told me your name that I realized you were Sir Leslie's daughter. And I only learned about Sir Leslie a few days before. Dekker discovered him and, believing in his innocence, made plans to have him released."

"So it's Dekker I should be grateful to, and Dekker I should consider marrying."

"Not damnably likely." From the corner of her eye, Lady caught Robin's mouth quirking on a smile. "Dekker's a rogue when it comes to the ladies, good wives, and serving wenches who catch his eye. Besides, it took both my efforts and his to gather the testimony and evidence required to have you father freed so quickly."

"Quickly!" She snapped her head in Robin's direction. "He was in the Tower for years!"

"Aye, but few knew that. Even you did not know that."

Lady said nothing, conceding that one point to Robin. She asked, "Why do you want to marry me? Before, you wanted me only as your mistress."

"Before, I was a fool."

"Good. I'm glad you realize it."

Robin chuckled. He stepped close to Lady again and placed one hand on her shoulder. He stood so near, when he spoke his breath tickled her neck. "You wanted to marry before, Lady. Why don't you wish to wed me now?"

She was no longer so sure that she didn't. But she said, "I thought you were a thief, an upright man, a padder. I loved the Falcon, that daring highwayman. But you, Sir Robert Moreton, I do not know. How could I want to marry a man I don't know?"

Robin nibbled her ear. Lady's face warmed as a tickling sensation ran down her neck and spread a blush across her bosom. "You know me, Lady," he informed her. "Better than any woman ever has."

Closing her eyes against his sensual onslaught, Lady said, "We're too different, you and I. Oh, I know it may not seem that way, since who we are by birth has come to light. But, truth be told, Robin, I despise what you do. Even if I didn't, what you do is dangerous—more so, even, than robbing passengers on coaches. I don't think I wish to be wed to a man who is always involved in intrigue and whose life is always at risk."

"I'll give it up."

"What?" His casual declaration so startled Lady, she

whirled around to look up at him and found herself pressed to his chest, Robin's hands on her back holding her close.

"I'll give it up. 'Tis really a young man's career, a young man with no family responsibilities. I'm not so young anymore, Lady. When I marry you, I shall have those family responsibilities as well. When I inherit, I shall have even more."

"What would you do?"

"Teach. I'm quite educated, dearling. My father insisted upon it, since he spent long years as an instructor at Gray's Inn. Besides, I've no real need to earn a living."

"Oh."

"You remain unpersuaded." Robin frowned at her. "I've responded admirably to all your objections. What else could possibly remain between us?"

Nothing at all, Lady thought, aware of Robin's maleness pressing hard against her belly.

"When I thought you were truly a highwayman, I really hoped that after you finished your business in London, we'd return to the north country. I love the country, Robin, and I do not care overmuch for the city. If I had not been reduced to scratching a living in the streets, perhaps I would feel differently. But Southwark changed me. I—I don't think I could live here happily ever again."

"Here?"

"London," she amended.

"But what about here?"

"I . . . don't understand."

"Could you live here happily?" Robin motioned with one arm to include their immediate surroundings.

Glancing toward the windows, Lady recalled the grounds that enclosed this great house. The place sat, indeed, in the middle of the countryside. "Oh, aye." She sighed. "I think I could."

"Then we will."

"How?" She peered up at Robin's face again.

" 'Tis mine," he explained. "In truth, it is still my sire's, but he would have no objection to our living here. And one day it will truly be mine. I've no brothers, only sisters, so I stand to inherit Moreton Green."

Lady said nothing. Earlier this morn, her prospects had been dismal. Now, her future had transformed into everything she might have wished for. It seemed too much. She felt afraid to speak, lest she break the magic spell.

"Have I done it? Have I managed to waylay all your fears and set aside all your complaints?" Robin asked curiously, both his eyebrows upraised as he smiled at her hopefully.

Still, she did not reply aloud. But she nodded.

"Glory!" Robin shouted. Then he scooped Lady into his arms and twirled her until she had no choice but to twine her arms about his neck lest she be flung from his embrace. He laughed and she giggled, and still he spun her around giddily.

"Robin, what are you doing there?"

Robin halted and faced the elderly gentleman who had entered unnoticed and now awaited an explanation as he rested his weight on a cane.

"I am . . . dancing with my betrothed, Father." He set Lady back down on her feet. "May I introduce Sir Leslie's daughter, Caroline Rose."

He brought her forward, and Robin's father said, " 'Tis a pleasure, my dear. May I say you are as fair as the finest English rose."

"Aye, she is," Robin agreed. "My own fair flower."

Lady slanted her gaze toward him. "And are you still my own reckless Falcon?"

Robin winked. "Of that, you are assured."